ered text: THE SECRETS THEY KEEP

Alison Haines

The Secrets They Keep
Guardians Society: Book One
By Alison Haines

THE SECRETS THEY KEEP

Alison Haines

To my husband, Jared.
Your support is the reason this book gets to see the light of day.

THE SECRETS THEY KEEP

Copyright © 2019 by Alison Haines

All rights reserved. No part of this publication may be reproduced, distributed, or transmitted in any form or by any means, including photocopying, recording, or other electronic or mechanical methods, without the prior written permission of the publisher, except in the case of brief quotations embodied in reviews and certain other noncommercial uses permitted by copyright law. For permission requests, email to the publisher, addressed "Attention: Permissions Coordinator," at the address below.

Printed in the United States of America

This book is a work of fiction. Any resemblance to persons, living or dead, places, or events is strictly coincidental.

Edited by Cecily Tartaglione of Red Pen Editor

Cover design by Germancreative
Book design by Valo Publishing
Font: Open Sans

First Edition

ISBN 978-1-9994829-0-9

Valo Publishing
valopublishing@gmail.com
Waterloo, ON, Canada

www.alisonhaines.ca

Alison Haines

Acknowledgements

Guardians Society book one has been a long time in the making: over ten years! I started writing this book with no intention of publishing, but because I love writing, and these characters demanded their story be told. I wrote and wrote all about Alex and Seth and their adventures discovering their true selves, something I feel everyone can relate to (even if we're not all shadowed by a secret society). The story grew and evolved, changing shape as the series emerged. Jared, my husband, was the first person I let read Alex's story. It took years of him asking what I spent so many hours writing before I worked up the courage to let him explore the Guardian's world; they are a secret society, after all! So, it's him I must thank first, for giving me the confidence and unwavering support to share Alex's journey with the world.

Next to read my book was Rowan Liddell, my lovely Critique Partner. She was the first person to actually have a dream about the world I created and the first to love my characters. She has unquestionably made my book better, and I am blessed to have found a critique partner for life. Having support from another writer who *understands* what

I'm going through has been invaluable in the editing and publishing process.

Michael Boik, my other trusty Critique Partner, is one of the best writers I have ever read. He was the tense checker and adverb police I so desperately needed. I am more grateful than I can ever express for his advice, humor, and patience.

Thank you to Scarlett, for teaching me to sprinkle, without crushing my baby writer's spirit. Thank you to ALL of my twitter writing family. You have shown me love, encouragement, support, and community.

To my parents, thank you for always supporting my dreams. You were absolutely no help in writing Alex's parents: a mom and dad who couldn't see their daughter's potential. My whole family: thank you for cheering me on but allowing me the time and space to finish my book.

I will forever appreciate Nana, for pushing me to write as a child and always showing interest in the stories I imagined.

I'm so grateful I found my wonderful editor, Cecily Tartaglione of Red Pen Editor. She helped me sort through commas, awkward sentences, and frustrating descriptions. You are a true gem.

And finally, to you, my readers. Taking the time to read my book is a precious gift. If you want to support me further, please consider reviewing this book. Reviews are the best gift you can give an author, and I appreciate each of you who takes the time to do so.

Alison Haines

THE SECRETS THEY KEEP

Alison Haines

PROLOGUE

17 years ago

"You can't tell me you haven't sensed it," Jack hissed.

Mark gripped his brother's upper arm, pulling him from his crowded dining room and into the adjacent living room. Mark returned his glare to Jack after casting a glance back towards the table; the kids were too distracted to notice their fathers' absence.

"Don't give me that *sense* bullcrap. She's just a little girl."

Jack sighed, looking back at their kids eating, laughing without any sense of the danger that lingered in their periphery. "Fine, don't take my word for it. If you can honestly say you don't see it in her, or any of the others, I'll drop it."

Letting out a breath, Mark bit the inside of his cheek, unable to completely discount his younger brother's assessment, as much as he wanted it to be wrong.

"We're going to have to move. If you're sensing it, even if you're wrong, someone else might as well."

THE SECRETS THEY KEEP

"Mark, are you sure we shouldn't let the kids decide if they want-"

"They are never to know about that world," Mark interrupted, voice booming. His wife Nicole turned, catching his eye from the table with a furrowed brow. Mark waved her off and forced a smile. "Jack, I mean it."

Jack looked into his older brother's eyes, opening his mouth as if to disagree. But as he took in Mark's expression, he thought better of it.

"I'll make the arrangements. Get your family ready." Before rejoining the festivities, Mark turned to his brother once more. "And don't tell Clarissa."

Alison Haines

CHAPTER ONE

I step out into the setting August sun, air still hot and thick with the smell of fresh-cut grass. Looking down the quiet street for a familiar car, I pop on my sunglasses. Mom is picking me up, but she's running late, as usual. I really didn't need to rush my shower. I spin my damp auburn hair into a messy bun with my ever-present hair elastic—the only accessory I wear.

"Are you the new 103?" An elderly woman asks, exiting the building with a yipping ball of brown fur.

"Hi. Yeah, I'm Alex." I reach down to pet the Yorkie, who promptly nips my fingers.

"Don't touch Winnie! She doesn't like strangers."

"Oh, sorry-"

"I live in 203, and I won't tolerate any tomfoolery. If you have a party, I *will* call the police."

"Right, well you don't have to worry-"

"You smoke?"

"What? No!"

"The last guy smoked." She leans closer, sniffing my tank top. "Winnie doesn't tolerate smoke, either."

"Fair enough."

"Your moving truck. It was too loud. You need to be more considerate."

I barely hold in a snort. "I assure you it won't happen again. Until I move out, anyway."

She glares at me for another minute through thick glasses and lets out a scoff as her eyes run down my jean shorts. "You kids and your refusal to cover your bodies. In my day..." she mutters as she tugs Winnie down the front walkway.

"Lovely to meet you," I call after her with a smile. She continues to mutter, tottering down the tree-lined sidewalk and clutching her sweater over her ankle-length floral dress. It's easily 30°C this afternoon; looking at her makes me sweat. *She's gonna be fun*.

My mom finally arrives, pulling to the curb and beeping her horn. I press my lips to suppress a laugh, my new neighbor jumping and turning to glare at the car.

"Who's that?" Mom asks through a forced smile as she waves at Ms. Grumpy-Pants.

"My delightful new neighbor."

She laughs. "Well, there had to be some downside to this beautiful building."

It's true; I'd been lucky to score this apartment. I start my job with the Toronto District School Board in a week, and I managed to find a place on budget in a quiet neighborhood in Markham.

"I thought Erik was with you."

"He and his mom are meeting us at the restaurant."

"Talia's coming?"

"Mom, we are *not* starting this again. Talia is *nice!*" I insist, checking my phone and channeling my anger at the red light. We're running late.

She huffs. "I *know* women like her. She comes from money and flaunts it. She thinks she's better than me, better than us."

My sunglasses mask my eye roll; Mom's clearly projecting. "You've met her once, and it was for, like, five minutes. I think I might know her a bit better than you. I swear, she's incredibly kind and generous."

"So, can I assume Erik didn't even help with the heavy lifting today?"

I groan, regretting inviting Mom to dinner already.

Erik and his mom are already seated when we arrive, only four minutes late.

"Sorry, sorry, sorry!" I say as I hurry to the table, darting past the hostess who attempts to greet us.

"Don't worry about it, honey. You're right on time." Talia smiles as she stands to pull me into a hug. She's wearing a beautiful blue sundress that makes her cerulean eyes pop. *Why didn't I wear something nicer?*

I notice with chagrin that this restaurant is fancier than Erik had let on when he invited us. The table is adorned with a cloth tablecloth and napkins, too much silverware, and sparkling glasses of water with extras for wine. This really isn't helping my "Talia's down to earth" case with Mom.

Erik greets my mom before pushing in my chair as I sit. Returning to his seat, he plants a kiss on my cheek. I smile shyly, looking into his gorgeous sparkling blue eyes. He gives me the half smile that melts my heart; *god, that smile.*

"Nicole, great to see you," Talia says. She reaches out to squeeze Mom's hand.

"And you, Talia," Mom responds, giving me a knowing look. "This is a very nice restaurant."

Please, oh please, let this lunch go smoothly, I pray, barely containing a grimace. Mom isn't going to make it easy.

"Happy moving day! How are you settling in?" Talia asks as she sips her water, mysteriously not leaving a mark on the glass despite her bold red lipstick.

"It's been a busy day. My brother-in-law helped Whit and I get everything moved in, and my dad installed new curtain rods for me." My eyes dart instinctively to my mom, who stiffens at the mention of Dad. I quickly push on. "It's a total mess right now, but I'm excited to actually *have* it." A shiver runs through me in the over-air-conditioned restaurant; I'd forgotten my sweater in the car in my haste. Before I can excuse myself to get it, Erik passes me his with a wink.

Smiling gratefully, I slip into his already warm hoodie. *It smells like him.* "How do you like Erik's new place?"

"Oh, it's nice enough. A little small, but nice," Talia muses. I ignore a kick from my mom under the table.

"Mom, I told you, that's what you get in the city. Besides, why would I need a bigger place? It's just more space to keep clean," he replies as Talia raises her dark eyebrows. "Hey, it's your fault for babying me and doing all the cleaning yourself."

"Yeah, thanks for that, by the way," I add sarcastically, causing both moms to laugh.

Erik also landed a job in Toronto, which was an amazing surprise. As excited as I am about having my own place, I didn't relish the thought of moving to a new city alone. We hadn't been dating long enough to even consider moving in together, but it would be nice to have him nearby.

He's a true city boy and found an apartment in the heart of downtown. His job as an accountant for a major firm also pays better than my starting salary as a substitute teacher, even in a busy school district. I'm sticking to the suburbs—more my style and price range.

Erik's eyes shoot to his vibrating phone sitting on the edge of the table. The illuminated screen reads *BLOCKED CALLER,* as usual. He reaches for it, but Talia gets there first.

"Mom, it might be-" Erik starts, but a look from Talia shuts him up.

"It's not as important as dinner with your girlfriend." She eyes Erik intensely for a moment before smiling at my mom and me. "Teaching your son manners is a never-ending pursuit. I apologize."

My mom catches my eye, brows raised, before returning Talia's smile, albeit a little forced.

Erik's fair cheeks burn red as he runs a hand through his short chestnut hair. Quickly regaining his composure, he smiles at me with *that* smile and takes my hand. "Sorry. Tell me more about your move."

After dinner, Erik promises to help me unpack in the morning, apologizing for about the tenth time that he couldn't get off work today.

Talia pulls me into a hug. "Alex, we must reschedule dinner with your father. I feel terribly about Michael canceling last Thursday."

"No worries. Let me know when you guys have a free night, and I'll check his schedule."

My dad had yet to meet Erik's, despite a few failed attempts. Michael is always away on business trips, which suits me fine; he makes me nervous.

"Oh! I nearly forgot. Please give this to your sister. It was so kind of her to invite Erik to the wedding, and he forgot our gift." She casts Erik another vexed glare as she hands me a thick envelope. "The pictures you shared online are gorgeous. Whitney's dress was stunning, and you made a beautiful maid of honor. I don't often see you that... formally dressed."

I blush. I really should put in more of an effort when I'm going out, but makeup has never really been my thing. Mostly because I suck at it.

Before we leave, I duck into the washroom. As I wash my hands, the sound of Talia's voice drifts through the door from the adjacent corridor.

"I don't care *what* other mission they offered you. This is a priority, and we're not done here."

"I'm ready to submit my report and wrap up. This was clearly a bust," Erik comments, his voice uncharacteristically petulant.

I see my brow furrow in the mirror as I listen.

"That is not yet the consensus..." Talia's voice fades away.

I try to unpack what I've just heard. I'm sure it was their voices... but it can't have been. Nothing they said made any sense, unless *mission* was just a poor translation from Talia's native tongue of Greek. Talia doesn't work with Erik though, so what were they talking about?

I dry my hands, half convincing myself it had just been two similar voices in the hallway. I'm certainly not going to tell Mom what I thought I overheard. She would latch onto it as an example of Talia being two-faced. Plus, she isn't crazy about Erik. She thinks he's too charming. Apparently, someone can be too chivalrous for her.

Alison Haines

The whole way home, I let Mom vent. She dissects the *true* meaning behind every word Talia said. She's still prattling on when we get to my place. I head straight for the wine: a house warming gift from Whit. I didn't think I'd be cracking it open quite this quickly, but after that dinner, I need a drink. Seemingly out of complaints, mom drops onto the couch and pulls her red curls over her shoulder.

For mother and daughter, we share very little in the way of looks. Where she is full figured, I'm slender and lack curves. We're both fair skinned, but I'm missing her red hair and charming freckles that add so much warmth to her complexion. We do share the same emerald green eyes, stopping me from considering too seriously that I was secretly adopted.

"Oh my gosh," Mom laughs as she pours herself a glass. "I just remembered that place we looked at, the one near the gas station."

I almost spit out my wine. "The one with *two bathrooms*, but one had a sink and a shower, and the other had a toilet and tub?"

We both laugh, trading stories of the worst units we'd seen. It's hard finding an apartment in a city you don't know well. I grew up in St. Thomas, a couple of hours from Toronto, and both my parents still live there. We didn't know the neighborhoods around here, so we'd wasted many summer days going through terrible apartments. It's disheartening what some people try to pass off as a habitable place for humans.

Mom reaches for the wine bottle on the floor, topping up our glasses. I take a drink, Talia and Erik's conversation I overheard at the restaurant pulling at my thoughts. Before I can replay the whole thing, my mom turns to me, eyes serious.

"Alex, this color really is too dark for autumn. I wish you'd let me book you in with my girl, get some highlights," Mom says, twisting a strand of my hair as I pull out my bun. "And you're such a smart girl. I really think you should look into law school again."

I clench my jaw, cheeks burning. "I know you do."

"I'm not trying to get you all worked up. I just want you to know I support you." She huffs, overshadowing my right to be angry with her indignance. "I just have a feeling that there is more for you than substitute teaching, and you know what Grandmother always used to say: *a woman's intuition is not to be ignored*."

"Thanks, Mom. That means a lot," I say flatly as I bite my cheek, trying not to cry.

She smiles, appeased, as she gets to her feet. "That's enough wine! I'm gonna get ready for bed."

I thank her for staying over with a tight smile; my irritation goes unnoticed or ignored. She leans down to kiss the top of my head, before stumbling to the bathroom. I take some deep breaths, pushing my frustration down. She hit a nerve that's still raw, yet she's like a dog with a bone, bringing up law school every chance she gets. Mom's never respected my decision to become a teacher.

I pop my head into the spare room, tossing a pillow on the air mattress I'd set up this afternoon. Truth be told, I blew it up for my little brother Caleb, but he had soccer practice tonight, so Dad took him home after we'd finished moving. I was starting to doubt my decision to use Mom as a back-up. I love her, but she knows how to get under my skin like no one else. Well, at least I don't have to stay alone.

*****

Whit yawns loudly, collapsing onto my couch, her impossibly long legs draping over the armrest.

"You're here for your muscles, not to lounge. Up!" I say, flattening another cardboard box and adding it to the teetering pile. Yesterday, Whitney came over to help me unpack with Erik, then I subtly manipulated her into sleeping over. It's one of the perks of being a little sister: your older sibling will instinctively protect you. In the last two weeks, since finding out my apartment application was accepted, I'd been so excited about getting my own place. Somehow, I'd ignored the fact I'd be living *alone. I wonder how long I can convince people to spend the night?*

"Hey, don't blame me! I had to share a bed with Kicky Mc. Ice Toes. God, do you even own socks?" Whit teases.

"My toes aren't that cold."

"I thought you died. I seriously thought I was sleeping next to a corpse."

I throw a pillow at her, trying not to laugh. "Whatever, at least I don't snore."

"That's true; Sam's like a freight train."

"I wasn't referring to your husband, Mrs. Freight Train." I drop down on the couch beside her, and a wave of discouragement washes over me as I lean my head on her shoulder. This place is a huge mess. "Plus, you could have slept in the spare room."

"I don't do air mattresses." Whit rests her head on mine. "Where's Erik, anyway?"

"Working. He has zero vacation time. He had to work super late yesterday just for taking the morning off," I explain with a frown. It sucks not having him here. He'd only spent a couple hours here yesterday before hurrying back to the office. To be fair, he did bring the most beautiful print of one of my favorite art pieces. He's always doing sweet things like that: remembering stuff I swear I've only mentioned once and surprising me with really personal gifts.

"Are you excited that you guys will be living so close now?"

"Yeah."

"Wow, with that enthusiasm, you'll be right on my heels down the aisle," Whit says, raising her eyebrows.

"Stop. I *am* excited."

"That's it. We're going to pick out china patterns right now!" Her smile fades. "Anything wrong between you two?"

"No, things are good. He's great. But with his crazy work schedule, we only see each other on weekends anyway, so it won't really make a huge difference. I'm going to miss seeing you and Caleb all the time."

"I get that, but this will be good for you."

"I worry about Dad. Will you visit-"

"Alex! He's an adult; he can take care of himself. You know I'll visit, but you need to stop coddling him."

I bite my cheek. I'd been living with Dad since the divorce, and I can't help but feel like I'm abandoning him. "Promise me you'll check in on Caleb. He needs homework reminders."

"Mom and Dad raised us; he'll be fine," Whit reminds me in her typical worry-free way.

"But we had each other."

She sighs, smiling at me indulgently. "Fine, fine. I'll keep an eye on Caleb, but only if you promise to let Mom and Dad deal with their issues. I know this sounds extreme, but *try* to start living your own life."

I glare at her as I pry myself off the couch, a familiar intricate knock saving Whit.

"I come bearing gifts," my cousin, Seth says with an elaborate bow, extending a box of delicious-smelling pizza my way as I open the door.

"I smell cheese. Gimme!" Whitney calls from the couch.

"Hi to you too, Whit." Seth shakes his head. "Sometimes I feel like you two only like me for my pizza discount."

"I mean, he's not wrong," Whit whispers loudly as I sit beside her, pizza in hand.

"I was going to share the precious *last slice* with you, but now I'm eating it myself."

"Where's Miles?" Whit manages as best she can with a full mouth.

"He got called into work."

I snort, reaching for a napkin. "Tell your brother I think he's full of crap and I'll remember this next time he needs help."

"Isn't our generation supposed to be full of lazy drifters who spend more time traveling to East Asia than actually working? Erik and Miles are a disgrace." Whit shakes her head, grabbing more pizza.

"Well at least we're here, in the middle of the afternoon on a weekday, eating garbage food and accomplishing nothing," Seth points out.

"Too true," I say, holding up a bottle of pop. "But seriously, I need you guys to help put my dresser together."

CHAPTER TWO

I survive my first work week, and the short drive makes the upheaval feel worth it. My first day of week two was made longer by an all-night marking session, leaving me dreaming of my bed. I'm supposed to be in orientation as a high school sub, but my preceptor is basically just using me as a marking assistant. Kelly loaded me down with an overwhelming stack of quizzes yesterday, having totally forgotten about them. She wants them returned to the students tomorrow, so I spent the night getting them done. Also, I may have been sucked into a Netflix binge session that made the whole thing take longer.

Just as I'm snuggling under the covers, my phone rings. I'm surprised to see my mom's picture smiling up at me. It's 8:30 in the morning—not her prime time.

"Mom? Everything okay?"

"Yes. Well, no. I was hoping you could watch Caleb? I forgot it's a PD day and I have a few appointments. You don't work today, right?"

"Oh, I kind of was up all night with work."

"I see." She pauses. "If you can't take him, I'll bring him with me. The waiting areas will have toys, I'm sure."

I picture her going into the doctor's office and leaving Caleb in the waiting room unsupervised. He could easily try to find a park when he gets bored. Who knows what could happen? My worrying mind gets the better of me.

"No, it's fine, of course I'll watch him. Can you bring him here, at least?"

"Can we meet halfway? I don't want to be late."

I shut my eyes, trying not to let frustration seep into my voice. *I'm just tired. I'll be fine.*

On the way to our meeting place, I hit the drive-thru at the nearest coffee shop to get tea and a donut. I have to get through this day somehow, and coffee isn't my thing.

"Seeeeeth" I whine, calling my cousin from the car.

"Whaaaaaat?" Seth laughs.

"Please tell me you have today off and access to a car."

"I'm heading to work now, but only for a few hours. What d'you need?"

"I was up all night, and I have to go get Caleb and watch him for the day."

"What? You do know he isn't your kid, right? Wait, he isn't, is he? I mean, I was only like thirteen when he was born, maybe I missed you getting super pregnant or something?"

I laugh. "No, he isn't mine. I wasn't a teen mom."

"Well, you kind of were… just sayin'."

"Don't trash my Caleb."

"Hey, Caleb is great, but why are you watching him when you should be sleeping?"

"He doesn't have school today; Mom forgot."

"Does your mom own a calendar? She's always calling you last minute to take care of the things that are her responsibility. You can't keep letting her do this, Alex," Seth says, sincere but stern.

I let out a sigh, knowing he's right, but my hands are tied. "I don't do it for my mom. I can't let Caleb suffer because of her irresponsibility."

Seth chuckles. "You're too good to that kid. I do have the car today. I'll drive to your place after work and bring my charming personality. But you owe me."

"Deal! Thank you, Seth. Seriously!"

When I arrive at our meeting place, a gas station definitely closer to my mom than me, I end up waiting twenty minutes for Mom to show up. Luckily, it's a sunny, warm day and the brightness perks me up. I fill my tank and buy a magazine to kill time, not unfamiliar with my mom's disregard for keeping people waiting. The new issue of Canadian Geographic has a wolf on the cover, so I get it for Caleb; he loves wolves. He calls them woofs, and I'm not going to correct that level of adorable.

"It's not my fault! Caleb spilled his juice box, and we had to get him changed," my mom says when she finally arrives. Her tone is flustered—it clearly hasn't been a very good morning for either of them. I open the back-seat door, and Caleb jumps out, hugging my waist; his smile chases away any lingering resentment.

"Don't worry about it. I'm just happy to spend the day with my favorite guy."

"Erik is your favorite guy!" Caleb says with a smile, crinkling his little freckled nose.

"No way, man! I have had way longer to build up love points for you." I tickle his tummy, laughing as he giggles uncontrollably.

He reaches up to take my hand. Mom stays in the car, distracted by her phone.

"Okay, we'll see you later, Mom."

"Hmm?" she mutters idly, finally looking up. "Have fun, baby. Did you get his bag?" She waves a hand towards the back seat. Caleb's overstuffed backpack is sitting on the other side of the car; he must have packed it himself.

I resist the urge to ask if she wants to get out and hug us, moving instead to get the backpack, Caleb's little hand in mine.

"Call me later."

She notices me looking in the passenger side window and jumps, her hand pushing a distinct carton back into her purse.

My heart sinks. "Mom, not again. You said you quit." I try to hide how dejected I feel. Caleb doesn't need more stress.

"I don't know what you're talking about. I have to run, honey," she says, avoiding my gaze.

"You're smoking again."

"Not with Caleb in the car. Don't lecture me," she tsks. "I have to go. Call you later." She rolls up the window and speeds from the lot. Pulling Caleb away from the car, I hold in a curse with clenched teeth.

"Alex, can we get a snack?" Caleb asks after only a few minutes.

"Didn't you just have breakfast?" I'm surprised. Caleb isn't a big eater.

"No, just a juice box. Mom said she was in a hurry and that you would feed me."

I let out a breath, but smile at him in the rearview mirror.

"All the better, I was hoping to check out one of the new breakfast places near my apartment."

Caleb's eyes widen, his smile lighting up his whole face. "Yes!" he squeals, excitedly.

We chat the whole way back to the city, and I pull into the only diner I've seen in my short time here.

I let him order chocolate pancakes and chocolate milk, but I also make him eat a fruit cup; *balance*. His mood is contagious, and I find myself glad to have him with me. As tired as I am, it's exciting to show him my new home.

When we get to my apartment, I open his backpack; it's not full of toys as I'd imagined. His homework folder is tucked along the back, but the main body is filled with a pair of PJs, a change of clothes, and his stuffed turtle. I shake my head at my own ignorance. This is way too well-planned for my mom to have put together last minute. There are even toiletries. She had set this up at least yesterday, clearly intending for him to stay over. I don't mind him spending the night, but the blatant manipulation pisses me off. I should have predicted it; it's her week with Caleb.

When Seth arrives, I direct him to a nearby park. He's over six feet tall, and Caleb looks so small holding his hand as they leave, Caleb skipping in excitement. I wave them off before collapsing into bed, setting my alarm for a couple of hours; left to my own devices, I'd sleep all afternoon.

Before the blaring buzzer sounds, my door slams, startling me awake. I'm disoriented for a minute before Caleb's giggle brings me back.

I furrow my brow, it's only been about 45 minutes.

"Back so soon?" I ask after pulling myself out of bed and stumbling to the living room.

"Seth says the park was a bus."

"Not a bus, a *bust*," Seth corrects with a smile. He meets my eyes with a serious expression and shakes his head.

I open my mouth to question him but think better of it. "Well, I'm glad. I was bored, anyway. Want to play with the new Lego set I got you?"

"Yes!" Caleb jumps before running to the spare room. "A dragon? Awesome!"

"We'll be there in a minute," I call, catching Seth's arm as he tries to walk past me. He looks at me blankly and I raise an eyebrow.

"It was nothing." Seth's eyes dart around the room.

"What happened?"

"I know it sounds crazy… It's probably nothing." Seth tugs on his collar. "While we were at the park, some guy took our picture. Well, it looked like he was taking our picture, maybe he was just snapping shots of the park." His troubled expression tells me he doesn't think this mystery man was taking a picture of the slide.

"Did you say anything to him?"

"I turned to push Caleb on the swing, and when I looked again, he was gone. I'm sure it was nothing, it was just… weird."

I bite my cheek, torn between reassuring Seth and wanting to protect Caleb. Dad had a friend on the police force run a record check of this neighborhood, and there wasn't an issue with predators.

"Like I said, I'm just being overly cautious. Just… be careful if you take Caleb there again."

"I will. Thanks for the heads up."

Seth stays the rest of the day. Even if he won't admit it, I know it's to keep an eye on us. More than once, I catch him peeking through the curtains. I try to make the best of our day, building forts with every blanket I own and making Rice Krispie squares. By late afternoon, I've convinced myself to let the park incident go. It was just a coincidence.

Caleb and I rent a movie and eat popcorn after Seth leaves, snuggling under blankets on my couch. My living room is a total mess of toys and sheets. Hugging Caleb tightly, I sweep his curly brown hair from his forehead. It's getting a bit long and falls into his eyes. I'll have to take him for a trim soon. A consequence of uncivil shared custody: my parents don't negotiate over small stuff like haircuts and new shoes. Those things end up falling to me. Just another reason I can't stop thinking about my plan, the one so big I haven't even told Seth. I'd taken the first steps, getting a job and a place of my own, but would a judge take my request seriously?

With Caleb here, it's so easy to picture this as our life. The spare room would make a perfect bedroom for him. He'd have to switch schools, but he was only in the first grade, so that wouldn't be the worst thing. I had done the same as a kid; he would make new friends. Maybe this really could work.

"Alex!" Caleb yells, and my eyes fly open. I must have nodded off. "You missed the best part! Now we have to watch it again."

"Nice try." I pull him closer, tickling him.

"St-Stop," he finally manages through fits of laughter. I stop tickling him to check my phone. Seven thirty and no missed calls from my mom.

"Hey, keep watching. I'm gonna get more water." In the kitchen, I slide the pocket door closed, dialing Mom's number.

"Honey, having fun with Caleb?"

"Yeah, are you planning to pick him up or what's the deal?"

"Oh, I had a thought! I wondered if you'd like him to sleep over?"

I roll my eyes. *You had a thought, eh?* "Is that why he had PJs in his bag?" I ask before I can catch myself. I'm tired; my filter's a bit broken. "You know he can sleep here. Will you be able to pick him up tomorrow? I have to work in the morning."

"Of course I'll pick him up tomorrow," she says indignantly. "I'll pick him up now if that's what you want."

"No, I'm happy for him to stay. We'll see you tomorrow."

"Okay, honey, if that's what works best for you. Have a good sleep. Kiss Caleb for me. Love you both," she adds before hanging up.

I let out a long breath to relax my clenched stomach, reminding myself I actually *do* want Caleb to stay. Getting him ready for bed is a bit of a challenge; he's so excited to be *"camping in his new room."* I read to him and tuck him in, reminding him I'm right across the hall and promising to leave the nightlight on in the bathroom all night. Caleb is so easy to love, I hate that I can't always be with him. It's weird to have a sibling that I don't spend every day with. Growing up, I'd been so close with Whit; I can't imagine how different our relationship would be if we hadn't had all that time together. I guess it's not the same with Caleb. Whitney and I aren't peers to him; we're so much older. He's basically an only child.

I go to sleep that night imagining this as my life, smiling at the routine I could provide for Caleb if I had custody. As I drift off, I wonder if it's something I should talk to Erik about. No, that's silly. We haven't been dating long enough; no need to talk about that much future stuff. He would probably think it was crazy, anyway.

*****

When I get home from work the next day, I wander to my kitchen, looking for something easy to cook for dinner. I had barely made it to work on time this morning; Mom was predictably late to pick up Caleb, and I'd been playing catch-up all day.

A staff meeting had dragged my stressful day even longer. Technically, I didn't have to go to the meeting. I'm just on orientation, but I desperately want a permanent position with guaranteed income. I worried that could only happen if I made a good impression on everyone. The logical side of my brain reminded me I was being silly. If an opening became available in my department, I'd have a good shot at it. The emotional side told the logical side to shut up and think of something smart that will *wow* the principle.

As I close the fridge, a flashing light on my phone catches my attention. I can't use my phone during classes, so I'm in the habit of leaving it at home. If I had it with me, I'd spend my lunch hours in the safety and comfort of an ebook. Not exactly helpful when you're trying to get to know people.

The blinking notification grates on my nerves: voicemail. I hate voicemail. I've repeatedly told my parents to text me or wait until I call them back. Yet still, they persist with the damn voicemails.

"Hey Alex, it's Dad. I was wondering if you've talked to Seth today? Jack says he doesn't know where he is and I thought you might have some ideas. Give him a call if you do. Hope work went well. Love you."

I furrow my brow. My uncle Jack isn't prone to worry, so it's unlikely he'd call my dad on a whim. I dial Seth's number, hoping to clear this up before my anxiety-prone mind is roused.

"Hey, you've reached Seth. Leave it, and I'll hit you back," his voicemail recites.

Okay, that doesn't mean anything, I insist.

I call my dad to find out what's going on, but it's a waste of time. He knows almost nothing and doesn't sound concerned at all. He picks up on the growing panic in my voice and tries to calm me, reminding me that Seth isn't a little kid anymore and he's probably just out with some friends. He's right in theory, but a bad feeling is nesting in the pit of my stomach.

Dialing my uncle's number, I try to ignore the tremble making its way to my hands.

"What's up, cuzo?" Miles, Seth's older brother, asks.

"What's going on with Seth?" I ask, not in the mood for pleasantries.

He pauses for a second. "He just left, I guess?" The distinct sounds of a video game explain his flat tone.

"What do you mean *he just left*?" I close my eyes, trying not to let frustration and panic show in my voice.

"He left a note, well an email I guess. He went to Europe."

"Europe?" My eyes shoot open. I didn't see that one coming.

"He's always wanted to go," Miles says, as if we're having a complete conversation and he isn't just spitting random bits of information at me.

"Wait, he sent you an email saying 'Hi, off to Europe' and your response is 'Okay, that sounds about right'?"

"I'm not his keeper. What d'you want from me? He's a big boy."

"Miles, pause your stupid game and talk to me!"

He sighs, but the rapid-fire machine gun and dubstep go silent. "So you're telling me that Seth went off to Europe out of the blue? That's not like him," I insist. That's not like most people. I mean sure, he's nineteen, but he's more responsible than this. The story isn't adding up. Unfortunately, as I'm now experiencing, Miles isn't the co-detective I need.

"I just saw Seth yesterday, and he didn't mention anything about this. He wouldn't just take off like that without talking to me, or at least someone," I say, in a final attempt to arouse suspicion in Miles. "Read the email to me."

"Lexie, let it go. He went on vacation. Good for him. He has wanted to go to Europe for years. Look, I just forwarded you the email so you can obsess over it some more." Miles chuckles. "You are so stubborn, hon, and too suspicious. I'm sure he's fine. I'll let you know if he emails me again."

I squint my eyes, irritation rising at Miles' use of *hon*. He's only a year older than me. "Put your dad on the phone."

"He's out for a walk with Mom."

I bite the inside of my cheek, wishing I had someone to share in my panic. Miles' condescending sigh on the other end of the phone makes my heart sink.

"You need to chill, have a drink or something. I'm sure he's fine. You aren't his mother."

"Yeah you're probably right," I lie. "Let me know if he emails or calls."

"Will do, cuzo, have a good night. Get that drink."

I hurry to the living room, turning on my irritatingly slow computer. It's unlikely I'm going to get any more clues from Seth's e-mail, but I have to read it for myself anyway. Miles is right about one thing: I'm obsessive. But come on, this situation is weird! On top of the fact that it's totally out of character for Seth to just take off, I also can't shake the bad feeling now deeply rooted in my gut. I hate that I already doubt myself, with Dad and Miles taking this so lightly.

It takes five password attempts before I get it right; my hands are shaking. My nerves twitch, like electric shocks are surging through me.

> Miles,
> I went to Europe for a while.
> Tell mom and dad. See ya later.
> - Seth

See ya later? Seth definitely didn't write this message. And who writes an email like this anyway? It's ridiculous. Something else is going on, but what? And how is Miles buying this?

Yelling in frustration, I get to my feet to pace my small living room. I call Seth again out of desperation, annoyed but not surprised when he doesn't answer. I try to come up with any plan that doesn't involve wearing a hole in my laminate floors. Turning to my phone, I call the first person who comes to mind.

"Erik, I need your help," I say frantically when he answers.

"You sound stressed. What's going on, baby?"

I tell him everything I know about my cousin's impromptu Euro-trip. "I just have a bad feeling about this."

He pauses for a little too long; my throat tightens as my small light of hope is extinguished. "You think I'm crazy."

"No, honey, not crazy. You care about your cousin, I get that. I just think..."

"I'm over-reacting?" I finish for him, crumpling onto my couch.

"He's young. He's had that job a while, probably been saving his cash. You said yourself that Seth has always wanted to go to Europe. I know you're worried, but baby, I think you shouldn't stress over this. He left an email, so it wasn't totally irresponsible."

I frown. *Not totally irresponsible?* "Maybe you're right," I lie for the second time tonight. Maybe Erik is right, but unfortunately for him and Miles, my crazy isn't that easily dissuaded.

"I'm sure I am." I hear Erik's smile as he speaks. "Have you talked to Whitney?"

"No, She's out of town for a couple days. Why?"

"I know how close you all are. Just thought she might have heard from Seth. I'm glad you called me, though. You know you can call anytime. Do you want me to come over?"

"No, no, I'm fine. You're right," I say lightly, putting my high school acting classes to use. "I have to work in the morning...oh, and so do you!" I cringe; Erik is super protective of his work nights since getting his new job. "I'm so sorry. You probably need to get to sleep."

"Don't worry about it, baby. Are you sure you're okay? I'm just returning some emails, but I can finish them later, come to your place right now."

"No, really, I'm just going to take a bath and go to bed."

Erik yawns. "Okay, if you're sure. I'll call you in the morning before work."

"Okay, yeah, okay." My mind is racing. I have a hard time keeping my composure. "I'll talk to you tomorrow."

I spend the next several hours lost in a haze, dissecting the email and replaying my conversations with my dad, Miles, and Erik in a loop. The more I do, the crazier I feel. Like Miles, Erik had taken the practical perspective, content to believe the email. Maybe I'm on my own, then? I just need a plan. A plan, and possibly some sleep.

I finally abandon my pacing and go to bed a couple of hours later, still without any rational ideas and having neglected to eat dinner. I try to reason with myself. Dad said Uncle Jack had called him in hysterics. I assume that the "in hysterics" part was an exaggeration, but Uncle Jack was worried. Seth never missed dinner without calling. He had never missed work, even when sick. Am I really being irrational in thinking something is wrong? Isn't the evidence supporting my theory?

I sigh, rolling over for the hundredth time, unable to find a position comfortable enough to soothe my pounding head. If I am right, why doesn't anyone else see it? And, more importantly, where is Seth? I remind myself that he's a smart guy, strong and clever. He can take care of himself. The weight in my stomach doesn't ease as I close my eyes, uselessly trying to shut out my thoughts.

CHAPTER THREE

At work the next day, I can't concentrate; I'm thankful, for once, that I'm still in orientation. Not only am I tired, but my emotional distraction seems to show. Kelly actually sends me home early, promising it's our secret.

"Alex, you are working so hard here, marking a ton and organizing everything. Those color-coded files you made me? They're brilliant! But starting a new job is right stressful. Plus, you just moved! That's a lot to be getting on with. Take a duvet day, and you can start fresh Monday," she says in her pleasant English accent.

I return her smile, barely holding in a humorless laugh. Her reasons would have been overwhelming enough, yet they seem like a vacation compared to my actual stressors. I thank her and hurry to my car, hoping the principal doesn't see me bagging off early, but in this moment, I'm too relieved to care.

I'm dead tired, but have no intention of going home. I use my newfound free time to take a road trip. My cousins live in Burlington, only about 45 minutes from my apartment. I have to check out their place, fully acknowledging I've passed obsessive levels of worry.

My uncle answers the door in a pair of sweatpants and a housecoat. "Lexie? What're you doing here?" he asks, surprise shifting to a smile. My uncle is such a soft e. He always wanted a daughter. He treats his sons like kings, but as his only nieces, Whit and I hold a special place in his heart.

"Hey, sorry, did I wake you?" I ask, the answer obvious by the crease marks on his face.

"No, of course not. I was just watching TV," he lies. "Come on in. I'll make us some tea." My dad's side of the family is British; tea is their answer to everything.

I follow my uncle through the foyer and into the kitchen, sitting at the counter as he fills the kettle. His home has always been the most comfortable place, with its soft butter yellow shag carpet and dependably-warm temperature. In the winter, it's made warmer still with the smell of cookies baking and an ever-present pot of soup on the stove. Aunt Cindy would sometimes tease Uncle Jack about the tattered furniture and outdated kitchen, but it seemed more a running joke than true annoyance. If she really wanted something changed, she'd only have to ask. My uncle would never refuse her anything.

"Aunt Cindy at work?" I ask as Uncle Jack pulls milk from the fridge.

"No, we didn't get much sleep last night; I suggested she take the day off. She's out walking the dogs," he says with a tight smile. "So, what brings you by? Settling in okay in Markham?"

"Yeah, I just... I wanted to see how you were doing, you know, about Seth?" I watch him closely.

"Oh, that. I'm sorry if I scared you with the panicked phone call. I don't check my email, well, you know, very often. I was just calling everyone I could think of to hunt him down. Your dad always helps me think through these situations, so he was top of my list. Though, I guess I didn't actually call you." My uncle looks up, finally meeting my eyes.

"My dad did. He asked if Seth had come by my place."

"Right, he was helping me call people. Anyway, when Miles got home and checked his email, he saw that Seth had left word." Uncle Jack shakes his head. "It's funny how out of control you can get when you assume the worst." Tea spills to the counters as he pours with trembling hands.

My dad has always been very much the older brother, the leader between him and my uncle. Still, I can't believe Uncle Jack is passive enough to swallow this story.

"So, the last time you saw Seth was when he came home from my house yesterday?"

"Yes. Well, I didn't see him get home, but he probably just got in late."

"He left my place really early."

Uncle Jack just lets out a sigh, staring at his tea.

"You really think he just went off to Europe?" I ask, trying to elicit a reaction to get a sense of his true feelings.

He smiles sympathetically, but the smile doesn't reach his eyes. "I didn't believe it at first either, but after I thought it through I realized that it really was the most likely explanation. He has wanted to go to Europe for a while, and I guess he had some money saved. I was a bit surprised that you weren't gone too, though."

My uncle's words combined with his intense look send a shiver down my spine. I stare at him, trying to decode the message he seems to be sending. It's like having a word on the tip of your tongue; I just can't quite grasp it.

"I mean," he continues, expression softening as he looks down at his tea, "I thought you two would go together. You had been talking about it this past summer at the cottage. I guess you just couldn't get the time off work?"

My eyes widen. In all my stress and confusion, I'd forgotten that Seth and I made plans to do Europe together. He would act as my bodyguard, and I would make sure that he didn't get himself in too much trouble. We had been joking about it and planning the last couple summers. This solidifies my suspicion; if I'd been seeking more proof, I found it. Seth didn't go to Europe on a whim. He and I are too close. He would never plan a trip to Europe, however short notice, without inviting me. It's against our unwritten code. I knew about his first kiss, he knew about the first boy who broke my heart, I knew about his first time getting drunk, he knew when I learned to forge my mom's signature and started ditching school. I talked him out of a tattoo, he'd talked me out of a bad haircut. It's what we do; our system.

I'm now more certain than ever that Seth is not on his dream vacation. The realization, however momentarily gratifying, leaves me nauseous.

I make a point of leaving before Miles gets home, not wanting to deal with his condescending remarks. Before I leave, I go to my cousin's room, telling Uncle Jack I'm using the washroom. When I open his door, it's the usual organized chaos that drives Aunt Cindy crazy. I don't even know what I'm looking for, but I certainly don't find it.

I flush the toilet for good measure before heading back downstairs; I'm nothing if not thorough in my façade.

When I'm getting ready to leave, I hug my uncle. This is my next clue that something's up. He grips me just a little too tight for a little too long. As I pull away, his glistening eyes search mine for a long moment, looking conflicted.

"Take care of yourself, kid," he says finally, turning back into the house and leaving me alone on the porch.

This last picture of my uncle clings to my mind as I drive home. He knows something. I'd wager my car he has a better idea than he's letting on about what's going on with Seth. And what's worse, he isn't going to tell me what he knows. Unless... he was trying to tell me something when he brought up my absence on Seth's trip to Europe. But why would he be so convoluted and not just come right out and say it? Is he being watched?

I shake my head, an embarrassed laugh escaping as I open my window for some fresh air. I'm letting paranoia run away with me. I had almost convinced myself a random black SUV was following me. Clearly I need sleep, but I still think Uncle Jack is hiding something.

If he isn't going to talk, can I get Aunt Cindy to spill? It's tempting. She might have more information, but the thought of getting between my uncle and aunt leaves a bad taste in my mouth. They've been nothing but loving towards me, and if Cindy thinks Seth is missing, she's probably even more of a mess than I am. I might make it worse by involving her. I begrudgingly put the idea of approaching her on the back burner. I trust that if she can fix it, she will. I'll give it some time, but if I don't have a plan in a week, I'm doing what I have to do. *Let's be real, five days tops.*

Three long days pass; I keep my body busy organizing and cleaning my apartment, but my mind is no closer to sorting things out in regards to Seth. I can't accept that he left for Europe on a whim. No one else shares my concern. Whitney's too absorbed in the news that Sam got a fancy new job, and they *finally* get to move out of their "crappy" apartment, the one that makes mine look like a hovel. She's obsessed with real estate, going to a new showing every day, frustrated that she isn't finding her dream home the instant she's ready to buy.

Dad remains no more helpful than Whitney and Miles. He's a firm believer in Occam's razor: the simplest explanation is most likely the correct one. He is convinced that my uncle was destined to raise a kid irresponsible enough to leave for Europe out of the blue.

With Erik, I keep the subject of Seth's disappearance to a minimum, not bringing it up unless he does. I'd complain that he hasn't texted me any pictures, or called to let me know how much fun he's having. I would wonder aloud what sites he's seen, or which countries he's visited. I'm not sure if Erik is buying my act of being unconcerned; I suspect he isn't. He's changed his rule about no work night hangouts, instead coming to my place every evening. He insists it's because things have calmed down at his work. I worry it's actually because he senses I'm losing it. Erik made it clear he doesn't share my suspicions about Seth, but it's a lot harder to hide my strain with him around all the time. I don't want him to think I'm a lunatic, although I am beginning to feel like one.

I've become majorly sleep deprived, feeling like a zombie most of the time. When I do sleep, I'm tormented by bad dreams. I wake up covered in sweat and shaking, but I can rarely remember what caused the fear. There's only one dream I remember. In it, I'm in my grandmother's garden. She sits with me on her big wooden swing. My grandmother died when I was twelve, but in my dream, I'm an adult. She reminds me that a woman's intuition is a special gift and it needs to be nurtured and respected. Then she looks into my eyes with intense scrutiny, opening her mouth to say something. Before she can speak, a shadow pours over us. She gasps, face turning pale, wide eyes looking just past my shoulder. I turn around, my body rigid with fear, before waking up. It felt so real, I had tears in my eyes as I sat up in bed. I chalked it up to my mind trying to release the stress I'm feeling about Seth and the frustration of no one believing me.

*****

"Hey, you okay?" Erik squeezes my hand. He'd brought over dinner from my favorite restaurant, something he used to do all the time before we moved. Maybe things really were just settling at his work. Maybe he really isn't hovering because he thinks I'm unraveling. Maybe Erik just wants to spend time with me.

We're sitting on my couch watching a movie, although I'm not really paying attention, my mind stuck on Seth.

I turn to him with a smile. "Yeah, fine, just tired. Haven't been sleeping well lately." *Crap!* "I mean, y'know how it is, moving and my new job. Just stressful trying to learn everything in such a short orientation."

I shift my attention to the movie: some romantic comedy that he obviously picked for me. His gaze stays trained on me. Reluctantly I meet his gaze, concern etched on his beautiful face. *Busted.*

"Alex, what's really bothering you?"

"What do you mean?" I bluff, putting on my doe eyes.

"Seriously, you've been off all week. Ever since…wait. Are you still worried about Seth?" he guesses, eyes narrowing in suspicion.

The direct question catches me off guard, and I pause for a second too long. He takes my hands in his and sighs, looking at me with a small smile. "Honey, I thought we talked about this. Seth is fine, I'm sure of it. You can't let yourself get so worked up about these things," he says soothingly.

I want to cry, but I hold back. "I know he's fine." An idea comes to me. "It's... no, it's silly." I shift on the couch, leaning my cheek against Erik's firm chest.

"Your feelings aren't silly," he says, rubbing my back.

"It's just... Seth and I were planning to do Europe together..." I trail off, hoping my true sadness will add sincerity.

His hand pauses for a second while rubbing my back. "Oh." *Nailed it!*

"I know. See, I told you it was silly!"

"Oh baby, no I just thought... well, it doesn't matter. I'm sorry Seth bailed on you for Europe."

Hook, line, and sinker. I smile inwardly. I don't like lying, but I've learned to follow my gut when navigating unknown waters. Okay, maybe I like getting away with a lie a little bit.

"Yeah, you're right, just bummed." I pull away from his chest, letting a weak smile play on my lips.

"Hey, I have an idea. Why don't we go to Europe together?"

"What?" is all I can manage. My elation from my minor deceit evaporates as I try to regain my footing.

"It'll be fun. I have family we can visit. We could use the vacation." His tone is casual, though his eyes polar his easy words, scrutinizing me. I try to figure out where this is coming from. It's like I've slipped into an entirely different game with no concept of the rules.

"Since when do you want to go to Europe? I thought you had no vacation time."

"I'll find a way to make it a work trip. We have offices in London and Prague."

"Erik, I don't have the savings for that. I just moved, and I have less than no vacation time."

"You're a substitute teacher." Erik scoffs, head tilting to the side as a small smile forms.

I look at him, my mouth literally hanging open, any attempts to decipher his motivations abandoned.

"Excuse me? What is that supposed to mean?"

He shakes his head. "I didn't mean anything. Just that, come on, you know, you can get time off whenever you want. They aren't exactly going to miss you."

My eyes narrow, but he continues before I can respond.

"That sounded bad; I didn't mean it like that. Just that you have the chance to get away now, before you get busier."

Seething and embarrassed, my cheeks burn, and my eyes sting with oncoming tears. I wrap my arms around myself, trying to hold in the rage that wants to lash out.

"You should go," I finally whisper, turning away from him. His warm hand rests on my shoulder, but I stand up to shake it off.

"I'm sorry if I offended you. Forget about Europe, it's fine," he says quietly.

I shake my head, not turning to face him as I scramble for an excuse to be alone. "No, I just... I have to get up early. Lost track of time."

Silence presses into my ears for a minute before the door creaks open. "Goodnight, Alex. Call me tomorrow."

I close my bedroom door, desperate for space and isolation. As I pull a pillow to my chest, tears pour down my cheeks, the weight of the past week finally squeezing out the fear and confusion I was forced to mask. My throat stings as sobs force their way from my body. How did my boyfriend inviting me to Europe turn into this?

Lying in bed a couple hours later, my face streaked with dried tears and unable to sleep, guilt seeps through me as I replay the fight with Erik. Maybe I'm being ridiculous. Why did I get so upset over him inviting me on a trip I wanted to go on? It was sweet of him to try and cheer me up with such a grand gesture. He knew I was upset and was just trying to fix it. It's not his fault I entered into the conversation full of anxiety.

Something in the back of my mind nags at me, but I brush it off. Erik is great. A trip to Europe is a wonderful idea. I'd been over-sensitive. I should've explained what I'm actually feeling about Seth; maybe his support is just what I need. If I present the evidence to him, he might side with me, maybe even help. I haven't given him a chance since the night Seth went missing, and I've learned more since then.

It's after midnight and Erik has to work in the morning; this probably isn't the best time to call with my conspiracy theory. That won't exactly portray the picture of sanity I'm going for. Instead, I text him:

> *Hey Erik, call me when you get a minute tomorrow. Just want to talk. Sorry about earlier, I was being weird <3 Alex*

Guilt appeased, I roll over and shut my eyes. I have my performance review first thing tomorrow with the school principal. Like I need another stressor to keep me awake.

THE SECRETS THEY KEEP

*****

I'm ripped from sleep, my room still pitch black. *What was that?* I peer at my too bright clock, totally disoriented. 2:36. In the morning?

BANG!

I jump as I instinctively turn to my window, a shadow visible just beyond the curtain. Someone is out there.

My heart pounds and I gulp for air; my body trembling from the shock of being torn from sleep so suddenly.

I'm completely paralyzed, trapped as the figure crouches, my window pane shaking as the shadow works to pry it open.

CHAPTER FOUR

Frozen and trying to catch my breath, I stare transfixed at my curtained window. Gravel crunches as the figure shifts into a deeper crouch. My mind orders my legs to run, but they refuse; I can't pry my eyes away.

A fist pounding on the glass shakes the window forcibly.

My heart pounds erratically. Before I can scream, the shadow speaks.

"Lex! Open up, quickly! We don't have much time."

Freed, I jump to my feet, recognizing the voice immediately. Running to the window, I throw it open, immensely grateful I live on the ground floor.

"Seth!" I yell, my voice hoarse from sleep.

He slides through the window and pulls me into a one-armed hug, covering my mouth with the other hand.

"Shhh, we need to hurry. A black SUV is idling out front... I'm sure it's them," he whispers into my ear.

"What?" I ask, but it's muffled by his hand.

"Whisper, Alex, they *can't* know I got to you first."

I nod, and he releases me. "Wait, who? Who can't know?"

"I haven't been in Europe." He pauses, shifting to look out the window. "Not yet, anyway."

"I know! I mean, I knew it. I've been going crazy worrying about you." I punch his arm. "Where have you been?"

"Ouch." He flashes a smile, the smallest glimpse of the Seth I know before his expression hardens. The moonlight casts harsh white light on his tightly clenched jaw. "It isn't my fault. They took me, and I've been trying to escape."

"What? Who? Who took you? Wait, who's out front?" My heart starts racing again, my head pounding. The relief of seeing Seth quickly dissipates in the awareness of danger. *What the hell is going on?*

"We don't have time, we have to get out of here. Now! Grab your shoes."

I stare at him, mind blank.

"Alex, shoes, now!"

I follow his direction, unable to process anything else. Hurrying through my living room to the door, I blindly grope for my shoes. My apartment is nearly pitch black— only a small stream of light seeps under my door from the building's hallway.

I swear under my breath and flick on the lamp. It swings precariously in my haste. Through the dancing light, I grab my shoes, risking Seth's wrath by stopping to pull a sweatshirt off the back of my couch before scrambling back to my room. Seth's intense gaze is trained on the window. His fists are clenched as tightly as his jaw, and he only spares me a brief glance as I clumsily pull on my shoes.

"Was hoping for more time," he mutters, sounding more like he's talking to himself than me. It's just as well; I have no idea what he means.

"Are you gonna tell me what's going on?" I ask again, tugging my sweatshirt on over my pajamas. *I don't think Seth's willing to wait long enough for me to change,* I lament.

"We need to run. Now. I'll explain later, just trust me."

I search his eyes, trying to get a sense of what he's thinking. All I see is fear, and it's enough to kick me into action. "Lead the way."

He nods, satisfied, and jumps smoothly out the window. Snatching my phone off the bedside table, I move to follow. I'm markedly less graceful as I try to pull my shorter frame over the metal ridges of the sill. Seth reaches in with both arms, grabbing my waist to help me through.

When I'm finally free, he presses against the rough brick of the building, still as a statue. The moon illuminates his tense frame. My brain is screaming for answers, but I stay silent, trusting Seth knows what he's doing.

After a few anxious breaths, Seth reaches down, taking my hand and pulling me towards the forest behind my building. The whole neighborhood is asleep, and our footsteps pierce the silence as they crunch dried leaves and sticks. Scents of bitter pine and sweet decaying leaves fill the air; our breath comes out in white puffs, shimmering in the moonlight.

Seth pulls me deeper into the canopy of trees until the sky isn't visible, the moon no longer lighting our path. The firm ground gives way to thick mud, slowing our progress. Feeling our way around ancient trees as we move in the darkness, he finally stops, tugging me to crouch in a small ravine. I grip onto a small trunk to keep my balance, legs trembling. The forest seems unnaturally silent as I strain to hear any sounds of danger. *Is it normal for these woods to be so quiet at night?*

"I think they're coming for you. They had a tracker on the email they wrote to my family from my account. Overheard them saying Miles forwarded it to you. Then I heard them mention your name a few more times. Knew I had to warn you. I was hoping for more time." Seth whispers, like he's been having a conversation in his head this whole time and finally invited me in.

"You're not making any sense. Who's coming?" My whole body is shivering, but I suspect it has less to do with the chill and a lot more to do with the adrenaline surging through my veins, making my heart race. I can barely make out Seth's eyes as he stares at me. He's so close I can feel his warm arm pressed against mine.

"I don't know. They won't tell me anything. I just pick up bits and pieces from their conversations. Has to be something to do with our dads. I don't know why it's me, not Miles. They know about him, but took me instead."

I let out a shaking breath. "We need to phone the police."

"No!" he hisses, grabbing the phone I pull from my pocket and throwing it deeper into the woods.

"Seth!"

"The police can't help us! You have no idea the reach... Listen, we just have to get away from here. They don't know about Caleb and Whit, or at least they didn't mention them. If we can hide you, maybe we can hide them-" Seth tenses beside me, the eerie forest stillness broken by a single cough.

Gripping my hand, he slowly pulls me to my feet. We take quiet steps deeper into the forest, away from the sound.

Seth swears. "We need to split up." He covers my mouth before I can protest. "I don't want to either, but if we separate ourselves, we separate them. It's our best shot at getting away and warning the others." Seth sounds so certain, I can't bring myself to argue.

I nod against his hand, even though I'm not entirely sure what he's talking about.

"Go further south. I'll go west. Be safe," he breathes before pushing me deeper into the thickening brush.

Stumbling a few steps, anxiety floods me anew. I turn quickly, but Seth has already vanished into the oppressive blackness. *Should've stayed with him,* I scold myself. The forest feels unbearably dark without him. Gritting my teeth, I focus on taking slow steps and reach blindly with trembling hands for a tree to help steady me. My legs tense to run, but I suppress the urge; running into a tree would be just my luck.

Loud pounding floods my ears, and I spin on the spot before realizing it's my own pulse. I imagine I wouldn't be able to hear my pursuer even if they were right behind me.

Turning again at the thought, light ignites the forest floor. Too close. My throat burns with a trapped scream. Backing away, I finally find a large tree to guide me. My hand slides around the trunk, moving swiftly. Squinting, I try to force my eyes to see something in the blackness. All I can make out is the outline of trees with no depth perception to help guide me to them.

Footsteps crunch in the distance and my pulse quickens. Darting forward, arms outstretched, I search for another tree. My feet start moving faster. Too fast. I try to force them to slow, but panic is taking over. I breathe heavily, heart racing, eyes blindly searching.

My hands connect with another large tree and feel their way around the rough bark.

Sickeningly, my foot drops through air where ground should be, propelling me forward into the blackness.

My arms fly forward to brace my fall as I land painfully on the root-filled ground. I groan, trying to sit up. The blackness is so consuming, I'm completely disoriented.

Heavy footfalls vibrate through the dirt, and before I can move, blinding light stings my wide eyes. I snap them shut, pulling my hands to my face and letting out a scream.

Hands grab me, pulling me to my feet, covering my mouth, squeezing my wrists, encircling my waist.

I try to scream again, but it comes out infuriatingly muffled.

"Relax," a quiet male voice coos in my ear. He's so close I feel his breath on my neck. "I'm not going to hurt you, just relax, Alexandra."

I stiffen at the sound of my name before kicking wildly. It's useless. I can hardly move anything, my ankles now bound together and the hold on my wrists tightens painfully. Darkness presses in and my eyes strain to find light. I try to scream, even though a hand is pressed firmly over my mouth; the logic side of my brain isn't exactly *driving*.

A strong arm wraps around my waist, pulling my back against a firm chest. Kicking both legs as my feet are lifted from the ground, I finally make contact with the man holding me. He lets out a grunt but doesn't loosen his grip. I take rapid panicked breaths as I wriggle, trying desperately to think.

A gasp escapes my lips as my body is thrown, landing on something soft. As soon as I move, I fall further onto a hard surface. The distinct sound of car doors slamming cuts the silence and I'm thrown back as the vehicle accelerates, my head smashing onto something hard.

I blink trying to clear my vision, but I'm still surrounded by oppressive blackness.

Hearing myself groan, I realize my mouth is no longer covered. I scream with all my strength before being pulled roughly from the hard surface and thrust into a seated position.

Light floods my world as something dark is pulled from my head. I blink hastily, taking in the lit interior of the vehicle.

"Enough with the screaming; no one can hear you anyway and I've already had a long night," a male voice says flatly.

My vision finally clears. I'm in the back row of what appears to be an SUV. An Asian man with jelled black hair sits in the bench ahead of mine, eyes locked on me. Beside him is another man, who turns away as I meet his shockingly teal eyes.

"Wh-who the hell are you?" I demand, shifting my attention from Teal-Eyes to the man still watching me. Hair clings to my face. Reaching to brush it from my eyes, I find my wrists heavily bound with duct tape. I take a deep breath to hold off a panic spiral that's threatening to overtake me.

"Name's Scott," the man finally says with a smirk after watching me take in my equally bound ankles.

"Okay, *Scott*, what am I doing here?" I ask, shock shifting to anger.

"Oh, apologies. I seem to have given you the impression you're in a position to ask questions. My mistake." His cocky smile makes my palms itch to punch him. My quick temper is always worse when I'm tired, and this situation is more than a little rage-inducing.

"I'll be honest with you, Alexandra. We came on a bit of a whim. The intel that you are gifted is spotty at best, but your lineage is impressive enough to give you a chance. My question is, how did you know we were coming for you tonight? You can't have been more than a few minutes ahead of us. What tipped you off?"

I stare at him. My breath is still heavy as I clench my teeth, forcing myself to stay quiet.

His smile only widens. "Fair enough. We all have our secrets. Either way, you've earned the pleasure of joining us on a little trip."

"Really, sounds lovely. Where are we headed?" I ask, voice dripping with as much sarcasm as I can muster.

"You'll find out in due course." He matches my sarcastic pleasantries. "Whether or not we do this the easy way is up to you. Cooperate and we'll have no need to involve anyone else in this, like your siblings." He's fishing for a reaction; I know this tactic. My dad used this on my sister and I growing up. His father was a detective, and the skill of interrogation had worn off on him.

I keep my face blank, focusing on my breathing. I so badly want to snap back at him, but I clench my teeth. He who speaks first loses.

He studies me carefully before continuing. "Which I'm sure your brother would appreciate." Again, I keep my face blank. He presses on. "Well, that's what was said to Seth. For you, I suppose I should say... your sister."

At the sound of Seth's name, a pang of rage shoots through my chest. Instead of breaking me, I use it to fuel my focus. I have to protect the family I still can. Seth was right: he doesn't know about Whitney and Caleb, and I need to keep it that way. He scrutinizes my face, eyes darting, searching for a tell.

I give him nothing.

I start to doubt my success until his eyes squint and his mouth purses in dissatisfaction, a look I rather enjoy seeing on his smug face.

"Drew, hand me that box, will you?" he says quietly to Teal-Eyes.

I can't help but watch curiously as *Drew* shifts his gaze to me briefly before reaching into the front passenger seat, pulling back a white box. It isn't particularly foreboding, reminding me of the kind of box you see in movies when people get fired and are told to *'clean out their desks.'*

As Drew leans back in his seat, I get a better glimpse of his face, realizing with some surprise that he's young, about my age, with smooth chestnut brown skin and dark curly hair.

"My associate took a tour of your apartment. I hope you don't mind—he borrowed a few…keepsakes." Scott pulls out a yearbook.

"I know your cousins didn't go to your high school, any other Chambers' in here?" he asks, eyeing me with his ever-intense stare.

I look at him, expression blank, and raise an eyebrow, saying nothing. On the inside, my stomach does a somersault.

He flips to the index, taking his eyes off me to scan the long list of students' names. "Hmm, I guess not." He opens two other yearbooks to confirm. "Surprising. I always thought Mark would have tried for a son." His eyes linger on mine, and I let out a breath as he turns to set the yearbooks down.

Whitney and I are only three years apart, but we'd gone to different high schools. Whitney was really into sports and had gone to a private school, full scholarship. I was not so athletically inclined, except in dance and gymnastics. Our local high school had a strong dance program, so that was good enough for me. *Lucky break*, I realize, struggling to keep my emotions in check.

"I guess you're out of luck. You can just drop me off here," I say casually, nodding towards the door. I can't see anything outside with the bright interior lights reflecting off the heavy window tint.

Scott lets out a bark of laughter, looking up from the photo album he's flipping through. I recognize it as one from my school trip to Ottawa. Hope he likes antique airplanes and political landmarks. "Didn't I tell you this mission would be fun, Drew? This one's gonna be a laugh."

Drew doesn't react to Scott's comment, focusing on a photo album of my high school friends.

"When the other team took Seth, they had Miles to dangle over his head, so that did help him cooperate," Scott says, recapturing my attention.

Glaring at him, a tingling numbness spreads down my fingers as I pull uselessly on my binds. "Don't even say Seth's name," I spit, unable to stop the words from escaping, all of my self-control spent.

He laughs again. "You *are* feisty."

"Scott, we're going to be hitting construction soon. Might be prudent to..." the man driving the car interjects.

Scott sighs. "As fun as this has been, we'll have to continue our discussion later." Turning around, he retrieves a small black pouch that I don't recognize. He slides it open, pulling out a syringe.

I gasp, unable to mask my fear this time. "No," I plead, pushing my bound feet against the floor to scoot as far back as the seat will allow.

"See, I wish I could trust you, but I get the sense you're a troublemaker. I'm not willing to gamble against it. This'll help you cooperate."

I jerk forward as the car pulls to an abrupt stop, smashing into Scott and Drew's bench. Drew grabs my shoulders, pinning me against the upholstery. I drop, my knees hitting the floorboard as my shoulders slip from his grasp. Twisting onto my back, I kick my tightly-bound feet in the air, connecting with Scott's shoulder.

Drew jumps over the seat-back to land on my seat and pulls me up by the shoulders in one fluid motion. I let out a frustrated growl as he pins me against his chest, his arms encircling mine. I try to kick off the floorboard again, but he's holding me firm.

"Get your hands off me!" Tears distort my vision as claustrophobia reignites my panic. I hungrily gasp for breath that can't satiate my frantic demand. My lungs burn in desperation.

"Scott, hurry," Drew grunts as Scott climbs to sit on the bench beside us.

"There's that feist, maybe this trip wasn't a waste after all," Scott says in my ear as a sharp pain shoots through my shoulder.

Tears cool my cheeks, washing my vision away with them. Despite my panic, my body relaxes into the collapsing darkness.

CHAPTER FIVE

Awareness slowly trickles through me. My cheek rests on something warm and soft, eyes heavy as sleep beckons seductively. I try to remember how I got here, but before I can untangle my dreams from reality, a voice interrupts my struggle.

"She hasn't moved in over an hour. Maybe you shouldn't have given her that extra dose before the border. You sure she's okay?"

I try to take a deep breath to clear my head, but sleep is tugging me further away from consciousness. *Is this a dream?*

"Relax, Drew. She was starting to move; I had to be sure she would cooperate. Based on her family reputation alone, she would have found a way to alert border control. I'll admit, I may have overdone it a bit, but I'm sure she'll be up soon."

I'm paralyzed with exhaustion, too tired for panic to take root. I strain to focus on what the men are saying, but

I'm distracted by a gentle bumping sensation under me. *Am I in a car?* A loud chime pulls me closer to the surface.

"Damn, we're going to have to drive all the way to plan C. Damian upgraded to top clearance only, which is a major pain in my ass."

"Be grateful we weren't assigned to the other target. Frane's having a hell of a time with him."

"I wouldn't underestimate this one just yet."

My limbs tingle gently as feeling and movement return. I scratch my arm reflexively. *Why does my shoulder hurt? That voice, I've heard it somewhere.* My thoughts are slippery, gliding away without a trace, leaving me blissfully disoriented. It doesn't last long. Consciousness solidifies and memory rolls through me.

Gasping, I shoot up in my seat. Seth, the forest, men grabbing me. The flashbacks are so gripping that I can't take in my surroundings. I draw a desperate breath as a wave of nausea overtakes me.

"See, she's fine," says the voice I begrudgingly recognize as Scott's.

Before I can process my current dilemma, the nausea intensifies, and I turn my head just in time to avoid covering myself in bile.

"Oh yeah, she's totally fine," the other voice responds.

Drew, I remember.

Vision blurry, I reach for the back of the seat in front of mine but fall short. Hands grip my shoulders, preventing my sprawling descent. I'm pressed back onto the soft pillow. Closing my eyes, I take a few deep breaths as vertigo slowly passes. I try to remember what was being said in the car as I was waking, but it's fading away like a dream. The tighter I cling, the quicker it evaporates.

"James, pull over at the next gas station," Scott says. I'm feeling too sick to snap at his irritated tone.

Opening my eyes, I blink against the relative brightness. It's clearly daytime now; a low sun filters through the left side of the vehicle despite heavy tint on the windows.

I sit up slowly, trying to block out the sickening scent of vomit that fills the air. Running a hand through my hair, I catch sight of my red wrists. I draw them closer to my eyes. Lines cut through the raw skin, reminding me they were bound tightly in tape before I lost consciousness. I flex my fingers into fists, looking around the tan interior of the three-row vehicle, trying to distract from my rising sense of confinement. I'm in the far back still, a pillow on the seat next to me. *Oh, look how much they care about my comfort*, I muse sarcastically. My inspection is stalled when I meet Drew's nervous eyes watching me from the bench ahead. His forehead wrinkles in a frown, dark eyebrows almost pulling together. His green-blue eyes widen as our gazes meet and he forces a neutral expression, quickly turning around without a word.

Scott, on the other hand, is unabashed about being caught staring.

"Where are we?"

Scott shakes his head. "Never you mind that; just focus on not puking in my car again."

I glare, shifting my attention to the driver who I'd ignored until now, distracted with more pressing concerns. All I can make out is the side silhouette of a man with short brown hair. In the rearview mirror, a pair of brown eyes scan the road. The distinct sound of a turning signal ticking breaks the renewed silence. I follow Scott's gaze—we're pulling into a service center.

"Drive over to the vacuums," Scott orders, even though the driver is already heading there.

The gas station we're pulling into is also a truck stop, with a coffee shop sharing the large parking lot. The only signage is branding for the gas station and coffee shop—no signs telling me where we are. There are a few trucks parked in the lot and only one other car at the pumps. Beyond the pavement to my right is forest, leaves starting to change color in the autumn sun. The brush seems reasonably thick, and my mind instantly shifts to thoughts of escape. I weigh my options. I'm not sure how deep the forest is, or even where we are. I don't see anyone near the big eighteen-wheelers. Even if I did see someone, the idea of making an escape with a random trucker seems unwise. I've watched way too many episodes of *Dateline* for that.

In the distance to my left is a car dealership, but about half a kilometer of flat paved lot and gravel separates me from that option. Even if I thought they could help me, I certainly can't make it there unseen by my captors.

James pulls to a stop and hops out of the car, letting in a beam of bright sunlight.

"Take Alexandra to the bathroom," Scott instructs Drew as he opens his door.

"I don't need a washroom chaperone."

"Fine," he says with a predictable shrug of indifference as he gets out of the car. He leans back in, meeting my defiantly narrowed eyes. "No washroom break for you, then. We won't be stopping again anytime soon." With that he slams the door, leaving me to regret my stubborn tongue.

"Here, come with me. James has to clean out the car anyway. I'll get you some water," Drew says, stepping into the sun and holding out my shoes.

THE SECRETS THEY KEEP

Eying the shoes with surprise, I realize I'm just wearing socks. A small piece of tape still clings to my cotton pajama pants. Claustrophobia tightens my chest as I reach to remove it. My breath catches in my throat as I feel the memory of my wrists and ankles tightly bound.

I grab the shoes, pull them on, and stumble out of the car. Taking a deep breath, I let the fresh air sooth my panic.

A gentle breeze lifts my wavy hair; the beautiful day is in complete contrast of my current predicament. Beside the car, James gathers supplies to clean up my mess; I can't bring myself to feel guilty. Scott's a few feet away, watching us while talking on his phone. This is a bad spot for them to stop. Well, bad for me anyway. Even if I make it to the forest, this is a terrible place to make a run for it; guaranteed Scott knows it, too.

"Come on," Drew prods, gently pressing a warm hand on my lower back but letting go as soon as I start to walk. He leads the way into the gas station, heading straight for the "Washrooms" sign on the back wall.

"Make it quick, okay?" he says, scanning the empty store.

I don't argue this time. For one, I need to pee. Secondly, I'm fairly sure Drew isn't in charge here. Given his stiff posture and avoidance of my gaze, it's clear he doesn't like this kidnapping thing; maybe I can use that.

The washroom is a single stall room with no windows and no emergency exit—just stark white linoleum floors and white walls. The lights are painfully bright, and my tired eyes squint against their harsh reflection in the small room.

As I wash my hands, I take in my reflection. I'm still in my PJs; my face is pale, and my pants are covered in dried mud, but otherwise, I look normal. How can I possibly look like myself when my whole life is in chaos? I don't know what

I expected, but the normality of seeing myself unchanged seems wrong.

When I come out of the washroom, Drew is waiting for me with a bottle of water.

"Here, we'll pick up some food later," he says, turning to leave.

The small store is still empty, excluding the heavy-set man behind the counter. He eyes us over his paper, thick eyebrows pulled together.

"Alexandra, come on," Drew hisses, turning back to face me. "Please." His eyes are wide, pleading.

I can't ignore that this might be a great opportunity to get help. Seth said no police and seemed certain, but I could so easily tell this man that I've been kidnapped. Surely, even if Scott gets me out of here before the cops show up, their vehicle will be caught on a surveillance camera, and the police could find me.

"Kids, let's go, let's go," Scott says, arriving in the store's doorway as if my defiant thoughts summoned him. He smiles at the guy behind the counter before turning to glare at me, stepping into the store.

My head is fuzzy from whatever Scott injected me with last night, distorting my thinking. I have no time to decide what to do. It's now or never. The employee lowers his paper, watching us with interest.

"We'll stop for lunch soon; let's hit the road. We don't want to be late," Scott adds.

The ringing sound of the door opening startles me. James enters, ignoring us and heading straight to the counter. The attendant takes his curious eyes off of us to talk to James and Scott makes his move.

In three steps, he's right in front of me. Grabbing my upper arm tightly, he drags me out of the store before I can so much as make a sound. He pulls me effortlessly back to the car, shock stunning me into paralyzing silence.

"Let's just clarify something, Alexandra," Scott says after roughly loading me into the far back seat of the SUV. He turns around in his seat, eyes locked on mine.

I'm mad at myself for letting shock get the best of me. I should have just screamed, ran... anything! Determined to show Scott I'm not scared of him, I clench my teeth, refusing to break from his intense scrutinization.

"Don't test me," he continues. "You pull another stunt like that, let's just say it won't end well."

I raise my eyebrows in defiance, challenging him. Based on the fact that I'm still alive, he wants me for something.

Scott leans over the seat to whisper in my ear, "And I don't mean for you. That poor gas station attendant probably has a wife and kids." He pulls away, watching my face closely as his mouth blossoms into his too-familiar smile.

My eyebrows drop as my eyes widen before I can regain control and glare back at him. By the stretching of Scott's smile, I know he didn't miss my surprise. I'm pretty good at reading people, and something in Scott's eyes tells me that he isn't lying; he really would have killed that man. If I had somehow been partially responsible for someone's death, I don't know if I could live with myself. I shiver as blood drains from my face. If I am going to escape, I have to do it on my own.

I jump as a door slams: James returning from the store.

"Who's hungry?" Scott asks, winking as he takes in my pallor. He turns back around, sticking his head beside the driver's seat to talk to James.

I try to take a deep breath, but my chest feels like it's bound with tight rubber bands. I look desperately at Drew, but he's dutifully avoiding eye contact, staring out the window. Sweat forms on my brow, my hands shaking uncontrollably as my nails dig into the flesh of my upper arms. It feels like the night Seth went missing; my nerves jump and twinge like electric shocks.

The seriousness of my situation dawns on me with harsh clarity. I'm in a car with three men I don't know. I have no idea where they are taking me, or where I am now, for that matter. They want me for something, and they are literally willing to kill to keep me. My life has changed too much in the last day to process. *This can't be real. Wake up. WAKE UP!*

Drew looks at me, eyebrows furrowed. I realize I'm hyperventilating again.

"Hey, Alexandra, just relax, okay?" he whispers. His eyes shift to Scott, who's still talking to James and ignoring our exchange.

"Where are we? Where are you taking me? What do you want with me?" I demand, louder than I should.

Drew swears under his breath, stress tightening his expression. "Calm down, Alexandra. Seriously, chill."

"Where are we? What do you want with me?" I yell, unable to control myself. Somewhere in the back of my mind, the logic side is tugging at me to calm down, but I'm too far gone to stop myself. I can't hold it in anymore; it's too much to contain.

My whole body trembles as I try to catch my breath.

Scott turns, shaking his head. "I saw this coming. She kept her cool longer than I hear Seth did. Hand me my bag, Drew."

"Just let her calm down; she'll be fine," Drew protests, keeping his eyes on me.

"Seth? Where is he?" Hearing his name only increases my panic. Had he successfully escaped or did they catch him, too? The car is suddenly moving too fast. *There isn't enough air in here. I can't breathe.*

"Pass me my bag, now!" Scott turns his attention from me to Drew. I stare desperately at Drew, but his gaze drops from mine as he hands Scott the same black bag he had used last night.

"No. No drugs! Just tell me where we are!" As always, my question is ignored, not that this simple answer would have been enough to calm me at this point.

"Pull over for a second, James," Scott says, voice calm.

I lean as far away from Scott as I can, pushing myself against the window on the right side of the SUV. Still trembling, my mind shifts into flight mode, searching for a way out. Time slows. Gravel crunches under the tires as we pull onto the shoulder of the highway. My eyes dart around the SUV; Drew shifts in his seat so he can't see me and James picks up his phone in the front seat.

"Now, don't go making this more difficult than it needs to be, Alexandra," Scott says like he's talking to a disobedient child. I'm so sick of my full name, I want to scream. No one calls me Alexandra. I hate hearing it, especially out of Scott's mouth, in his ever-calm voice. I want to kick him, anything to rattle his sense of control. Smiling bitterly, I see my opening.

He moves to get beside me. As he straddles the seat, I kick him right in the groin. A grimace twists his expression as he falls, hitting his head against the driver's seat.

"Hey!" James protests, jarred by the impact. Drew turns to help Scott and I make my move in the chaos.

I scramble up and reach for the door, a path cleared by Drew's shift to help Scott. Falling out of the SUV, I jump to my feet and take off in a full sprint. Dense brush and forest lie ahead, similar to the gas station. It's my only option. I don't even care where we are; desperation for escape is my only thought.

"Get her, now!" Scott yells from the car. Feet trample the dirt in pursuit, but I keep pushing forward as fast as I can. A kind of sick satisfaction twists my lips into a broad smile, hearing the panic in Scott's voice.

My pulse pounds in my ears as I push my legs to run faster through the patch of damp grass.

Only a small field separates me from freedom.

"Alexandra stop, please," Drew pants from behind me, too close. *Damn, he's fast!*

I throw myself forward faster, almost tripping, my legs growing numb. Just as I enter the tree-line, a heavy mass slams me to the ground, forcing all the air from my lungs. Two strong arms turn me onto my back and a weight pins my hips to the cold dirt.

I open my reflexively closed eyes to find Drew looking down at me. I fight desperately to catch my breath, gulping in air. My heart races and I try to turn onto my side to relieve the pressure. Drew holds me firm.

"Get off of me!" I finally puff out, voice raspy.

"That was really stupid, Alexandra!" Drew chastises between heavy breaths. "Are you okay? You could have been hurt." Swearing under his breath, he wipes his brow that's glistening with a fine mist of sweat. "Did you really think you could just run away from us?"

I don't know what to say. He's right; the odds of me out-running and being able to hide from three people in a small forest were below slim. It was a pure sympathetic response that pushed me to run. Now, as adrenaline trickles from my veins, I feel like an idiot.

The cold, hard ground quakes as someone jogs towards Drew and me.

"Nice run, Alexandra. I should have warned you though, Drew's pretty fast. But I guess you know that now, so we won't have to repeat this; what a relief." Scott's composure has returned, which pisses me off. Drew finally gets off of me, reaching down for my hand. Still furious, I take his hand, but when he pulls me to my feet, I stick my foot behind his and body check him to the ground. He lets go of my hand to try and catch himself, leaving me standing freely. Scott reaches for my arm, but I dodge him and take off again into the forest.

Scott laughs jovially as Drew once again tackles me to the ground. The second fall doesn't wind me but hurts like hell. My shirt soaks through instantly from the mossy forest floor.

"Damn Alexandra, you really never quit, do you?" Drew asks, easily flipping me over again, a slight smile playing on his lips. "Nice trip though; didn't see that one coming."

I don't have a chance to reply before Scott comes strolling towards us, smiling down at me.

"Very feisty," Scott says, holding a dreaded syringe.

For the first time, I realize my sweatshirt is missing, leaving me in just a tank top. I hadn't considered *easy access to my upper arms* a factor when picking my pajamas last night.

Scott covers my mouth as a scream escapes my lips. I yank my arms free to pull his hand away, but Drew gathers both my wrists with one hand while keeping my waist pinned; I can't budge my upper body, causing panic to surge through me again as tears blur my vision. I uselessly kick my legs, trying to connect with one of my captors. I manage to knee Drew in the back a few times, but he hardly budges.

A needle pierces my skin, making my stomach roll. Branches of the towering trees sway in time with the breeze, dropping colorful leaves around us—unaffected by my panicked struggle. My body relaxes against my will and my feet fall to the spongy forest floor with a gentle thud. I groan weakly as Scott removes his now sweaty hand from my mouth.

"Get her back to the SUV," Scott says, his voice pulling away. "Let's hope no one saw her great escape." Light streaming through the trees blurs and dims as I sink into the soft moss. Drew scoops me into his arms as I'm swept into darkness.

CHAPTER SIX

Letting out a groan, I force my tired eyes open, finding myself in the dark. My whole body hurts, courtesy of Drew. Who tackles someone in real life? If you can even call this real life.

Blinking, my surroundings come into focus. I recognize the hotel room I woke up in last night. It had been disorienting, waking up in a hotel after passing out in a forest. I'd searched the room, looking for any clues as to where I was. The only piece of info I'd gleaned is that we were in a busy city, based on the traffic I could see from the window. There was no TV in the room, and someone had even gone to the trouble of removing the label from the tiny shampoo bottle. I wondered if it was just Scott messing with me, trying to drive me crazy. I was only up for long enough to search the room and eat a cold hamburger they'd left for me before exhaustion dragged me back to bed.

Stretching, I roll my head to the right and jump, clasping a hand over my mouth before a scream can escape. Someone is in the other bed. Squinting in the dim light, I recognize Drew's face, relaxed in sleep. I dart from the bed, backing into the wall. The thought of someone watching me sleep sends shivers up my already trembling body. I guess when you get kidnapped you can't really expect respectful consideration of your *boundaries.* The sky outside the parted curtains is still black, but there's no way in hell I'm going back to sleep now.

Drew's chest rises and falls evenly; clearly, he's still asleep. I move to the only exit in the room: a door that seems to lead to a larger hotel suite. The faint sounds of Drew, Scott, and James having a discussion had traveled from there last night while I searched the room. I'm not surprised to find the door locked. Grimacing, I shake out my stiff muscles and walk down the short hallway to the bathroom. Even though I have nothing to change into, I head for the shower. My body is filthy from both forest incidents, my hair heavy with mud. Plus, I'm freezing.

Hanging on the hook behind the bathroom door is a backpack. Drew must have put it there after I fell asleep; I hadn't noticed it in my room search. Inside is a pair of jeans, one of my t-shirts, and my favorite sweatshirt. I take out the clothes, including a pair of my underwear and a bra. I blush at the idea of these men going through my underwear drawer. Admittedly, it's a weird thought to have, given the circumstances, but lately, I've had very little control over where my mind wanders. It's strange to think my kidnappers care enough to put all this together for me. They must want me for something, so I guess it's in their best interests to at least keep me clean and healthy. I can't let myself think they're doing anything for me out of kindness.

Starting the shower, I step into the steaming water, letting out a heavy breath as the muddy water cascading off of my body begins to clear. I stay in for a long time; it feels good to do something mundane like wash my hair. In the warm steam, I close my eyes. I let myself imagine I'm back home, safe; free. A loud bang on the bathroom door pulls me from my fantasy, a small shriek escaping my lips.

"Alexandra, are you okay in there?" Drew's muffled voice slips under the door.

I shut off the water, shoulders tightening. *Back to reality.*

"Yeah," I sigh. Wrapping a towel around my body with shaking hands, I step out onto the mat. The chilly air is sharp against my steaming skin.

"You were in the shower a long time."

I don't respond as I run another towel through my hair and hastily pull on my clothes. I feel completely exposed talking to Drew while naked. My hair is too tangled to even try taming, so I gather it hastily and wrap it into a bun.

"Alexandra?"

"What?" I snap.

"Nothing, just checking," he mutters, sounding sheepish.

"Checking what?" I yank the door open. Drew, as expected, is standing directly on the other side. "There are no windows in the bathroom. Did you think I escaped through the drain?" I push past him, seeing the clock glowing in the dark room. It's 6:45.

"Drew, I'm sorry... I woke you up." My manners get the best of me. I want to slap myself for apologizing to him. He's literally kidnapping me. *Damn, I have Stockholm syndrome already!*

"Don't worry about it," Drew says slowly, following me back into the bedroom as he watches me, head tilted to the side.

I flick on the lamp to break his gaze.

"Sleep deprivation comes with the job," he says through a yawn. "Okay, if you're up, I might as well get us some coffee...well, me coffee. You don't drink coffee. I'll get you a tea." He pulls a key out from its hiding place in his track pants pocket, shutting the door quickly as he leaves.

How long were these guys stalking me? They know I like lettuce and ketchup on my burger, they know I hate coffee; what's their deal? I sit back against the headboard. *I need a plan.* Biting the inside of my cheek, I scan the room for inspiration. On the bedside table, just in front of the clock, is a phone. Drew must have left it. My breath catches as I grab it, eyes darting to the door nervously. I freeze, pulse hastening. *Who should I call?*

I shove the phone under my pillow, certain Drew will come back for it. My mind spins; I don't know who I can trust not to be involved in this. These guys just know so much about me; the information must have come from somewhere. My dad has to be involved somehow. Does that mean I can't trust my own father? I can call Mom, but what would she be able to do? What can anyone do?

Erik or Whitney, I finally narrow it down. Erik is the obvious choice, right? He's my boyfriend. Something holds me back. I don't want to get him wrapped up in this. *Same goes for Whitney then,* I reason. Tears fill my eyes as realization hits me like a bucket of ice water. No one's coming to save me.

I slam the phone back on the bedside table. Digging my nails into my upper arms, I stomp back to the bathroom to retrieve my sweatshirt. I have no idea how to get out of this mess, especially knowing the lengths these people will go to keep me. I have to watch for an opportunity. The only way to do that is to avoid being sedated by Scott.

"Good morning," Scott calls cheerily, coming into the room. *I have to stop thinking about Scott; it seems to summon him.*

I step out of the bathroom and fold my arms across my chest again, saying nothing.

"I hope you like eggs. What am I saying, I know you like eggs," he says, goading me.

Keep it together, Alex. Deep breaths. I distract myself, still not saying anything. Silence is the only way to keep my mouth from acting out my overwhelming desire to rake Scott over the coals.

His smile widens, seeming to enjoy my pained silence. "Not feeling chatty this morning, I see. That's fine, not all of us can be morning people. Breakfast should be up in a few minutes. Drew will bring it in."

When Scott leaves, it takes a few minutes of pacing for the urge to punch him to fade.

As promised, Drew arrives with a tray a few minutes later, leaving me to eat in peace. I pick at my toast, more anxious than hungry. Drew comes to get me when they're ready to go. James must have gone to get the car, as the suite is empty save Drew, Scott, and me. This must be an expensive hotel room. A large living room dominates the space. On the other side of a formal dining table is another open door; the second bedroom. Drew hands me my shoes and I put them on obediently, wondering if Scott is actually going to let me go to the car conscious.

"Alexandra, I trust you remember what I said to you at the gas station?" Scott asks, his dark eyes burning into mine.

I say nothing, nodding. My jaw is clenched so hard my teeth hurt. Something about Scott brings out my temper like no one else.

"Wonderful. Drew, hold her hand just to be sure she doesn't forget."

I turn my attention from Scott to Drew, eyes wide. Drew stares at Scott intensely. His knuckles crack as he clenches his fists. I look away from their silent exchange awkwardly. Drew had literally carried me yesterday. I know why I don't want to hold his hand, but why does he care?

Drew says nothing as he reaches down and laces his fingers through mine. I don't protest, greatly preferring this to the alternative of being sedated.

I'm on my best behavior as we make our way to the car, keeping my head down and my hand in Drew's. He all but ignores me, and I try to ignore that it actually feels nice holding his warm hand. That's delusional Stockholm Alex thinking, and she can't be indulged.

I don't look around for clues as to where we are; I'm certain Scott's watching me to see if I really am going to behave. I'm not going to help him make the distinction. I'll look for signage when we're on the road.

The rest of the morning goes by in a blur of road passing under tires. In my usual position in the very back of the SUV, I keep an eye on the clock; time is moving excruciatingly slowly. Who knew one could feel bored while being kidnapped?

I spend my time thinking of ways to escape. *When we stop for gas, I can fake feeling sick and run when Drew takes me to the washroom. But he's so fast!* I remind myself. *Okay, ask him to buy me water, and sneak out while he's distracted at the till,* I muse. *Or when we stop for gas, I'll get out, like I'm heading for the bathroom. Then I'll run back and highjack the SUV! Maybe James'll leave the keys in the car. But if he doesn't, I'll be worse off than I am now; Scott will lose it.*

As I plan, I keep my eyes peeled for city signs. After driving a short time, a billboard welcomes us to South Carolina. I let out a small gasp, covering it with a yawn when Scott's eyes dart to mine. *South Carolina! What the hell are we doing here?* I've never been this far south. It's hard to imagine we've driven so far in such a short time. An hour or so later we enter the city of Columbia. I have to admit the scenery is beautiful, from farm fields to forests threaded with rivers. We don't stop anywhere. James must have filled up the tank before we left, crushing my escape plans.

The drive is mostly a silent one, with Drew and Scott both distracted by their phones. Scott finally breaks the monotony after a few hours. "Are we still on track, timing wise?"

"At this rate, we'll likely arrive early," James replies.

Scott returns to his phone, selecting a contact that I can't read from my position.

"It's Scott, may I speak with her?" he asks when a female voice answers.

After a pause, "I wanted to give you an update, Mrs. Castleman. We'll be there before lunch," he says in an almost reverential tone. It's so unlike his usual tone I almost laugh.

"Yes, all is going well today. No issues," he adds with a smile that fades as the woman, *Mrs. Castleman*, speaks. "No, we haven't acquired any new intel. Very well, see you shortly." He hangs up and a pit forms in my stomach. Wherever we're going, we'll arrive before lunch today. It's already almost 11:00.

Where could we be going? Who was Scott talking to? My mind races. I'm not sure I want to meet someone who makes him that nervous.

As is always the case, time races as I begin to dread the destination. It's hard to believe an hour ago, I was bored. *Fool.* The only thing that pauses my stress spiral is the view as we drive over a large bridge that crosses a wide river. The sun sparkles on the deep blue ripples of the water's surface; the view is breathtaking.

Shortly before noon, we pull into a gated driveway. We entered Mt. Pleasant maybe fifteen minutes ago. I'm desperately clinging onto the *pleasant* part being a good omen.

The gate buzzes open, and we drive down an intricately stoned drive, arriving at the largest house I have ever seen. The SUV slowly curves past a sparkling fountain before pulling to a stop in front of an ostentatious double staircase, leading to a massive set of rounded double doors.

Drew sticks his head back in the vehicle when I don't follow him out.

"Come on. We're here," he says, as if that explains anything.

I take in the beautiful tan stucco home with its multiple balconies and large windows. It's hard to think of this place as menacing. The warm wood tones and gently swaying trees are so welcoming. I get out of the SUV, justifying that really, they would get me out one way or another. Not to mention, my curiosity is starting to get the better of me. *What could people like this possibly want with me?*

CHAPTER SEVEN

As I exit the car, a warm breeze meets me, carrying with it the distinct smell of sea air. Gulls caw in the distance, making this place seem even more benign. It's a drastic change from the cold autumn weather of Toronto.

I follow Scott up the stone steps, Drew close behind me. Scott's shoulders are tense as he knocks on the large oak doors with intricate fogged windows, obscuring our view of the house within. I can just make out the blurry form of a figure walking towards us.

"Please, come in," a young woman says, gesturing for us to enter with a small smile. She looks to be in her mid-thirties, wearing black slacks and a tan polo shirt with a sensible pair of flats. I'm not one to judge a book by its cover, but she isn't what I expected. She certainly doesn't strike me as intimidating.

The inside of the home, on the other hand, is exactly what I expected: extravagant. White stone pillars frame the foyer, and marble staircases to the right and left lead to an expansive balcony above. The white and gray marble floors reflect sunlight from a vast expanse of windows; wood accents in the furniture and staircase banisters provide a sense of warmth to the otherwise cool-tones. A subtle scent in the air tugs at my subconscious: like cinnamon mixed with wildflowers and clean laundry. It's almost familiar, but not placeable.

"Oh good, y'all made it," another woman says, pulling me back from my gawking.

An older woman with smooth silver hair stands between two pillars. Now *she* has presence. Confidence shines through her, not daunted by her advancing age. Her posture is perfect, as are her pearls and purple dress with matching heels. Something about her proud face is familiar, like the scent, but I still can't place it. I can't imagine where I would've seen her before.

"Scott, I'm sure you got business that needs seein' to. Leave Alexandra here with me," she says in a thick southern accent, assertive without raising her voice.

Scott nods. "Drew, let's go," he says before stepping closer to me. "Don't think because I'm gone, you're not being watched. Mrs. Castleman's security is more than capable of keeping an eye on you."

"Oh now, hush, and go on," Mrs. Castleman tsks.

Scott's smile drops as he hurries out of the house. I kind of love this woman already. Drew follows Scott out, leaving me alone with Mrs. Castleman and her supposed security, but, scanning the space, I see no sign of them.

"Now, that takes care of them. Come on through," Mrs. Castleman says, giving me a warm smile. I smile back nervously, still totally confused and more than a little apprehensive.

She leads me past a large living room area and through a set of doors at the back of the mansion. My mouth literally drops as we step out onto the large slate veranda. Immediately in front of me is a large infinity pool that is a perfect cerulean blue. Past the pool is a long dock leading to a wide stretch of beach. The wetlands between us and the sand provide a beautiful touch of green to complement the blue water and sky. This property is stunning. Another stark contrast from where I grew up, and certainly from the basement apartment I now call home.

Lounge chairs and a large covered eating area surround the sparkling pool.

"Make yourself at home, darlin'," Mrs. Castleman insists, gesturing to a chair at the table that faces the stunning view. I don't object, feeling the need to sit. This place is too much. As soon as we settle, the woman who let us into the house appears with a large, frosty pitcher and two glasses.

"Sweet tea, miss?" she asks, looking at me. I nod vaguely.

"Lunch will be right out, if that suits, Mrs. Castleman?" she asks after pouring us both large glasses and leaving the pitcher on the table. Sweat rapidly pools around the base.

"Thank you, Marcy. I hope you're hungry, hon."

Mrs. Castleman smiles, eyes warm but intense. I look away, unsure what to say. I had a million questions before we arrived, but my mind's gone blank sitting out here on this beautiful veranda at this ridiculous house. It just doesn't feel real.

"You have a lovely home," I finally say, manners filling in for actual conversation.

Her smile widens, seeming to take more from my statement than I sent.

Alison Haines

Be brave. I force myself. "Um, Mrs. Castleman, is it?"

"Call me Clarissa, sweetie."

"Okay, Clarissa," I amend with a tight smile, looking down again. Her gaze is so fierce I have a hard time looking directly at her. "Where am I?" I finally blurt out.

"Oh, for heaven's sake, where are my manners?" She breaks into a light-hearted laugh. "We are at my home in Carolina, near Charleston. That's South Carolina, to be clear," she says, giving me only what I had gleaned from signage on our way here.

Before I can ask anything else, Marcy returns with a large tray. She sets out green beans, potato salad, and the most amazing smelling breaded pork chops.

Clarissa piles food on my plate like I'm a child, but I don't have the heart to turn her down. I'm having a hard time processing this scene. Here I am, looking at the ocean, cicadas singing in the heat, drinking *sweet tea* like this is a freaking picnic instead of a kidnapping.

"Why am I here?" I demand so suddenly that Clarissa stops chewing for a moment before regaining her composure.

"I reckon this is real confusing for you, sweetie, and I'm truly sorry 'bout that. We don't have enough time for me to explain everythin', but I'll try to give you enough information so you don't go losin' your marbles on us." Her smile takes on an air of sadness as her eyes soften.

I wait with bated breath for her to tell me something; anything would be more than Scott had been willing to share.

"I'm fixin' to explain. It's hard to know where to begin. Do you remember your life before y'all moved east?" she asks.

My brow furrows, confused at this change in direction.

Clarissa lets out a little laugh. "Well now, I guess you wouldn't; you weren't but knee-high to a grasshopper, and I'll bet your parents don't gab about it much." I want to ask her how she knows all of this, but I bite my tongue, watching her pause to eat. When I was eight, my family moved from Calgary, Alberta to St. Thomas, Ontario. I remember vague details about Calgary, but it's a time I rarely think back on. I haven't stayed in touch with any of my old friends, so there isn't much to anchor those memories or stir me to recall them.

"Your family didn't move for your daddy's promotion. That's just your daddy tellin' tales. They moved to get away, escape a past they no longer wanted to be part of and that they certainly didn't want you young'uns involved with." She pauses, fork halfway to her mouth and winks at me. "You *and* your sister."

"My... sister?" I'm too startled to pretend Whitney doesn't exist. Clarissa doesn't sound like she's fishing. She stated it so matter-of-factly; *who is this woman?*

"Yeah, I know you have a sister, darlin', even though you were able to pull a fast one on Scott. I tell you what, sometimes I've a mind to tan his hide, but damned if he ain't a hell of a recon man," she adds distractedly. "As I say, I knew y'all quite well back when you were young'uns. Y'all spent vacations in this here house."

Suddenly I remember where I know her face from. She's in my parents' wedding picture. I'd seen it just last month when my mom and I were going through pictures for my sister's wedding slideshow. When I asked my mother who she was, mom just said that she was an old friend and changed the subject. I remember it because I had thought it was strange; it wasn't like my mom to resist a chance to tell a story.

"You're in the wedding picture" I mutter, attempting to piece this new information into the patchy story that's beginning to form.

"Your daddy's? Yeah, I was there." Clarissa's lips purse and she looks down. "Before they up and moved we were real close. Sadly I'm part of the past y'all are runnin' from."

My shoulders tense in the silence until it's more than I can take. I'm thirsty for answers, and Clarissa is the only one willing to indulge my curiosity.

"So why did we move then? And what does it have to do with me being here?" I urge.

"You used to do gymnastics."

"Yeah..." I manage, trying to keep up. Is Clarissa trying to distract me?

"You quit when y'all moved."

"My dad enrolled me in dance instead; he thought it was less dangerous."

"Well, he was dead right in one respect. You were real good, and that was bad for y'all keepin' a low profile. They didn't want you competin' no more; that was an easy way to hunt y'all down."

"Hunt us down?" I ask, just above a whisper, shivering despite the warm South Carolina air.

"You even changed that last name of yours when y'all moved."

I shift back in my seat; we *had* changed our name. My dad told us that one of the gangs who dominated the area where we used to live was not too happy with him. As a paramedic, he often had run-ins with gang members while working. He had been unable to resuscitate one of their members but had been successful in reviving a man from a rival gang. He had already been in their bad books for refusing to do transport favors for them. They had taken it as him choosing sides and vowed to get revenge on him and his family. So when we moved, my parents changed our surname from Conry to Chambers, just to be safe. We were told not to tell anyone our old name. I stare at her, stunned by this rewriting of my past.

"Why? Who didn't they want to find us?" I ask, voice shaking. A chilling realization dawns on me; whoever my parents had gone to great lengths to hide us from had found me, and Seth too.

"Darlin, y'all are from a rather unique bloodline. Your family is destined for certain greatness. You are genetically wired with special gifts. See, they are stronger in some than others. Now I don't know the whole story, but I'd wager you or Whitney went on and showed some of those traits as a young'un, and your daddy wanted you protected. Your sister was a real sporty little thing if I 'member right, and what with you and your gymnastics. This ain't in and of itself particularly unique to your bloodline, but when your parents up and moved y'all away, they marked you and your sister. They made the Guardians suspicious."

Guardians, marked, unique bloodline, gifts... it's too much. What were my parents protecting me from? I don't have any special gifts! My heart begins to race again, pounding against my ribs uncomfortably. What will these people do with me when they realize I'm ordinary?

"Now you got to understand something. The Guardians ain't bad people, and we ain't gonna hurt you." Clarissa continues, beginning to sound far away. I do my best to pay attention despite my growing anxiety.

"Your daddy chose a life in which we ain't welcome, and you will have that choice...one day." Clarissa pauses, looking at me with pursed lips. "I was dead set against having y'all kidnapped. Mind you, I was outranked, which seems to be the damned way of things lately. When y'all were found at the end of last year I wanted to call your daddy and reason with him, see if he and your uncle would agree to send you kids to Sweden. Let y'all see for yourself what the options are. Bryce and Damian wouldn't have none of it. They reckoned that if y'all were tipped off, they would pack you up and move again. The trackers would'a had to start from square one to find y'all." She let out a breath. Clearly, this is painful for her to talk about but I'm too stunned and desperate for information to ask her to stop. Her southern accent grows incredibly thick as her temper rises.

"So, instead they had you, your sister, and your cousins followed, investigated. They reckoned that only one of you from each family would have gifts, if even one, being that your daddies didn't marry within the bloodlines. The Guardian who tailed you thought ya mightn't be gifted until Seth was taken. Your instincts were so strong, and you followed them even when no one else supported your theories. That's what gave you away to Scott. He told Bryce, and well, he said to bring ya on in. The Guardian houndin' your sister was unconvinced one way or another, but her current lifestyle, being married and such, made her a tough take. Bryce called off the investigation and decided to focus on you and Seth, at least for the here and now. He reckons your sister will be easy pickin's now he's got you."

"Seth?" This whole conversation is so confusing, I pick a detail that seems most pressing. Seth is still out there; the other information can wait.

"Yes, ma'am. Seth, like you, seems to have gifts. Miles just might not, at least in early investigations," Clarissa says with a nod, her face drawn.

"Where is Seth?"

"Now that, I don't know. I ain't seen him yet. Although he was taken before you, which is strange; I keep my hand outta that cookie jar. If Damian and Bryce are going to do as they please..." she shrugs, waving her hand as if waving away a fly.

"Who are the Guardians? What gifts do they think I have?" I ask, questions spinning around my head as I try to pluck them out one at a time. I have not forgotten about the fact that my parents are involved in this, but I push it aside.

"The Guardians are a complex web of powerful people. As for what gifts you have, I can hazard a guess, but that conversation is out of my wheelhouse. Just 'member that y'all get to choose in the end, just like your daddy and uncle did. They chose love and family over their gifts."

I bite my cheek, holding in my observation that despite what my father had chosen, his kids weren't safe. Did he really have a choice?

"Where do my parents think I am?" I ask instead. I don't want to try and open the whole *"your dad was part of a secret society and kept this world from you your entire life"* can of worms right now. I skirt around the emotional landmines. Already at the edge of panic, I'm desperately trying to cling to this conversation.

"Oh, by now I reckon they've pieced it all together. I thought your daddy woulda done called by now, madder than a wet hen, demanding we go on an' bring y'all home," she says with a smile that doesn't reach her eyes. "Might just be they hollered at Bryce or Damian, I don't rightly know."

Marcy gently knocks on the French door, startling me. She's holding up a phone, trying to catch Clarissa's eye. Clarissa stands up and walks towards the house. Before entering, she turns back to me.

"Scott and Andrew will be along to collect you soon, I reckon. I pushed to show you some southern hospitality for a couple days, but Damian prit'near pitched a fit. Said you needed to be gettin' along," she says, looking troubled again. "You go on and rest out here a spell; I've got business."

"Collect me? Where are we going?" I call, but she's already inside. I guess we still haven't arrived; another pit stop.

I let out a frustrated groan. I'm alone again, trying to process scattered bits of information. Looking down at my plate of nearly untouched food, I spear a green bean with my fork and pop it in my mouth before realizing I'm not hungry. I still have so many questions. Letting out a breath, I try to calm my nerves; my hands are shaking and head is spinning. I'd yet to see the so-called security Scott warned me about. Glancing at the house, no one appears to be watching me. I casually make my way around the pool, walking towards the long dock. As I exit the shade of the veranda, I'm startled by a large man standing on the far side of the pillar to the right, facing the sea, wearing a dark pair of sunglasses. Standing at the pillar on the left is a well-muscled woman with a matching wide stance. Both are wearing black slacks and black t-shirts. The sun is quite warm now that I'm out of the shade and I wonder how they can tolerate it. Do they just stand there all day, or were they placed there for me? Neither say anything, so I start down the dock, curious how far I'm allowed to roam. When I'm about ten feet away from the pillars, both wordlessly move away from the wall, shadowing me. I sigh, looks like running here isn't going to be easy; they both look in excellent shape. Also, I have to admit that my intrigue about who these *Guardians* are has quelled my desire for escape, at least for now.

"Alexandra?"

Drew stands at the edge of the veranda, shielding his eyes from the bright sun. I look longingly at the beach before turning back to the house.

"Oh, there you are. We are heading out soon," he says, looking relieved.

"Alex," I blurt.

"What?"

"My name, it's Alex. No one calls me Alexandra." I'm not sure why I have the sudden urge to correct him.

"Oh." He looks at me, eyebrows pulled together. "Sorry."

In the awkward silence that follows, I cross my arms and look away towards the pool.

"Right, well, um, the car's out front so... we should go," he mutters, turning to the house. I glance to see if the two guards are still behind me. I can't see them, so I assume they've returned to their posts behind the pillars.

"Drew, what took you so long? Take Alexandra to the car. I'll be there in a moment," Scott says in a dismissive tone as we enter the house, turning to resume his conversation with Clarissa.

"Goodbye, Lexie," Clarissa says, ignoring Scott's attempt to re-engage. "Y'all come back real soon." She takes a hesitant step towards me but stops, eyes narrowed in a pained expression. I smile at her tentatively as Drew puts his hand on the small of my back, leading me outside.

Lexie? It was weird hearing that name from her. Drew and Clarissa both acting awkwardly does nothing to help my already frayed nerves. My stomach hurts, and I wonder if it's just stress or lack of food. Nerves and food don't really mix for me.

As I step out of the house, I turn to admire it one more time. It's seriously breathtaking. I wonder what Clarissa had done to become so wealthy. Two town cars with tinted windows wait for us on the intricately stoned driveway. Drew leads me to the first car and opens the back door before making his way around the car and getting in on the other side. The sweatshirt I left in the SUV is waiting for me in the backseat.

"So," he starts, conversationally. "Did you enjoy the visit with your aunt?"

"I didn't see my aunt here. Which aunt?"

"Clarissa..." he adds, pulling his eyes from his phone. "She's your aunt. Well, your great aunt."

"What? No, she isn't," I say, although I can't be sure; it certainly wouldn't be the weirdest part of my day.

"Yeah, she is. She didn't tell you?"

"It didn't come up," I add this to the growing list of things I need to process. They really should have provided a notebook. Clarissa being my aunt would explain why she's in my parents' wedding picture. She must have been my dad's aunt, if Drew isn't just screwing with me. I haven't ruled that out.

A couple minutes later, Scott arrives, getting in the car behind ours. I wonder briefly why we were taking two cars and where the SUV is but I don't linger on the thought. I'm too preoccupied with all the information I'm still trying to process from Clarissa. Biting my cheek, I try to pick through the finer details. First thing that comes to mind is no mention of Caleb. She truly must have lost touch after our move; Caleb was born several years later. This provides a small raft of comfort to my ocean of concerns.

The rest of the drive we don't talk, or maybe Drew does, and I don't hear him. I'm so absorbed in my thoughts, I don't even notice the car has stopped until someone opens my door, startling me.

"Alexandra, let's go." Scott holds my door open, looking irritated. I wonder if it's me or his conversation with Clarissa that has him so grumpy. Either way, it's satisfying.

We're at a small hanger of some sort, and a private plane waits for us on the steaming tarmac. Scott walks ahead of me and Drew comes to my side. The driver and front seat passenger of our car get out to follow Drew and me closely. *Wow, they're really not going to give me any chance to escape.* It's slightly humorous; as if I need this much security. I couldn't even outrun Drew alone.

Boarding the plane, my sense of awe returns. "Drew, how rich are you guys?" I ask, looking around. The hotel room was fancy, but a crazy loaded private jet?

"By *you guys*, you mean us. You're part of this now. This money is your money, too," he says. *What the hell is going on?* I wonder for the millionth time.

Soft tan leather chairs and a leather couch fill the roomie space. The plush, white carpet makes me feel self-conscious in my dirty old sneakers. Drew guides me to a pair of seats in the back, surprising me by dropping into the chair beside mine. The two men who followed us out of the car don't board the plane. *Not much risk of me escaping now, I suppose.*

"Well, well, well. You had me worried we wouldn't get you here safely, feisty girl, but here we are. I trust I don't need to sedate you for the flight? You don't have the sudden urge to jump out of a plane without a parachute, do you?" Scott smiles. I glare at him, swallowing back nausea. Scott's watching me like I'm a new toy on Christmas morning. He laughs at his own wit and turns to the cockpit.

"Is he a pilot?"

"No, he just likes sitting up front, you know. Feels more in control that way." Drew's tone is lighter, his posture noticeably more relaxed since boarding the plane.

"I have to ask... why did we drive for, like, two days if we were just going to take a plane? Is this thing not allowed in Canada or something?"

"Nah, we do fly to Canada, but this mission required top-level clearance. We don't have that at every airport, and Damian didn't want to risk an international incident. We usually fly out of Breslau or Ottawa, but there were complications." He shrugs. My body is pressed into the soft seat as the plane accelerates forward.

"How long's the flight? And where exactly are we going, assuming you can tell me now?" I ask hesitantly. I've gone so long with my questions unanswered, I'm afraid to experience the antagonizing silence again.

"Guess there's no harm now," he says, stretching his well-muscled arms above his head, seeming more at ease by the minute. "It's not like you're going anywhere until we get there. We're going to Gavleborg, Sweden, which is the home base for the Guardians. I guess you don't really know much about that though?"

"No," is all I say. Not only had I never heard of Gavleborg, but I also know next to nothing about this *Guardians* thing. I don't feel the need to elaborate on my ignorance.

"Well, the Guardians are an organization, so to speak. The full name is Guardians of Enlightenment, but that's a bit of a mouthful. My parents are part of it, and your dad and uncle used to be members as well. You still have some family involved, like Clarissa. It's made up of a fairly large group of main families, as well as other individuals identified for special skills or abilities, then their children often become Guardians. Outsiders are essential for breeding reasons, of course, or you would likely be my cousin and my aunt."

"Am I your cousin?"

"No, no. You and I are from two different lines." He looks at me intently for a moment before shifting his view out the window, the plane gliding smoothly off the ground.

"Okay," I say, ignoring the unwelcome wave of relief that rushes through me. "So what do the Guardians do?"

"Everything, really. They, or more aptly *we,* are a group of people with widely varying gifts posted all over the world."

"What *gifts?*" I demand, frustrated with how much I still don't understand. "Do you have, like, magical powers?"

Drew lets out a laugh before taking in my narrowed eyes and burning cheeks; I hate being teased. "Sorry, I shouldn't laugh. No, we don't have magical powers. I hate to disappoint, but you aren't a wizard or something. The gifts are more subtle than that." He pauses, biting his full lower lip. "So, Scott, for example, is a combat expert strategist: great at planning missions and doing reconnaissance. Don't let him hear you say the words *expert* and *great* when describing him. His ego doesn't need the boost."

I can't help but laugh at that. *Is having a massive ego a gift? Because Scott has that in spades.* "Okay, fair enough, what else?" I ask eagerly, surprising myself with my intense interest. I am sure I don't have a gift, and part of me still worries what they'll do with me when they realize I'm not special, but hell if I'm not curious about what the gifts are. Even if I'm not special, apparently my dad and uncle are.

"James is a tracker. He's really good at following trails and finding people. Your dad was an intellect. He could have helped plan missions or been placed as a military strategist or within a corporation. Your uncle was a sensor: he could identify gifts in others."

My uncle, a sensor? Does that mean he watched us for gifts?

"And you?" I ask, trying to shift my thoughts away from my family. A sharp, hot barb stabs through my stomach every time I think about my dad keeping this from me.

"I'm really fast," Drew mutters, tone flat.

"I know," I say with chagrin, which makes him smile.

"I'm training in combat. I'll be part of recon teams probably."

"Like kidnappings?" The words fall out of my mouth before I can stop them.

Drews smile falls, and his face pales. "This was just a favor, not my future."

"So, if you aren't magical or superheroes, are you, like, a secret society? Like the Skull and Bones?" I ask, trying to change the subject. *Why am I trying to make him feel better?* I want to slap myself.

Drew's face remains serious. "Basically. Guardians date back much further than the Skull and Bones, although we don't have quite so many freaky blindfolded robe-wearing traditions. Not anymore, anyway."

"Right," I mutter, trying to wrap my head around this. I'd been kidding when I asked. If Drew is being honest, I'm part of a secret society, so secret I didn't even know it existed.

"Guardians are in high political positions in almost every country, members of boards for top banks and corporations, involved in spy operations, military groups, you name it," he recites casually. His tone implores me to believe him, but what he's saying seems impossible. How can a group involved in so many high-ranking organizations go unnoticed?

As Drew speaks, he fingers a pendant around his neck. The chain is long enough that it likely resides under his shirt when not being toyed with. My hand reaches for it without my permission.

"This is interesting. What's the symbol?"

Drew looks down at my hand, and I suddenly realize how close we are. Dropping the pendant, I shift away, blushing.

"It's the Guardian crest. It dates back over a thousand years," he says, graciously ignoring my embarrassment. I try to examine the image without getting so close to Drew's chest. There's a scroll at the base with some symbols etched on the surface that I can't make out. Standing atop the scroll is an upright image, half of which is a sword, the other half's a flower.

"What does it mean?" I breathe, so intent on the symbol I start to lean in again.

"It's representative of the Guardian values. Well, at least those of the founders and early members. The scroll represents knowledge; the sword, strength; the lotus flower, beauty," Drew explains in a soft voice, barely rising above the quiet whisper of the plane's engine. His eyes watch me intently. I shift my focus back to the symbol, his gaze causing me to blush again. I think about what Drew said as I look at the pendant. Knowledge and strength make sense, given the limited information I have about the Guardians. "Beauty?" I ask, looking up again, brow furrowed in disbelief.

Drew gives me a half smile. "Never underestimate the power and influence of beauty."

Looking into his gorgeous eyes, I grimace, unable to refute the point.

CHAPTER EIGHT

Drew falls asleep shortly after we're served dinner. Who knew you could get seriously delicious sweet potato fries on an airplane? I'm ruined for flying commercial now, although I'll never admit it.

I sneak past Drew and move to the couch, watching the sky turn black and begin to lighten again prematurely. The timezone shift is disorienting, like the hours are fading too fast. Drew has the right idea, but despite my exhaustion, sleep evades me. I try to keep my eyes from shifting back to Drew's relaxed face. I can't get a clear read on him, and I hate that it makes me want to spend more time with him. Sometimes he seems sweet, other times he's tackling me or trying to trick me into exposing my secrets. I should leave him alone. I should.

Drew wakes with a start, and I tear my wandering eyes from him again, focusing on the window. In my periphery, I catch his confused expression as he glances at my empty seat before he finds me. He digs his ringing phone from his pocket, moving to the back of the plane and shutting the compartment door without a word. Using your phone—another private plane perk.

"We're landing in a few minutes," Scott says, stepping out of the cockpit for the first time in several hours. "Better buckle up. They're letting me touchdown for the first time; might be a bit bumpy."

I roll my eyes as he shuts the cockpit door, not totally sure if he's kidding. I move back to my original seat as Drew returns from the back. He hesitates, opting for a chair across the aisle.

"We're landing soon," I say, trying to catch his eye.

He nods but focuses on the window. *Maybe he's not a morning person.* He certainly isn't the friendly, laid-back Drew who chatted with me earlier in the flight.

Once we touch down, as smooth as the takeoff had been, Drew gets to his feet, moving to the door even though the plane hasn't stopped rolling.

I miss Scott's comment as he returns, lost in thought. Wracking my brain, replaying the flight, I try to remember what I had done to piss off Drew. Nothing comes to mind, so I force myself to let it go. There are much more important things to worry about. Two men board the plane and Drew pushes past them to get out. The men step out of his way, watching me stumble to my feet. I hurry after Drew, who isn't waiting for me. Bright sunlight blinds my tired eyes as I exit the plane. Cold air stings my cheeks, the strong wind cutting right through my sweatshirt.

I'm about halfway down the steps when something stops me, the chill completely forgotten.

"Erik?" I stammer, voice cracking. A million thoughts race through my mind, but none prepare me for the reason he's here.

"Hi, baby." Erik smiles as if it isn't absurdly ridiculous for him to be standing in front of me. He shrugs off the shiny Audi he's leaning against and opens the back-seat door. Searching for anything that makes sense, my eyes land on Drew. He looks at me for a moment, his expression unreadable before nodding to Erik and getting in the back of a matching black Audi.

One of the men standing behind me clears his throat, bringing me out of my stunned state. I slowly descend the rest of the stairs; Erik's casual smile is unmoved by my panic. *Maybe I actually did fall asleep. This has to be a dream.* "What are you doing here?"

"Sorry I couldn't tell you," he says, his gorgeous almond eyes meeting mine as he tries to pull me into a hug. I put a hand on his chest, holding him back. Awareness trickles through my veins.

"You knew? You knew about all of this?" I whisper, sympathy finally twisting his too calm expression. "Wait." With unexpected force, realization pushes through me. "You're one of them!" Gasping, my chest tightens, stealing my breath.

"Honey, calm down," he says, his posture stiffening.

"Careful with that one; she's got a lot of fire in her," Scott warns Erik as he jogs down the plane steps, moving to the third car.

"Alex? I think I can handle her," Erik scoffs. Erik's amused tone is infuriating and awakens my frozen muscles. He's looking at Scott as I lunge for him, pushing him to the tarmac. Caught off guard, he stares up at me, unmoving.

"You jerk!" I yell, slamming his head on the ground as I pound on his chest, straddling him. Two pairs of hands pull me up from behind. Screaming, I struggle to free my arms;

I need to hit him again. "How could you keep this from me? How could you let me go through that?"

"I told you to watch out for her," Scott muses loudly as he saunters towards us. I turn, fighting to free myself from the two men holding me firm.

"Please, no," I beg as Scott stops in front of me with a syringe. Looking to Erik, he raises an eyebrow.

"Just let her calm down," Erik huffs and pulls himself back to his feet.

"If you're sure," Scott shrugs. "Just to be safe, put Alexandra in my car."

"We'll talk at the house," Erik calls as I'm towed away.

"Like hell we will." I cross my arms tightly over my chest as I'm pressed into the back seat, my jaw clenched.

Scott opens the other backseat door. "On second thought, I'll sit in the front," he says with a laugh as he takes in my expression.

I roll my eyes, not in the mood for his cheek.

"Am I not allowed to be mad anymore?" I demand as Scott and the driver get in, the car pulling away from the hangar.

"Of course you are; I love your scrappy ways." Scott smiles and turns in his seat. "I just can't let you kill Erik. His dad would be displeased if he got hurt and I don't want to piss off the boss like that."

"Erik's dad?"

"I believe you've met him, haven't you?"

"Yeah, but I didn't know... I thought he was a businessman."

"He is, in a manner of speaking."

"Right. And I bet Erik's really an accountant."

Scott laughs. "No, that was a lie. He's actually crap at maths."

"I'm guessing that isn't all he lied about," I spit, seething.

"Okay sensitive subject. I get that, but give him a break, alright? This wasn't his idea," Scott says, an uncharacteristic hint of sympathy in his tone.

I'm definitely not planning to *give Erik a break*, his idea or not. Letting out a sigh, I turn my thoughts away from Erik. "Where does everyone think I am?" I ask, curious if I get a cover story like Seth did.

"Soul searching your way through Europe; it's the standard story for people your age." Scott shakes his head. "What a ridiculous North American notion, *soul-searching*. You know, not everyone feels the need to blow through their parents' hard-earned money to try and find their bliss."

"Yeah well, not everyone has the required hardware; your lack of soul finally plays to your advantage. Besides, what do you know about hard-earned money?"

"You should have slept on the plane. You're in no mood to meet everyone today."

"Doesn't mean I'm wrong."

Scott laughs, turning back around. "This is going to be hilarious."

I spend the rest of the drive fuming about Erik. My mind shifts between visions of attacking him and rehearsing tearing a strip off of him. So consumed with my anger towards Erik, I didn't even take in my first glimpses of Europe through the speeding car window. I take a minute to look out the window now that we've stopped. We're in front of a massive, castle-like estate. Stepping out of the car, I stare at the sprawling house in awe. It's undeniably beautiful, built with light grey stone, looking hundreds of years old. It's exactly the type of building I always pictured touring on my dream Europe trip. Doors slam shut as another car pulls up behind me.

"You look like crap," Erik says right behind me.

"Wow, thanks, Erik." Turning my attention from the house, I cast a glare at him.

"No, I just mean, you look like you could use some sleep," he amends with an exasperated sigh. *Erik thinks he's annoyed?*

"I almost had a great nap back there, thanks to you." I let my anger pour through in my tone.

"Thanks to me? I have you to thank for this goose egg on my head. I'm the reason you weren't sedated!"

"I suppose you want a thank you, too?" I match his tone before turning away. He doesn't get the hint and walks around me to regain my attention.

"Come on kids," Scott calls from the door.

"We'll be there in a minute," Erik replies, not taking his eyes off me. "Listen, Alex, I get that you're upset, but it's not acceptable to attack me like that. I was given a job to learn about you. It wasn't my choice."

"Oh, so I was your job?" I look at him, eyebrows raised. "And it's *unacceptable?* Who do you think you are?"

"What's gotten into you?" he asks just above a whisper, forehead wrinkling as his eyes search mine.

I let out a humorless laugh. "Oh, I don't know, maybe my cousin disappeared and I confided in my *boyfriend*. This *boyfriend* assured me everything was fine, even though he knew what had happened and that I might disappear, too. Then I was taken by force and kept in the dark about what was going on when my *boyfriend* knew all along. After that, I was driven across two countries, drugged multiple times, and flown to another continent, all to have you asking what's gotten into me?"

"Calm down," Erik demands, as he reaches to take my arms.

"Don't touch me!" I hiss, seething with anger and pushing his hands away.

"Alex."

"No. Stay away from me."

Erik growls, gripping my wrists painfully.

I gasp in surprise as pain radiates up my arms. "Let go!" I try to pull away. He steps towards me, face tight with anger. Fear floods me and momentarily quells my rage as I stare into his narrowed eyes.

"Hey!"

"Drew, not now." Erik looks up at him with irritation, but his grip loosens.

"Get away from her." Drew glares down at Erik as he walks towards us from the broad front steps. I hadn't realized how tall Drew really was until now; he towers a good five inches over Erik.

"What are you talking about?" Erik scoffs, as his anger shifts to indignation.

"She said to stay away. I suggest you listen to her," Drew replies, articulating each word clearly.

My eyes dart between the two boys. The familiar sense of confusion returns. Both of their jaws are clenched, fists balled; any anger I lost seems to have seeped into them. *Are they about to fight? They seemed friendly enough at the airport, how well do they know each other?* Maybe this feud has nothing to do with me. It's disorienting seeing my two worlds collide like this. Erik and Drew are from different realities, yet they're more connected than I ever could have imagined.

"Erik, Andrew, enough!" another familiar voice calls from the door. Erik's dad, Michael, stands in the open doorway, arms crossed. The boys stare each other down for another minute before Erik stomps towards the house.

"Alexandra, come inside, please. Andrew, you too," Michael adds, his voice sounding strained. I walk towards the building behind Drew, having a hard time comprehending him standing up for me so fiercely. Even more startling is that I needed defending from Erik; he's always been gentle and reserved. Drew avoids my curious gaze as we make our way to the door.

"Thank you," I mutter. Drew doesn't respond, walking so fast I have to jog to keep up.

"Alexandra, welcome." Michael smiles as I walk past him into the foyer.

"Andrew, Erik, go wait for me in the study; now," Michael demands, voice stern. Neither argues, leaving without so much as a glance in my direction. I take in the entryway for the first time. It's unquestionably the largest entryway I have ever seen, with a wide staircase dominating the space and a hallway splitting off in two directions on the upper landing. The floors, including the stairs, are dark hardwood with a red carpet runner. A large brass and crystal chandelier above my head reflects on the shiny floor, making the room exceedingly bright. *Ostentatious much?* I thought Clarissa's house was ridiculous! It could be a shed for this place.

"I hope your trip was comfortable," Michael says formally, turning his attention back to me. Erik's dad has always made me uncomfortable; it never bothered me that he was often away on business. I could never put my finger on the reason, so I chalked it up to the pressure of trying to impress him. I felt like I needed to prove to him that I was good enough for Erik. That thought is laughable now.

I have always gotten along much better with Erik's mom. I don't even want to think about Talia being involved in this.

I swallow hard, not sure what to say to Michael. Am I expected to make pleasantries with the man who seemingly arranged this fake relationship and my abduction?

"I believe a proper introduction is in order. My name is Damian, not Michael."

I let out a breath. This shouldn't even register when compared to all of the lies I've been told. I suppose I should just assume everything I thought I knew about Erik and his family isn't true.

"I prefer to keep my first name when undercover, but your father knew me well in our youth. My name isn't the most common, and Erik looks enough like me that I didn't want to arouse suspicion," he explains conversationally.

"Right," is all I can manage. What does he want, a compliment on his clever deceit of my family?

"This evening I will introduce you to the Guardians who reside in this estate. For now, I'll let you get settled," Michael, I mean *Damian,* says, turning to wave over a woman standing near the stairs.

"Rosalita, please take Alexandra to her room and get her something to eat," Damian orders. The woman who looks to be in her early forties nods meekly.

"Dinner will be at seven in the main dining room. Rosalita will help you get ready." Not waiting for a response, Damian turns, leaving me alone with Rosalita.

"Right this way, Miss Conry," she says, heading towards the stairs. It's strange being called by my old surname, but I don't feel the need to correct her right now. From the stairs, I turn back towards the door. An overly-muscled guard is standing in front of the now-closed set of double doors. I bet Damian thinks I want to make a run for it. Frankly, I'm too tired to even consider that option right now. What the hell would I do if I did manage to run away? I'm in Europe with no money, phone, or ID.

As we walk up the stairs, I run my hand on the ancient wooden banister. It's just as silky smooth as it looks. Rosalita turns to the right, then down the hall, and up another large set of stairs. The hallways all look disorientingly similar with their red runner carpet and wainscot walls matching the entryway. Some have variations in the upper wallpaper, but it's of no help to me; I would never be able to retrace my path back to the main entryway.

"Don't worry," Rosalita says, reading my mind, or perhaps my panicked expression. "You get used to it."

Rosalita adjusts the tuck of her white dress shirt and shifts her navy skirt discreetly. She has a slight accent that I can't yet place, and she's quite full figured. Her auburn hair is twisted in a stylish knot. With her back to me, she reminds me so much of my mom that I have to swallow down the lump that fills my throat and force my eyes to look away. She finally stops at the end of a long hallway and opens a door that looks like all the other's we've passed. We step into a gorgeous bedroom with a huge four-poster bed. Light green fabric is drawn to the posts with silk ties. Light fills the room from the large floor to ceiling windows dominating the far wall, covered with sheer curtains.

"They said green is your favorite," Rosalita comments as she enters the room.

Her shoes click on the dark hardwood floors as I follow her in. She makes her way around the bed and opens another door leading to a massive marble-tiled ensuite, complete with soaker tub, separate shower, and large vanity.

"I will let you freshen up while I get you some breakfast. There are clothes in the closet that should fit you. I'll arrange a shopping trip in the next few days to get some clothes that are more your style," she adds, switching on the cascading tap of the tub.

As she speaks, I realize she has the same faint accent as Drew. *Is that a light Swedish accent?*

I stand frozen in the bathroom as she leaves, the distinct click of a lock echoing loudly in the silent space. *Why even lock me in? It's not like I could find my way out of this labyrinth, even if I tried.* I watch tears trickling down my cheeks in the mirror.

Taking a deep breath, I try to persuade myself that the lock doesn't make me feel like a bird in a gilded cage. I turn my attention to filling the tub. The thought of a bath is too appealing to resist; my body's still stiff from the last few days.

Smiling as I sink into the steaming water, my mood is brightened knowing Erik will be feeling the hard landing I gave him this morning.

Thinking of Erik is an inevitable misstep. My mind overflows with images of him standing outside of the plane; anger courses through me again, my bath becoming oppressively hot. My cheeks burn in a surprising wave of embarrassment. I'm a fool. I'd trusted him completely. How could I let someone convince me they liked me when they were just a spy? Am I that naive? *Yes,* my inner voice answers quickly. I shake my head, forcing my inner voice to shut it. I'm reminded of the Guardian crest, the *lily* suddenly making more sense. Erik's beauty had disarmed me. I try to reason that this isn't my fault. I know, in theory, that people are tricked by jerks all the time. *It doesn't make me stupid. I was manipulated*. I bite my cheek, forbidding my silent tears to turn into sobs. Flashbacks take my sight: Erik and I laughing as we walk, talking for hours, going to the movies. I had told him everything, opened myself up completely. *What an easy mark I am.*

Bath ruined, I get out and tie a towel around myself. As I towel-dry my hair, I wonder how I'm going to hold myself together today. I just want to curl up in a ball and cry, but it doesn't sound like that's on the agenda. The thought of sitting through a dinner with my kidnappers is absurd. *It's that, or sit around pouting, not learning anything about why you're here.* My inner voice is being a real bitch today.

Peeking into the bedroom, I find it empty. I search for a wardrobe or sliding closet doors, but I don't see either. As I turn, I spot a door beside the bathroom. Inside is a walk-in closet as big as my bedroom back home. *Should have guessed.* Rows of neatly hung clothes, a wall of dressers, and a full-length stand-up mirror surround the space. There's also a padded bench that creates an island in the center. One whole wall is dedicated to shoes and accessories, with lots of space to add more to the already considerable collection. I have no idea where to start, so I grab the first shirt I see: a long sleeve t-shirt. Moving to the dresser, I find a pair of jeans. Both are a little loose and long for me, like when I try to borrow Whitney's clothes.

"Oh, hi," I say, startled by Rosalita as I leave the closet.
"Ma'am," she replies, setting a tray on the desk.
"Thanks, um, Rosalita."
"Actually, Miss Conry, it's Rosalie or Rose," she says.
I smile. "In that case, please, call me Alex."
She looks at me, eyes wide before a smile spreads across her lips. "Alright, Miss Alex. Enjoy your breakfast. I'll be back shortly to get you ready for tonight."

"Wait," I call before I can stop myself. I don't want to be alone. I don't want to go into another Erik spiral, which is exactly where my mind is itching to return. "Can you stay?"

"Stay?"

"Oh, sorry," I blush, realizing I'm being rude. "You don't have to. I mean, I am sure you have better things to do." I make my way to the desk, dropping into the chair. I just want to curl up in bed and forget about everything that's happened today.

"No, I, well... I am not used to being asked to provide company for Guardians."

"I'm not a Guardian."

"Yes, you are, miss Alex," she smiles. "Being a Guardian isn't a choice; it's a birthright. Albeit you are not the typical... well, anyway, don't take it as an insult. Being a Guardian is about what you do with your gifts."

I turn to my food and take a bite of the croissant and egg sandwich, mulling over what Rose said.

"I apologize. That was not my place."

"You know a lot more about this stuff then I do. I appreciate your input."

"it's strange how much you remind me of your father."

"You knew my dad?" I ask. A surprisingly strong wave of homesickness fills me. I feel like an unstable weather system of emotions, unsure if sobs or screaming will escape when I open my mouth.

"Yes, we both grew up here. He was very kind like you, as was his brother. I was actually quite sad when they decided to leave, but I respected their decision. Not everyone could leave all of this for love." She looks around the room before giving me another assessing look.

"My dad grew up here?" I mutter more to myself, trying to picture it. "And so did you; are you a Guardian, too?"

"No, my family has served the Guardians of Enlightenment for many generations," she clarifies. Uncertainty must be showing on my face because she smiles. "It's a great honor, really. The Guardians are responsible for some truly amazing things in this world. To be fair, they are responsible for a lot of terrible things as well, especially as of late." She freezes, eyes wide as she stands abruptly. "I should not have said that."

"It's fine, I won't tell anyone. Your honesty is refreshing." I smile as she sits back down on the chair tucked beside the desk.

"Rose? Can I call my parents?"

She looks away for a moment, seemingly lost in thought. "To be honest, I don't know. I will ask. In the meantime, I'll keep you busy getting ready for the remainder of today."

This stupid dinner party. "Could you maybe find a way for me to call them? Tomorrow?" I don't want to get her into trouble, but I really need to talk to my dad. He has a lot of explaining to do. I cling to my anger towards him; it drowns out the sadness about Erik. Anger I can work with. Anger won't leave me in a heap of tears, unable to function.

Rose gives me a mischievous half-smile. "I think I can make that happen."

CHAPTER NINE

I want to know more about this new world I've been dropped into, and I sense Rose is going to be a great inside source. Unfortunately, after I finish eating, another woman joins Rose to get me ready, and our conversation has to end.

I've never had two people dressing me before; it's a weird feeling. The other woman is a seamstress who fits me into a beautiful red dress. Rose helps her with the fitting, as well as discussing hair options, doing my nails, and helping with makeup. I'm not really one to wear a lot of makeup, so I'm embarrassingly unhelpful. Rose kindly takes over after noticing my blank stare as I try to interpret the contouring kit.

When Rose finally settles on a pair of shoes, the first three rejected by me for their ridiculously high pencil-thin heels, the seamstress gets to work finishing my hem.

"Do they dress like this for dinner every night?" I ask, trying to imagine spending hours every day just getting ready to eat.

Rose smiles up from her post at the hem of my dress. "No, Miss Alex, just on special occasions."

"What's tonight's occasion?"

"You. Your arrival has been greatly anticipated. There will be another celebration when Mr. Conry arrives."

"Did they find Seth?" I ask, Rose pulling my attention from the amazingly fast hand sewing of the seamstress.

She stands up to meet my curious eyes, the seamstress taking over her section of the hem. "I know they had caught up with him, but I believe he again evaded capture. You Conrys are very spirited, but then again, so were your fathers; I guess we shouldn't be surprised. We have been very entertained by tales of Scott's team trying to keep you from escaping and Frane trying to catch up with Seth." She and the seamstress share wide grins.

A knock on the door startles me, and I move to answer it.

"Megállás!" the seamstress protests as the dress is tugged from her frantically stitching hands.

I freeze. "Sorry." I step back onto the stool as Rose hurries to answer it. I can't see the door from my position in the closet, but I recognize the voice instantly. My teeth clench and shoulders tighten.

"Is Alex ready?" Erik asks.

"Not quite, Sir. She'll be about five more minutes," Rose replies formally.

"I'll be out here when she's ready."

Rose comes back to the closet. "Erik looks very handsome."

I glare at her, causing her smile to fall and brow to pull together.

"I don't want to see him," I assert, crossing my arms. I'm so mad at him. More than mad; I'm heartbroken.

"I don't understand; you and Erik are a pair."

"A pair? You mean we're dating? Yeah, well that was before he lied to me."

"You're all set," the seamstress says, standing and giving me the once-over. She gives a satisfied nod before leaving.

"Thank you," I call after her before turning back to Rose.

"No, Miss Alex, you two are a pair." She takes my hand, eyes imploring me to understand. "You two have been chosen for each other."

"What, like an arranged marriage?" I scoff.

"Not exactly, but that's the general idea. You two have been matched as ideal partners; you will create gifted offspring," she replies casually as if what she's saying doesn't sound absolutely absurd.

"That's ridiculous," I enlighten her. "I'm not marrying a man just because someone feels we will make perfect little babies."

"Well, I can't make that decision for you," Rose says, looking down and smoothing her already wrinkle-free skirt. "But you are going to be late, so let's get your jewelry on. Erik is waiting."

I let out a breath. This isn't the time, or even the person, to talk to about this. For tonight, I have to go to this dinner. I need to get my bearings here, and I can't do that if I stay in my room, refusing to see Erik. Even if that's exactly what my heart is screaming for me to do. I squeeze my eyes closed and push my feelings down. I don't have time to indulge my sadness.

Rose and I move to the full-length mirror. A gasp escapes my lips. I can count on one hand the number of times I have gotten this dressed up. It always makes me feel like an imposter, but I have to admit, Rose did an amazing job.

"You look beautiful." Rose smiles as she clasps a silver necklace with a red stone around my neck. My hair is piled up in an elegant updo, showcasing silver dangling earrings that complement the chain. The princess cut red dress fits me perfectly, thanks to the hours spent with the seamstress. I look like a completely different person than when I arrived this morning—my dark circles and overly-pale complexion corrected with the magic of makeup, my green eyes sparkling.

Rose lifts my wrist gently, holding a bracelet. She draws a sharp breath, and I follow her gaze. A deep bruise is setting in. I pull my wrist closer, examining the distinct finger outlines. The sight makes my stomach roll; I clutch the wall to steady myself. I have never been physically hurt by a boyfriend before.

"It's alright, Miss Alex. I will cover it with some concealer," Rose says in a comforting tone, hurrying out of the closet.

"No," I call out.

She peeks her head back into the closet.

"We aren't covering this. Erik can see what he did. I'm not hiding it to save his pride." Shock lingers, making me feel sick, but I dig down to pull my anger back out.

"Are you sure? It might be best if we-"

"Yes, I'm sure. I am not covering it," I insist.

A mirrored bruise is forming on the other wrist. I take a breath, trying to steady myself and ease the nausea; the tight corset of my dress is making me even more light-headed.

I walk to the door in my elegant dress with my high heels, feeling like I'm in another person's life. Maybe this feeling will help me cope with everything tonight? Maybe I can pretend this is another role I'm playing? High school drama class all over again. I can pretend I'm a spy who needs to keep her cover. Anyway, that's closer to the truth than anything else.

Opening the door, I predictably find Erik. I can't deny that Rose was right; he looks good. It pisses me off. I don't want to think of him as anything other than the lying dog he is. He stands in front of me with his perfect smile, wearing a charcoal suit with a black shirt and a red tie to match my dress. His blue eyes sparkle as he smiles.

"Wow, Alex, you look beautiful," Erik says, stepping towards me and planting a kiss on my cheek. I freeze. He reaches for my hand, but I pull away.

"Oh, come on Alex. You aren't still mad?"

"No, I got over everything you lied to me about in the last five hours," I spit, rolling my eyes.

"Fine, I'll give you some time, but at least let me escort you to dinner?" he pleads, looking at me through his beautiful dark eyelashes.

"Well, it's not like I can find my way there without you." I glance at his hand that's reaching to take mine. Sighing, I turn to walk in the direction of the main entrance. I'll *try* to play nice, but I'm not going to hold his hand.

"I don't know what's happened to you the last few days; you are like a completely different person. You are so...so..."

"Feisty? Yeah, I've heard." *Okay, maybe I'll have to settle for playing civil. Nice might be a bit of a stretch.*

He gives me a searching look, like he's trying to figure me out in an instant. Turning away, I focus on the stairs ahead. I can't handle looking into his eyes right now. Despite my anger, they still tug painfully on my heart.

As we enter the lobby, I look longingly at the front doors. Escape would be stupid, but damn if it's not tempting. Carved in the ancient wood above the door is a large crest that I hadn't noticed this morning. I recognize it as the Guardian crest Drew wore. I suppose that's one small piece of insight I have about this place, assuming their core values still mean anything.

Erik guides me to stop at a set of large double doors on the main floor, two men flanking them. As we approach, one of the men slides into the room beyond, closing the door before I can get a good look. It's Erik's turn to avoid my curious gaze.

The man returns after a moment, drawing both doors wide with the help of his friend. Erik links his arm through mine, expression blank as he pulls me forward before I can protest.

I take in the massive dining room as Erik stops us just inside the doorway. An expansive T-shaped table dominates the space, three massive chandeliers sparking whimsically above. The white table linens are contrasted by deep crimson napkins and shiny silverware. Dozens of people get to their feet, watching Erik and me with a blend of expressions my darting eyes can't process.

"Everyone, I am pleased to introduce Alexandra Conry, escorted by Erik Jonasson," Damian boasts from the front table. Of course, Erik hadn't even told me his real last name. Applause fills the room, and I begin to blush. *Why are all of these people clapping? This better not be a trick wedding.*

Erik leads me up to the front of the table. As we walk, I hear voices, but the clapping drowns out their words. Two empty seats wait for us at the top of the T. Erik pulls out my chair before taking his place between his mother and me.

Everyone sits as we do, except Damian, who remains standing. Watching me with a smile, his eyes narrow in a way that makes my stomach clench.

Talia leans around her son. "Hello, Alex. Lovely to see you, koukla mou."

"it's Greek for doll, or something," Erik whispers.

I smile back stiffly. I can't help but hold resentment towards Talia, too. She's clearly played a part in this deception, even if she'd been nice about it.

Last time I had seen her, she'd acted so normal, and that was only a few weeks ago. A small gasp parts my lips, a memory stepping onto center stage of my thoughts. The conversation I'd overheard in the restroom between Talia and Erik. They must have been talking about *me*! Erik squeezes my hand, eyes tight with concern, and I realize Damian's speaking again.

"... thrilled she had a safe journey all the way from Canada, and we are pleased to hold this dinner in her honor," Damian announces as if I decided to make this *journey* on my own. Part of me wants to stand up and point out this inaccuracy, but a bigger part of me is too distracted, trying to pull back the memory of the conversation I'd overheard weeks ago. *What exactly had they said? Why had Talia been so mad at Erik?*

Damian looks at me, smiling widely. "Alexandra, welcome. We are all delighted to have you with us. You look lovely."

Applause fills the room.

I have that awkward feeling you get when a restaurant full of people are singing you "Happy Birthday." Taking my eyes off the staring crowd, I look down the front table. Just past Erik and his parents is a young girl who looks unmistakably like Talia. Past the young girl is a man and woman around my parent's age, then Drew. I stop there, unable to look away. Our eyes meet briefly before he shifts his gaze to the far end of the room. I can't read his expression.

"Now, I'm sure you are all eager to introduce yourselves to Alexandra and get to know her better, but we will save the mingling until after dinner. Let's eat!" Damian adds with a warmness I have never seen from him; I can't decide if it's fake.

Erik reaches for my hand, brushing my wrist in the process and causing me to jump. Brow furrowed, he picks up my hand, taking in the bruises for the first time. He looks at me as confusion contorts his face.

I raise my eyebrows, watching realization twist his expression.

He swears under his breath "Is this from... this morning?"

"From you? Yes."

He pales, looking into my eyes. "I'm so sorry," he whispers.

I look away, uninterested in his apology, suppressing the inner voice that feels bad he's hurting.

A door to the left of the table opens and people dressed in white, pushing trays, exit what must be the kitchen. My nausea lifts slightly at the mouth-watering smells that waft in through the open door.

They present us with salad, then soup, followed by pasta, and the best roast beef I have ever had. The meal is topped off with chocolate cake for dessert. The food is amazing, and as usual, all of my favorites. As I eat, I watch the other Guardians, gaining a better understanding of Erik's impeccable table manners. Growing up in this place could refine almost anyone. Despite everything, it feels weird not holding Erik's hand or leaning my head on his shoulder as we eat. I catch myself several times turning to tell him something about Scott or Drew, but stopping before the words can escape. He's not that person to me anymore. That's been shattered. Tears sting as I look to my lap.

When dinner is finally over, I just want my bed. I'm physically and emotionally exhausted, my resolve hanging by a thread. Unfortunately, my night isn't over yet.

"Everyone, drinks will be served in the lounge," says the man sitting beside Drew. I look between the man and Drew, wondering if they are father and son. Drew has a darker complexion, but the eyes are a match. That teal can't be a coincidence.

Fighting the urge to demand to be escorted back to my room, I remind myself I need to get a better feel for this place. I close my eyes. My dress is even more constricting now that I've eaten, making deep breaths painful.

"Shall we?" Erik asks with his perfect smile and mesmerizing eyes. For the first time since I met him, they don't hold the same power over me. I'm not mesmerized. Something about that gives me strength.

Talia comes to my side, giving her son a hard look as she links her arm through mine. Her stare is enough to send him along without me.

"That dress is lovely," Talia dotes as we walk. Everyone from the body of the table is standing but waits for us to pass.

"Thanks, um, yours too."

"She's such a doll." Talia beams at the smiling woman who walks behind us as she pats my hand. "It's wonderful to have you here." She places a hand on my cheek. "You're like family now, remember that."

I open my mouth, unsure how to respond to Talia's odd comment, but I'm saved by Erik's return.

"Take good care of our girl," Talia warns as Erik hands me a glass of champagne and escorts me through a wide doorway into what must be the *lounge*. Dark wood walls and a lush red rug stretch the length of the dimly lit room. A few seating areas dot the space, but it's mostly open, clearly meant for mingling. *Who has a place in their house specifically for mingling? I guess people who own a castle.*

The other dinner guests filter into the room and over the next hour, I'm greeted by the other dinner guests. They're all formally dressed like Erik and me, so at least I don't stand out. As everyone introduces themselves, I don't retain a single name or story about how we're linked; there's just too much information. That, and when I'm nervous, I have terrible retention. Erik stays at my side, ignoring my signals that I want him to go away. I hate that I'm slightly relieved to have him here. Even though I'm furious with Erik, facing all of these people alone would be torture. At least I have someone to help me make small talk. My eyes feel like sandpaper as I try to blink the crushing exhaustion away. *How long have I been awake?*

Scott catches my eye as I scan the room, winking and raising his glass. Based on his red cheeks, I'd say that drink isn't his first.

Drew seems to be the only person who doesn't greet us. I spot him sitting on the arm of a sofa, eyes on the floor and arms crossed tightly over his chest. *Is he still fighting with Erik?* I still want to thank him for stepping in this morning. Before I can make my way to him, the man I guessed to be Drew's dad steps in my path.

"Alexandra, so nice to finally meet you." He hands me a drink. "Bay breeze." He nods at the glass; my favorite of course. "My name is Bryce. I believe you met my son Andrew on your way here." Again, referring to my *trip* as if I had come along willingly.

"Thanks," I say, holding up the drink.

"I have to say, I am very intrigued by you. I have heard... interesting things from Scott about your trip here. And the way you were actually able to deceive him about having a sister? Incredible; he is not an easy man to lie to." He smiles at me, teal eyes narrowed as he looks me over.

I press my free arm across my stomach, sipping my drink. I feel suddenly exposed under his scrutinizing gaze.

"Oh, yes. This is my wife Gabriella," Bryce says, stopping a beautiful woman with curly black hair and a smooth dark complexion. I recognize her as the woman sitting beside Drew at dinner. He guides her towards us.

"Pleasure to meet you, Alexandra," she says with a kind smile. She looks so much like Drew that I can't help but smile back.

"Erik, may I have a word? Excuse us, ladies," he adds before Erik can reply. Bryce and Damian seem to have a pretty strict rule over Erik and Drew.

"You are lovely. You take after your grandmother very much." Gabriella sips her champagne. She has a sweet accent, different than Drew's. It sounds almost Australian, but not quite.

I nod shyly. "Thank you."

Gabriella shifts her dark eyes to look at Erik and Bryce, talking in the far corner of the room. "Alexandra, I am very sorry about all you went through to get here. I know our methods were not... orthodox," she murmurs, just above a whisper. "I want you to know that I am here if you need to talk. I came to be a Guardian in a similar way you did, except I was an outsider. It was terrifying."

She pauses for a moment, eyes on the floor. Taking a deep breath, she straightens up. "I was upset when I heard they had used similar methods with you. I only hope that I am able to help change your opinion of the Guardians. Tonight is no doubt overwhelming, but we will speak again soon." She gives me a soft smile and squeezes my hand before turning to join another group. I take a long gulp of my drink, my mind too tired to even attempt understanding Gabriella's comment.

Realizing I'm alone, my eyes search again for Drew. He's getting up from the couch and heading towards the door.

"Drew?" I step into his path.

"Alex," he sighs, trying to step around me.

"Wait," I say, stepping in front of him again.

He looks at the ceiling. "What, Alex? What do you want?"

"I just... I wanted to say thank you for today," I stutter, hurt more than I should be by his tone.

Drew looks down at me, his expression mirroring my pain. "I'm sorry, Alex," he mutters, stepping past me. Drew turns at the door. "You really do look beautiful."

Watching him leave the room, I'm stunned into silence. A pair of arms encircle my waist from behind. My body trembles as the feeling of being pulled from the dark forest near my apartment floods through me. I gasp, my mind certain a hand is covering my mouth.

"Relax Alex, it's just me," Erik says, searching my panicked expression. His eyes soften as he grips my shoulders, steadying me.

"Right," I manage, breathing rapidly. *What just happened?* The feeling's gone as quickly as it came. My shoulders ache, and my lungs burn for the deep breath I can't manage in this dress.

"Can you take me back to my room?" I ask, voice trembling. I don't have it in me to play nice anymore with strangers who pretend to know who I am because they know my name and favorite dessert.

"Of course. Are you feeling alright?"

"Let's just go," I say, heading to the door. He follows me, directing the way but thankfully keeping his hands to himself. I'm in no mood.

Out of sight from the lobby, Erik lets out a long breath and removes his jacket. Slinging it over his arm, he reaches to remove his cufflinks and fold his sleeves up to his forearms. It's annoyingly attractive. Distracting myself, I remember something I wanted to ask him.

"Who was that girl? The young one sitting beside your dad?"

"I meant to introduce you guys. That's my sister, Chloe," he says nonchalantly, rolling his now free shoulders.

"Another lie."

"What? She really is my sister."

"No, not that." I stop to glare. "You told me you didn't have any siblings."

"Oh, come on, you can't be mad about that. It was my job!"

"Yeah, so you keep saying. I don't even know the real you." I want to yell, but I don't have the energy.

"Alex, please. I'm sorry that I had to lie to you, but I didn't lie about my feelings. I really do care deeply for you." His eyes implore me to believe him. Letting out a breath, he leans against the wall of the hallway I've stopped in. "I didn't want you to go through so much trauma. I tried to bring you in myself."

"You... what?"

"When I invited you to come to Europe with me."

I open my mouth to refute this, but then I remember our fight the night I was taken. Letting out a humorless laugh, I turn to face him. "Wow, you really gave it the old college try, didn't you? Asking me to go to Europe with you totally out of the blue. So weird that didn't work!" I take a few steps before stopping so quickly he almost runs into me as I turn. "And what a white knight you are, trying to kidnap me yourself."

"I can't do anything right, can I?" Erik groans as I storm down the hall, stopping at my door. I recognize it because it's at the end of the hall with the peach wallpaper.

"Yeah, I guess I'm just too damn hard to please."

Erik's jaw tightens. "I'll come in so we can talk."

"No." I open my door and slam it shut in his surprised face.

I scream as frustration floods out of me before realizing I'm not alone.

"Miss Alex?" Rose jumps, looking up from the far side of the bed where she's turning down my sheets. Her brow furrows as she hurries towards me. "What's happened? Are you alright?" Her hands rest on my upper arms.

I shake my head, desperately wanting to be alone, to not have to explain myself. "No, I'm fine. I just... I want to go home. I can't stay here. I can't breathe!" I burst into tears, finally breaking down, letting go the fraying strands of my sanity I've clung to all evening. My breathing is ragged, the dress like a vice on my ribs. I pull on the fabric, trying to free myself.

Rose moves my hands from the sash and turns me around to unlace the dress, her practiced fingers working quickly. I gasp grateful breaths as the gown falls to the floor.

THE SECRETS THEY KEEP

Rose sighs, eyes pained as she steps around to face me. "Miss Alex, I know it's hard at first; you just need some sleep. Everything will seem better in the morning. I promise tomorrow will be much less hectic. No big party, no long list of people to meet."

I let my head hang for a minute, taking deep breaths to try and slow my sobs.

"Come, we'll get you into some pajamas and take all that makeup off."

Gripping my hand with a smile, she leads me into the bathroom. She helps me out of my slip and into a soft pair of flannel pajamas. I brush my teeth while she pulls a million bobby pins out of my hair. I keep nodding off until she's finally done removing my makeup and I'm allowed to get into bed. I don't even remember her leaving; I'm out the moment my head hits the pillow.

CHAPTER TEN

Okay, being kidnapped: decidedly not fun. But, I can't deny that this bed is the most comfortable thing I've ever slept in. Rolling over, I try to sink back into sleep. Before I can, my mind erupts, a landslide of memories and emotions filling every space. Erik, the feast, the mansion, Erik, Drew, being involved in a secret society, *Erik*.

I jump out of bed, feeling strangled by the sheets. I hurry to the heavily curtained window in a panic. Pulling back the heavy drapes, I discover large balcony doors. I yank them open, stepping out and breathing in the crisp, damp fall air. I clutch the sturdy stone railing; the cool rough rock soothes my burning hands.

My heart begins to slow, and my breathing eases. The view is spectacular. Mist hovers over a nearby lake framed by towering trees. Green lawns stretch out to either side, and colorful farmland extends as far as I can see. It reminds me of home; the familiarity calms me.

My anxiety fades, leaving me with more peace than I had last night. A good night's sleep really did seem to help. Not about Erik; the thought of him still makes my face burn with embarrassment and anger. But about the rest of my situation? I guess that's complicated. Now that I'm here, my curiosity pulls more forcibly than my fear. I'm mad at the way they went about things, I'm not going to forgive that easily, but I'm also hopeful that I will finally get some answers to questions I've obsessed over since Seth's disappearance. Answers I have been unknowingly seeking since childhood.

The thought of Seth causes my empty stomach to clench. Our last encounter was so chaotic; his panic had been palpable. Where is he now? Is he still safe? Still so scared?

A noise inside my room catches my wandering attention. Snagging the billowing curtain, I pull it aside to see Rose carrying a tray of food.

"You're finally up, Miss Alex," she says with a smile as I come in from the balcony.

"You missed breakfast; I thought I would bring you up some lunch."

"Thanks. Sorry about last night, by the way," I grimace, ashamed of my outburst.

"What?" she looks up at me with a furrowed brow as she sets the tray on my desk.

"Yelling..."

"Oh, honey, don't worry about it. Around here, as far as freak-outs go, that doesn't even register." She laughs, waving her hand. "Also, I have a delivery."

My forehead knits together as she opens my door, returning with a massive vase, flowers towering from the intricate crystal. It's comically large.

I reach for the card nestled amongst the purple and blue petals. Opening the small pink envelope, I read:
You looked so lovely last night.
-Erik

Rolling my eyes, I toss the card in the nearby trash. Rose flinches. I recognize the small purple flowers as salvia, one of my favorites from my grandmother's garden.

"Do you know what the blue flowers are?" I ask Rose.

"Morning glory, I believe."

I look at the bouquet for a moment, biting my cheek. I have never liked cut flowers. It made me sad that they were just here to die so I could look at them.

"Any word on Seth yet?" I ask, turning my back to the blooms.

"No gossip on Seth today; when I hear anything, you'll be the first to know."

Well, no news is better than bad news. "Oh, and Rose? Any possibility of sneaking me a phone?"

"Certainly. Your father has already spoken with Damian, so he knows you are safe. I'm sure no harm can be done by you speaking with him."

"Rose," I stop her before she gets to the door. "Can you get those out of here?" I gesture to the flowers. I don't want to look at them.

As she leaves, I turn to my food: delicious pasta with shrimp, butter, herbs, and parmesan, a meal I often ordered at my favorite restaurant. I stop chewing, mouth suddenly dry as realization strikes. That restaurant was a typical date spot for Erik and I. That's how they know so much about me. Erik must have kept notes about our dates, if you can even call them dates. They were more like catered intelligence gathering sessions. Embarrassment heats my cheeks, robbing me of any appetite.

Rose returns shortly and hands me a cordless phone. She grips it tightly when I try to take the receiver, her lips pursed. "You didn't hear this from me, but just a point of fact, I wouldn't say that is the *most* secure phone line."

I sigh, nodding in understanding. She smiles and leaves to give me some privacy, as much privacy as one can have when making a call on a bugged phone.

I stare blankly at the keypad. I have been aching to call my dad since I pieced together his involvement in this mess, but sitting here with a phone in my hand, I don't know what to say. After a few moments contemplation, I decide to wing it; not sure how long I'll have the option to call him.

"Hello?" my dad answers, voice groggy.

I hadn't considered the time difference. *What time is it in Ontario?* "Hi...dad?"

"Alex!" he exclaims, voice clearing. "Are you alright? You have no idea how worried I've been. I can't believe they would stoop to this level. I didn't even realize they had tracked us down."

I have literally never heard my dad this high strung. Tears fill my eyes, extinguishing my anger. "Dad, I'm fine. I...I..."

"Oh, Lexie, it's okay. They won't hurt you. They haven't hurt you, right?"

"No, I'm fine, just...in shock. Why? How could you keep this from me?"

"I was trying to protect you, keep you from them. I didn't want that life for you." His voice is tight, and I can picture his raised shoulders.

"You should have told me," I whisper.

"You're right," he agrees quietly. I don't know if he's serious or just placating me. "I was trying, well... I did what I thought would protect you. I'm so sorry, Lexie. Let me come get you. Just tell me which house you're in."

Yes, my internal voice replies immediately. I swallow the lump in my throat and focus on stopping my tears. "Seth... he isn't here yet. He's still on the run. I'm not going anywhere 'til he gets here. Plus, if you come get me, they'll probably just track me down again. I'm not going to live on the run from these people," I answer, my words sounding a lot more mature than I feel. I want to beg for him to take me home. I can't decide if my concern for Seth or my anger towards my dad actually tips the scales in favor of staying.

"I wouldn't let them take you again," he insists.

I clench my jaw, barely resisting the urge to tell him that he can't protect me from this. That won't accomplish anything but hurting his feelings. Part of me really wants to hurt him, though. "What is it about this place that you hate so much?"

"that's... complicated."

"Seriously? I'm here, and you aren't even going to tell me what to watch out for?"

"I've already offered to come get you. That's the best I can do. Look, your mother... well, she's worried. You should give her a call."

"Mom? You talked to her?" The fact my parents spoke is almost more bizarre than this whole Guardian situation. I don't think they've exchanged more than a glare since the divorce.

"Don't be ridiculous, of course we talked. You were missing!"

A small smile parts my lips. It's nice that if nothing else, my disappearance can make them behave civilly. "Okay, I'll give her a call. And I guess I'll talk to you later." I have so much more to ask my dad, but I just can't right now. My head is pounding, anger itching to control my words.

"Alright then... and Lexie? I really will come get you, if you want me to."

"Thanks, Dad. Umm, tell Whitney I love her, and try to keep her out of this."

"Don't worry, I already talked to Damian about that. He knows she's off limits."

Anger flares at his words, surprising me. Was my dad more concerned that his precious first born might be taken than about getting me back? I know that my dad loves me, but I'm not Whitney.

"Did you at least tell her what's going on?" I ask, anger seeping into my tone.

He doesn't respond.

"You have got to be kidding me! What the hell did you tell her?"

"Alex, it's fine. I told her that you went to catch up with Seth in Europe."

"Dad!"

"There is no reason to worry her."

"Oh, I think what happened to me proves there is every reason to *worry* her."

"Please, honey, I will take care of it."

I shake my head, stunned by what I'm hearing.

"Just leave it to me," he adds.

Like hell I will. I change the subject; I can just tell her myself.

"Speaking of Whit, do they not know about..." I pause, hoping my dad understands I'm asking about Caleb. In my whole time here, no one had mentioned him, even when they spoke of Whitney.

"No, they do not; let's keep it that way," my dad says seriously, seeming to catch my meaning.

I sigh, feeling a rush of relief.

"Please tell... everyone I love them and miss them. Goodbye," I whisper through a new stream of tears. I hang up, not wanting to let myself think about little Caleb. I miss him so much but feel beyond relieved that he's safe, at least for now. A flash of fear seizes me, stealing my breath. *Erik.* Erik knows about Caleb. Hasn't he mentioned him? If not, how do I go about convincing him not to tell his dad about Caleb?

I get to my feet and resume pacing, trying to distract myself. I grip the phone tightly like it's an anchor to the real world. I'm furious and so scared at the same time, a clammy sweat making me shiver. For the second time this morning I feel trapped, like I can't breathe. I splash cold water on my face in the bathroom. Looking at my pale reflection, I try to reassure myself. *You're fine. They won't hurt you. Caleb is safe.*

Caleb. There's nothing I can do for him right now. Rage grips my chest at the thought of him being kidnapped like I was. I have to trust my dad to watch over him. But if he is taken, there will be hell to pay.

I dial my mom's number, admittedly not in the best head-space for a conversation with her. Her cell phone is off, so I leave her a message, even though I hate voicemail. Desperate times and what not. I let her know I'm physically unharmed, my tone making it clear I'm pissed. My mom certainly knew about the Guardians and chose not to tell us.

Whitney is next, who also infuriatingly doesn't answer. What I have to say to her isn't exactly voicemail-appropriate information. I leave a quick message saying I'll call her later today if I can.

A numb yet wired energy fuels me as I pace. The call with my dad didn't go how I thought it would. I had rehearsed this conversation several times since I was taken. Sometimes it was filled with angry words, other times with desperate pleas, but this? I don't know. He had known this was a risk but still chose not to tell Whitney or me about this world. In his defense, he had moved to try and hide us, but clearly that hadn't been enough. The fact that he *still* isn't telling Whit is inexcusable.

When Rose returns, I'm relieved to see her. I don't want to think about my family anymore, so I ask a question before she can inquire about the phone call or comment on my tear-streaked face.

"Hey, is Drew around?" In desperate need of distraction, I try to focus on something solvable: clearing the air with Drew.

"I did see Mr. Jonasson at breakfast," she responds in a measured tone, eyeing me with concern before glancing at the phone I'm still clutching.

"Is there any way I can find Drew? I mean, how do you find someone in this place? I really need to talk to him."

"Miss Alex, I don't know if that's a good idea."

"Why not?"

"I shouldn't be talking about this," she says shaking her head.

"Please, Rose, I just want to talk to him somewhere alone. I need to clear the air."

She looks into my still tear-filled pleading eyes. "Oh, alright, I'll see what I can arrange."

"Thanks. Really, thank you." I smile.

Rose takes the phone, moving to the door. "Please stay put, Miss Alex, I'll be back soon." I hear my lock click. *Why bother telling me to stay put?*

I eat some cold pasta while I wait, before getting dressed and resuming my pacing. I know the house is big, but seriously? It's been almost an hour! Thoughts of Erik, Caleb, Whitney, and Seth spiral around my mind, making me nauseous. I force my thoughts back to Drew. He brought me here, then shut me out. During the flight, I had seen a different side of him. He was kind, funny even. I bite my cheek, wondering if I'd imagined it.

No, what about him defending you with Erik? My inner-voice chivalrously reminds me, preventing another panic spiral.

I certainly hadn't imagined that. I just want to thank him for standing up to Erik. That's the only reason I want to see him.

Sure it is.

Begrudgingly, a conversation I had with Drew on the plane comes to mind.

"Hey, I wanted to ask you something," Drew said, his bright eyes meeting mine. "I left my phone in the room this morning. You didn't even try to use it. Why?"

I furrowed my brow. "How do you even know I noticed it?"

"Call it an educated guess. Why didn't you call someone?"

"You left it there on purpose?" My heart sunk.

He bit his lip. "Maybe."

"Why?" I already knew the answer, but hoped I was wrong.

"I wanted to see who you would call. I know you're hiding something. I took a risk to see if I could find out what it was." He surprised me with his candor, but I'd been right. He was testing me.

Anger surges through me again, remembering how foolish I felt. Why did I even want to thank him? He was part of my kidnapping! I'd half convinced myself I don't want to see him when Rose pushes through my door.

"We are going shopping."

"What? What about-"

"*We* are going shopping..." she interrupts, eyebrows raised.

"Right, okay then," I say, catching her meaning. I was livid with Drew a minute ago, but I find myself desperate enough for a distraction to do just about anything.

Rose stops when we get to the front foyer, Damian waiting for us.

"Ah, Alexandra," he says with a smile. "Erik had some business to attend to today. I'm sure if he knew you wanted to go shopping, he would have stayed."

I have trouble making eye contact with Damian. He makes me feel uneasy, and today my nerves are already fried. After a brief silence, he continues.

"Anyway, Andrew will accompany you with some extra security. Just to make sure ...everyone gets *home* safe."

My eyes shoot to his half smile and intense gaze. I recover quickly and shift into an easily accessible glare. My anger towards my father is still just under the surface, and ready to be used on any available target.

"Cars are out front," Drew says, stepping in from outside, completely avoiding eye contact.

Rose slips her arm through mine. "Easy, Miss Alex. Relax the death stare on Damian," she whispers as we walk towards the door. Rose is probably giving wise council; I have very little to gain by pissing him off.

Outside, Drew waits for me to pick a car before getting into the other one. *Great; he isn't going to make this easy.*

Rose pats my lap after we both take our seats in the roomie back of the sedan. "I'm sorry, honey. He is just trying to be good. Do the right thing, you understand."

"No! I really don't," I groan, frustrated.

"Miss Alex, you and Erik-" She starts, speaking calmly.

"What about Erik and I? Is this about the pair thing again?"

"Well, yes-" Rose tries again.

"It's ridiculous! And does that mean I can't talk to another man?" I spit.

"You may see it as *ridiculous*, but I don't think Andrew does."

I can't stop myself from rolling my eyes. "Oh, come on, he's avoiding me because I am supposed to marry some other guy?"

Rose purses her lips. "No, not *some other guy*. Honey, Andrew and Erik are cousins."

My anger deflates. *Crap.* That does complicate things. I open my mouth, but I have nothing to say.

"They grew up together, practically brothers. To be honest, I have never seen them really mad at each other, except for the fight over you yesterday."

The now familiar sense of nausea washes over me. I didn't realize that I was causing so much trouble for Drew. "Oh."

"Now you know why I was so reluctant to let you talk with Andrew, but I think it's better this way. Maybe you two can smooth things over; you're destined to be family, after all. Also, we get to go shopping." Rose smiles. I try to smile back, but this situation sucks. Drew had made me feel safe in rough waters, but if I'm honest, I don't even know him; even if I felt like I did. Any feelings I've tangled around thoughts of him are just projections. I'm still pissed at Erik; any guy seems great in comparison.

But it's Erik, your Erik, a voice inside presses.

The cars stop after about thirty minutes, pulling over on a busy street bustling with pedestrians. Tightly packed shops tower over us.

"I love this part of my job!" Rose almost squeals in excitement. She reminds me so much of my mom that a painful lump returns to my throat. I need my mom so much right now.

One of the guards I recognize from the airport opens my door. Taking a breath, I shake off thoughts of my inaccessible family and get out of the car. I let the warm air and bright sunshine lift my mood. *You're shopping in Europe... You're shopping in Europe.*

I have no intention of testing my luck today; too heavily guarded. That, and I know nothing about this city. They would find me in a heartbeat. That doesn't mean I can't use my time to get a better idea of the surrounding area.

Throughout the afternoon, Drew keeps his distance. He politely takes bags back to the car from the clothes Rose picks out, but he otherwise ignores me. This woman loves to shop and ignores my protests that we're going overboard. Drew and my armed babysitters wait patiently in comfortable leather chairs outside of the dressing rooms of the many posh stores that Rose drags me to.

After the first store, I'm barred from looking at price tags. I attempted to leave when I found a grunge-inspired cotton t-shirt for 95 euro. Rose scolded me, saying that money is no object to *my family*—read: Guardians—and reminded me to settle down or I'd be dragged back to the estate.

Finally, around five, we stop for a break. Rose leads us to a cafe with the most amazing-smelling cinnamon rolls. She drops into the chair across from me and asks a guard to get our order.

"So, have you talked to him?"

"You're joking, right? You've been holding me captive in dressing rooms all afternoon!"

"Oh, right. Well now's your chance," Rose says with an encouraging smile as Drew enters the shop, having just taken a load of bags to the car. "Mr. Jonasson, will you keep Miss Alex company? I have to go pick up some things next door."

Drew hesitates then takes her seat. "Alex, I-"

"Drew, I'm-" We both speak at the same time, looking at each other and smiling awkwardly. Then I try again.

"I'm sorry if I put you in a bad position. I didn't know that Erik was your cousin, and Rose just told me last night that Erik and I are...paired. Just for the record though, I think it's ridiculous, and there is no way it's going to happen."

Drew shakes his head with a laugh. "You are so stubborn. You like Erik, you're even dating him, so why would you care that you two are matched? Just because someone tells you to do something doesn't automatically make it wrong."

My mouth hangs open, anger prickling through me again. "Correction, *Drew*. I *did* like him, I *was* dating him. Erik lost my respect when he lied to me. Our whole relationship was a scam. I can't forgive him for that."

"He had to lie to you; it was his job."

"Exactly. I was his job, he was my boyfriend. Can't you see how that would change things between us? He didn't have to take the job. Would you have done it?"

Drew watches me, biting his lower lip. His eyes dart between mine before sighing. "I don't know. I don't know what would I've done."

"I don't think you would have," I say, taking a deep breath to ease my anger.

"You don't know me, Alex."

"I know that you're kind."

"Look, I was nice to you because of Erik. Getting you was a favor for him. You're important to him, so I had to make sure you got here safely. That's it." Standing abruptly, he adds, "I'll be in the car."

I watch him leave. His words freeze my burning rage, and I'm left feeling foolish again. Of course he wasn't actually worried about my wellbeing when I was kidnapped. He didn't even know me. Was anyone in this place actually who they seemed?

CHAPTER ELEVEN

I spend the rest of the week sleeping too much and crying often. The disastrous conversation turned argument with Drew seemed to push me over the edge from coping to broken. I'd clearly misjudged him and his motivations, and his assumptions about my character hurt. As if the only reason I was pissed at Erik was because our relationship was meant to be an arranged marriage. I mean, okay, that didn't help, but it was nothing compared to how betrayed I felt.

My days are spent in bed, or on my couch watching TV, despair levels at an all-time high. My mind tortures me with memories of simpler times. I flash back to playing dolls and eating cookie dough for dinner with Whitney, swimming in our backyard pool with a group of friends, and summers at the cottage with Seth; getting into trouble but always worming our way out of punishment.

More painful still are thoughts of Caleb. I worry about him incessantly and wish more than anything I could call and check in. I always stop myself; talking about him on the phone would draw dangerous attention his way. The only times I do any real activity is when I'm pacing, trying to think of a way to get back to him. I worry about his homework, if he's eating enough, and most of all I agonize about what he thinks happened to me. Does he think I abandoned him? The last thing he needs in his life is more uncertainty.

Rose tries to be comforting, seeming desperate to end my funk. She nudges me to tell her what's wrong, or what I need. I insist I'm just having a hard time adjusting; it's clear Rose doesn't believe me. She finally relents, leaving me alone; delivering food and snacks frequently, but otherwise letting me wallow. She also commandeers a phone again so I can call my mom and Whitney. My mom is all tears and apologies, not something I have the emotional energy to deal with.

The conversation with Whitney is a lot of "wait, what?" on her end, which honestly just makes me realize how little I know about this place. I can't answer most of her questions and end up sending her to talk to Dad, which she adamantly assures me she'll do. I have a feeling she'll get more out of Dad than I had gotten out of anyone. She'd be more informed about the Guardians than I am, and I'm freaking living here.

I spare very few tears for Erik. Even my cruel mind knows he's not worth it. When he does come to mind, it's usually wonderings about why he hasn't tried to see me or fear he'll cast light on Caleb. I'm no closer to a plan to keep him quiet when I wake up about a week after the shopping trip, but for the first time, it doesn't paralyze me. A pang of sadness tightens my stomach when I wake, but mostly I'm restless; a welcome change.

After a shower, my first in too many days, I find Rose in my room, tidying as always.

"Nice to see you up so early, Miss Alex," she says, taking me in with a scrutinizing eye.

In reality, it's almost ten, but compared to the rest of the week, this is early.

"Any chance breakfast is still on in the dining room?" I ask as I braid my hair, the bathroom door open letting shower steam into the bedroom.

"Yes, of course," she says, a little too excitedly. "It's Sunday, so many Guardians eat late. Before we go down, I have news about Seth."

I step hurriedly from the bathroom. I have asked Rose every day, many times a day, about Seth, but there had been almost no news in the last week.

"They tracked him down last night. Yes, he's fine," she adds before I can ask. "And if they are able to keep hold of him this time, he'll be here in a day or two."

I pull her into a tight hug, which seems to surprise her. "Sorry," I say, shaking my head "I'm just...so relieved." A few tears slide down my cheek. *I'm going to see Seth soon!* As much as I hate that he was caught, I'm selfishly so glad that he's going to be here. It will be easier to work out a plan with his help.

Unfortunately, my trip down to breakfast comes at a price. Drew's mother, Gabriella, is still having coffee when I arrive and requests a private meeting in the lounge when I finish eating. I stall as long as I can, but when I'm done eating, and my tea is stone cold, I begrudgingly make my way to the lounge.

Taking a deep breath, I step into the room, reminding myself that Drew's mom had been nice. Somehow it doesn't soothe me. The room looks so different without the mass of formally-clad aristocrats. There are no windows, but it's well lit, feeling warmer yet no less intimidating than it did a week ago.

Gabriella looks up from her notepad at the sound of the door creaking. Smiling, she gets to her feet. She's so tall and thin, her high heels seem superfluous.

"Please come in, and shut the door behind you if you don't mind." She beams, gesturing to the seat in front of her. "Thank you for agreeing to meet with me, Alexandra. Or, apologies, Alex."

I nod, swallowing a lump in my throat. *Drew probably told her I was stalking him or something*, I realize, feeling sick.

I've avoided Drew all week, mostly because I stayed in my room. I was still hurt from our talk during the shopping trip, but when I thought about that conversation with a cooler head, I realized that from his perspective his argument probably made sense. Not the part about the arranged marriage, of course; that was just ridiculous. But his thoughts that I was only shunning Erik because the Guardians wanted us together. He hadn't experienced what I had; it wasn't fair to expect him to know how I felt. Admittedly, it took me several days thinking way too much about Drew to come to this conclusion.

"I am truly sorry, again, that you had to go through such trauma in order to get here," Gabriella says, pulling me back to the present. "I hope that I can help change your mind, show you that not all Guardians are quite so aggressive. We're all so happy to have you here. I'm not sure if you've heard, but your cousin is also due to arrive in the morning."

I smile, unable to contain my excitement.

"He and the recon team are somewhere in Northern Ontario; they fly out tonight. Before he arrives, I was hoping to get this chance to speak with you. We know that like you, your cousin will have a lot of questions when he arrives. Damian wanted me to sit down and answer some of your questions so you can help him along."

I bite my cheek, uncertain. She seems sincere, but her mention of Damian has me thinking otherwise. My gut says this has less to do with squelching my curiosity and more to do with Damian's fear that Seth and I will conspire. He just wants to avoid a double escape attempt. I'm keeping my options open.

Clearing my throat, I press on. "Can I ask you something?"

"Of course."

"My job, my apartment, even my car... what's happening with that?" In the last week, I had finally gotten around to thinking about the smaller logistics of the life I'd left behind, or more accurately, been stolen from.

"You are responsible. I sensed that about you." She nods, making a note in her notebook. "We have taken the liberty of resigning from your orientation program on your behalf. We noted you took on a full-time job elsewhere and thanked them for all of their support. I can forward you a copy of the email if you wish to review it. Your things have been packed and placed in storage, and we had your lease terminated, with payment in full so there will be no hard feelings or credit issues, I assure you. Your car, I am not sure, but I assume it is also in storage. Does it have sentimental value? We can have it shipped over if you would like.

"No, I just... I wanted to make sure it was taken care of, I guess." Biting on my already raw cheek, I add, "It's just, I worked hard to get that job and find that apartment."

She nods, leaning in. "I understand that. I'm sorry for how displaced your life has become. The timing was terrible. I can't change anything about that, of course, but I can personally assure you that if you decide to leave the Guardians, I will connect you with a job and accommodations that suit you." She pauses, reaching to squeeze my hand that's resting on my lap. "I know it doesn't fix everything, but I want you to know you have options."

"Thanks." A slight sense of relief loosens the knot in my stomach as I sigh. I hadn't realized how worried I've been about that, but I'm glad to know I'll have the chance to start again if I leave.

"It's the least I can do," She adds with a kind smile, Drew's smile.

Gabriella straightens back in her seat "Now, Rosalie tells me you are aware that members of the Guardians of Enlightenment all possess certain gifts. I was asked to speak with you because I'm in charge of profiling gifts of the Guardian's head families. That is one of my gifts; I'm able to sense abilities in others and pinpoint their gift. You, my dear, provide a bit of a challenge. It's always easier when someone grows up here, and we can assess their talents throughout their childhood. Obviously, we didn't have that luxury with you, but I am confident you are a rightful Guardian, as is Scott, for the record."

Gabriella pauses, scanning her notebook intently. "Interestingly, Erik wasn't convinced. He was ready to withdraw and thought perhaps..." Gabriella freezes, eyes wide as she looks up. "Well anyway, all of this to say-"

"No, go back. Erik thought what?"

"It's not actually relevant-"
"What did he think?"

She presses her lips together but sighs when my sharp expression doesn't falter. "He thought perhaps your sister... well, may have been a more fitting target," she finishes softly.

My face burns as tears sting my eyes. I didn't think it was possible for Erik to hurt me more. *Story of my life; Whitney has always outshone me.* I forcibly block my mind from going back over our dates to see if Erik asked about Whitney a lot. I hadn't noticed, but maybe I was just used to everyone talking about her.

"Alexandra, I shouldn't have said that. I apologize for my phrasing. Let me clarify: Erik really cares for you. He called Scott every day to make sure you were okay."

Wow, a phone call every day? After he found out I did have a gift? What a prince. A flare of anger towards Erik rekindles, hardening some of my pain.

I can't talk about this if I want to keep my cool. Shaking my head, I push us back on topic. "Anyway, you were saying."

Gabriella watches me, expression tight. She searches my eyes, mouth opening and closing as she seems to struggle with what to say next. Finally, she continues her story. "As I was saying, after Seth disappeared, you didn't let it go. That had us intrigued. Scott and Drew were sent to investigate. They followed you for a few days. It was obvious that you saw through our cover-up. I had a feeling about you, and so did some of the others, including your Aunt Clarissa. She remembers you as a child, and she had always seen something in you. Erik was asked to escort you... well, it ended up falling to Scott and Drew to bring you in." My eyes shoot from my lap to meet a pitying expression. She must be referring to Erik's half-assed attempt at talking me into a Eurotrip.

"Bryce and Damian were also quite impressed with your ability to deceive Scott about your sister." Gabriella continues before I can spiral further down the Erik well. I go with it, not wanting to waste time adding fuel to the already raging fire.

"About that, you must have known about Whitney. How was I able to trick Scott?"

"Yes, we did know you had a sister, but it's Scott's standard practice to know as little as possible about his target's history. With less information, he is less likely to make assumptions, and he's able to uncover more than we even knew. Typically, that is," she says, giving me a curious look that has me squirming in my seat. I'm not used to being the center of attention, but here, everyone is always watching me, expecting something I'm sure they won't find.

"I studied acting in high school and college," I say with a shrug, "That isn't a gift; it's just training."

"Or are you an accomplished actress because of your gift?" she counters.

I open my mouth but have no rebuttal.

"Moving forward, one way I do my job is looking at your genealogy. Often offspring have similar gifts as their parents or other relatives. We know your father and uncle's past and their gifts. Your father excelled at combat, as well as evasion. Your uncle was a gifted sensor, with effective combat skills. They were troublemakers when we were kids." She laughs warmly. "They constantly pulled pranks, but always managed to avoid getting caught by their parents."

Seth. That sounds just like him, maybe that's his gift? "You knew my dad?" I ask, changing the subject away from thoughts of Seth. A tension headache forms as I desperately try to steer my runaway thoughts.

"We grew up together at the UK house. Believe it or not, it was a pretty amazing place to grow up."

I do believe it. If that house was anything like this place; not that *house* is necessarily the most appropriate word. "I thought you were an outsider." On my first night here, Gabriella told me that she had come here by force, like I did.

"Indeed I am," she says, watching me with a renewed smile and writing something else in her notebook. "But I came here as a young child. My great aunt was a Guardian, and sensed my talents. She had my brother and me taken from our home in South Africa and brought here," Gabriella explains, looking past me, like her past was etched on the far wall.

I'm speechless. As traumatic as my abduction had been, Gabriella was only a child. She solved my conundrum by shifting back on topic.

"So, that is your dad and uncle, they were excellent at conman missions. I don't know that those are your gifts, though. Your father was also brilliant, a typical Conry trait, which is his core bloodline. I do believe you have inherited that, which could manifest in a variety of traits." She watches me, head tilted while biting the end of her pen.

I look down at my hands, feeling uncomfortable; the comment reminded me of an old memory. My mind travels back to third grade when our school underwent testing. The day the results came in, I was called into the principal's office. Both my parents were already there. I can still feel the fear that ran through me as I sat in front of her towering desk, my feet dangling from the large chair. I watched as my parents exchanged glances, first curious, but they shifted to something else as the principal spoke. She gushed about how I had aced the test. I was accepted to a private school in the next township on a full scholarship. My parents stayed silent, occasionally sharing a look that I didn't understand then, but now, maybe I do. Maybe private school would have brought too much attention to our family?

At the time, however, I thought that I had somehow pissed them off. My parents sent me straight to my room when we got home, saying they needed to talk. I remember hearing their raised voices through the vent. They never brought up private school again. From then on, I made sure to stay under the radar at school. I never wanted to upset them like that again.

I let out a breath, dragging myself back from thousands of miles away. I hadn't recalled this memory in years. What else in my past had unknowingly been altered by the Guardians?

"I do not believe that is all you are gifted with," Gabriella continues after making some notes. "You are truly stubborn and full of gumption when it is required of you. Also, you have an aptitude for hiding your emotions, making you an excellent deceiver. Your mother, although not a Guardian, is Irish, I believe?" she asks rhetorically. "I would love to look back in her genealogy. I bet I could find a link to one of our lines. In the Irish line I suspect you descend from, we also see fierce loyalty and a quick temper." Gabriella, writing excitedly in her notebook, doesn't notice my startled reaction. I take a deep breath to clear my face before she looks up again.

I can't argue with her observations, but they do surprise me. She really must have a gift in seeing remarkable traits. She could have just as easily assumed I was lazy or intimidated by my behavior this week. "Are all gifts culturally related?"

"Well, generally we do see patterns with different cultures and gifts, but more in families from those cultures. It's not a guarantee, of course, rather a helpful jumping off point. I have actually been studying a fascinating phenomenon of a shifting in the lines, probably due to breeding variations. I have started drawing up new traits for some families, labeling them as new cultural lines." She pauses, shaking her head with a smile. "Sorry, back on topic. An example might help. Take your Erik for instance. He has the insight we see from many Greek lines, although I am starting to question his innate perceptiveness. He wasn't able to see your clear intellect. He also has the beauty and persuasiveness of the Swedish line he descends from." I blush at that. I had been a total sucker for Erik's beauty and charm, that's for sure.

"He's not *my* Erik."

Gabriella's brow furrows sympathetically. "Yes, I did hear my nephew has earned your ample temper against him. He *is* a good boy, you know."

"I don't even know the real Erik," I mutter, more to myself, and Gabriella has the grace—or perhaps wisdom—not to argue.

"So," Gabriella reviews her notes, "that's a start, anyway. We'll just have to see what develops during your time with us. I don't mean to put any pressure on you, dear, but many Guardians expect a lot from you and your cousin. Your family has quite a legacy."

Expect a lot from me? They don't even know me. I clench my fists, feeling the familiar sensation of my nails digging in. I can't let myself care what these people expect.

"My hope is that after your cousin gets settled in, we can start the two of you in training. That way we'll be able to see what other strengths emerge. Now, there are still a few minutes until lunch service begins, and I'm sure you have questions. Feel free to ask, and I will answer as best I can," Gabriella says as she places her now closed notebook on the couch beside her.

I take a breath, trying to sort through which questions are most pressing, and which Gabriella might be able to answer. "Okay, so I understand that everyone here has gifts, but what do you do with them? What do the Guardians of Enlightenment stand for?" It's like I have a bunch of puzzle pieces but no idea what picture I'm supposed to put together.

"Oh, yes, good question. I wish there were a more straightforward answer, but the truth is we do a bit of everything. The overarching goal is a vague one, and open to interpretation. We are tasked with keeping track of and gaining knowledge. Many see this as encompassing a need for power, to create change that follows the knowledge we have."

Gabriella pauses for a moment, biting her pen. "You see, our gifts are so diverse that having one common goal couldn't possibly encompass everyone's unique abilities. At any given time, we have many open projects. There are people like me, for example, who are gifted in sensing others gifts. Many of us travel the world trying to find others to join us. There are trackers like Scott who we send out to bring people in, like he did with you. Those who are athletically gifted, like my Drew, often end up on missions with trackers, or on recon missions to investigate various global crises. We have a whole team of agricultural scientists who are working on creating drought-resistant seeds. We have charismatic Guardians placed in high political positions in many countries who are able to help us create political change when necessary. Erik is a great candidate for that role."

Reaching for her teacup, Gabriella asks, "Have you perhaps heard of the society, the Illuminati?"

"Yes, of course."

"Well, they often get credited, or sometimes blamed, for Guardian actions. It's rather convenient for us—keeps eyes focused on a completely different entity," Gabriella explains. My mouth literally hangs open.

"Aren't you afraid they will out you guys?" I ask, shocked. I've heard about the Illuminati and how they supposedly have a hand in everything from entertainment to politics. I'd always brushed it off as conspiracy, but sitting here in the mansion of a counter secret society, one who kidnapped me and easily erased my existence, it seems a lot more feasible.

Gabriella smiles indulgently. "It's unlikely they will make a statement of any kind; that would only fuel the fires against them."

"Are they a rival secret society?" I ask, suddenly worried. Have the Guardians put the rest of my family in danger?

"No, not the Illuminati."

The sound of a dish smashing next door breaks our focus, and Gabriella turns towards the dining room, startled. "We shall have to continue this conversation another time, my dear." Her smile falters as she takes in my expression. "Alexandra, forgive me, but is there something else troubling you? I understand this is a lot to process, but it seems you are holding onto something."

My eyes widened in surprise. I had been thinking about Caleb, wondering if he's *Guardian* gifted and whether he's going to be targeted by the likes of the Illuminati. Either way, I'm not ready to put him on their radar.

"Just processing." I force a smile.

Gabriella's mouth purses as her brow knits together for a moment before she nods with a small sigh. She's so perceptive, I have to remember to be more careful around her.

I make my way back to my room, still full from my late breakfast. As nice as it was to have some questions answered, it feels like I'm left with more unknowns than when we started. I focus on what I've learned. *Still no mention of Caleb*. Maybe Erik hadn't bothered to mention him because he didn't even find *me* worth investigating?

CHAPTER TWELVE

The day they find Seth is the first day they stop locking me in my room. Maybe it's because they sense I'm too depressed to plan an elaborate escape, or that knowing Seth is on his way will keep me here. Perhaps my terrible sense of direction also plays into my decreased threat level. Either way, it feels less like a prison now that I can open my bedroom door. Since I feel less like spending the day crying in my pillow, greatly assisted by the news of Seth's upcoming arrival, I decide to do some exploring. This beautiful mansion must hold a ton of secrets. Rose had given me a tour but based on the outside proportions, I've only seen a small fraction.

Unfortunately, my excursions have to wait. Rose and the seamstress catch up with me just outside of my room. Seth arrives tomorrow morning, which means another formal feast, and *another* dress fitting. This one is faster, as the seamstress knew my measurements. The beautiful royal blue dress is already a close fit when she starts, but she pins it still, wanting perfection. Then the manicure, pedicure, facial, and waxing take up a large chunk of my day. I still think the Guardians go way overboard for these dinners, but it isn't the time to start tearing into traditions. Except for the arranged marriage one... that's going straight to the shredder.

I do have time to hit up the obscenely large library before bed. It isn't quite *Beauty and the Beast* size, but it's just as whimsical. Like any inherited library this grand, it's filled with beautiful leather bound books hundreds of years old. Most aren't in English, but I can still appreciate them. Luckily there is also a section of *modern* novels, meaning from the early 1900s, which are English. The historian/librarian also shows me the overwhelming catalog of books available at other estates that I could have sent over. I peruse the list, mostly just to try and find out how many e*states* the Guardians have. At least five have lendable libraries in Europe, but they use library names and not locations. I make a mental note to ask Rose, before grabbing a fiction book to sink into. I need something to kill time before Seth gets here; idle wandering is only fun until my mind takes its own trip and I end up in another thought spiral about Caleb and Whit, with an irritating splash of Erik.

The next morning, I wake up smiling for the first time in way too long. I hurriedly shower and get ready, not knowing what time Seth will get here. He shouldn't have to be alone when he does.

I make my way to the front lobby with only a few wrong turns, and yes, maybe following a pastel-clad family that looked like they're heading to breakfast. Descending the main staircase, I'm stopped too late by the sight of Damian and Bryce standing in the lobby. The laughter of the three pastel-perfect children catches their attention, and Damian shares a disconcerting smile with Bryce as they catch sight of me. I'd been successfully avoiding them since my arrival banquet. During one of our many talks or my Guardian lessons, as I thought of them, Rose had filled me in on the basics of the power structure around here. The Guardians had several head families, and each line had a certain number of seats and different responsibilities, but all held *voting rights*. Damian and Bryce, both holders of head seats, were basically in charge of this estate. I suspect they're in charge of more, but Rose didn't get into it. Seth and I would also be head seat holders, once we were *adequately acclimated* to Guardian customs. I wasn't totally clear on everything, but it was clear that Damian and Bryce were pretty highly respected in the organization, which didn't exactly comfort me. I wanted to know what this meant in regards to Erik, but I was too afraid to ask.

"Alexandra, lovely to see you, as always," Damian says.

I grit my teeth, trying to find my chill. Eyeing a couple of well-muscled guards flanking the front entrance, I take a breath and give a tight smile to the brothers. I descend the remaining steps as slowly as I can manage, searching for an excuse to sneak away.

"Seth will be delighted to see you, I'm sure."

I nod, hesitantly, saved by Damian's phone ringing. The cool air meets me as I step out onto the front steps. There is no one else in sight: not a single guard, staff, or overbearing parent. I smile at the realization I am actually alone.

The moment is short-lived as the door clicks behind me. "You know, I may not be as young as I used to be, but Andrew does get his speed from me," Bryce muses, shattering my solitude.

"Good to know," I say flatly.

"Seth will be arriving in a couple of minutes. I'm so glad you have come around, by the way."

I turn to look at him, confused. He just watches me intently. I wonder how I ever missed that he and Damian were brothers; the resemblance is uncanny. They both look so much like Erik: dark hair, fair skin, and perfect smiles but they share Drew's teal eyes.

"You know... about the Guardians. You haven't tried to run away once this week."

Another thinly veiled test. I can see right through it, though. I smile at him and turn back to face the gate. Two can play at this game. I have to keep it together. Seth is almost here, and I need to see him. I can't let my anger get the best of me, or I'll likely find myself waking up in a few hours after attacking Bryce. I'm sure Scott's lurking around here somewhere with his syringes.

The door behind me closes again.

"Alright," Damian says quietly, "Seth is apparently quite agitated, so we need to be sure he sees Alexandra; that will keep him from bolting."

"Wait," I whip around "I'm not a prop for you guys to use." My carefully suppressed anger bubbles up within me.

"Too late, my dear. They're pulling up." Damian puts his hands on my shoulders, spinning me to face the main gate. A pair of black cars pull onto the pebbled drive. Stopping a few feet from us, two large guards exit the first car and open the back door of the following vehicle.

As soon as the door opens, I'm running before I even realize I've seen him.

"Seth!" I shout from behind the guard who is attempting to restrain him.

He stops fighting. "Alex?" His head peers around the massive body between us.

The guard stumbles backward, narrowly missing treading on my feet as Seth shoves him to pull me into a crushing hug.

"Are you okay?" I whisper.

He sets me back down, hands still on my shoulders, and looks me over. I do the same, taking in his filthy sweatshirt and jeans, the same clothes he was wearing when he came to my apartment over a week ago. He has some small scratches on his face but looks otherwise unharmed.

"I'm fine. Well, as fine as I can be considering the circumstances. Are you okay? Did they hurt you? I swear if they hurt you-" Rage floods his voice as he looks up at the guards.

"Seth I'm fine. Damn, it's so good to see you." I pull him into another hug, scared he's going to slip away again.

"Well, this is great! The Conrys reunited," Damian says from behind us. Seth takes a step away from me as Damian puts his arm around my shoulder. "I don't believe we've been introduced. My name is Damian, Erik's father."

What is he doing? I'm stunned for a moment, but quickly recover, pulling away and glaring up at Damian. Seth's knuckles crack.

"Let's go inside and talk," I say, taking Seth's hand.

Seth's overprotective in everyday situations, and this could easily send that instinct into overdrive. As momentarily satisfying as it would be, punching Damian won't help us right now.

"Yes, let's all head inside. I'm sure you are hungry from your trip, Seth." Damian extends his hand towards the mansion. When neither of us move, he simply smiles and walks to the door. The familiar throat clearing of a guard rings from behind Seth.

I roll my eyes. "Come on, Seth, these men don't mess around. You should have seen them after I tackled Erik. They were on me before I could get any good hits in."

"Wait, Erik... as in *your* Erik?" he asks. Before I can answer, we enter the foyer, and he's justifiably distracted. "Wow, this place is..."

"I know, right? It's crazy. Seth this is Rose," I say as she makes her way towards us. "She has helped me keep my sanity this past week."

Rose smiles as Seth nods, eyes still darting around the massive space.

"Rose, is there any way Seth and I can get some food up in my room so we can talk?"

"Of course. We can show Mr. Seth his room after you eat. Then you will both have to get ready for dinner," she reminds me before heading for the kitchen.

"What is she, a servant?" he asks as I lead the way up the broad staircase, distaste in his tone.

"Well, I don't know what you would call it, but yeah she works for the Guardians. I guess she's *staff* here."

I take in his expression, a mix of dislike and surprise at my response. "I think it's weird too. Don't worry, I haven't completely changed in the last week."

"What is this place?"

I bite my cheek, wishing I'd gained more information to answer that question. As we walk, I let him take in the elaborate furnishings. It's hard not to be impressed by this place, even if you want to hate it. I'd made a mental note of the wallpaper changes on my way to breakfast, so perhaps we take the *scenic* route, but we get to my room nonetheless. He's as awed as I had been by the size and amenities. I sit on my couch, Seth collapsing beside me.

"Okay, enough ogling. What happened? How did they find you?" There is so much for Seth and me to talk about that I hardly know where to begin. His face shifts to the serious expression he wore at my apartment: eyes wide, jaw tight.

"I should have trusted my gut. You remember that day I took Caleb to the park? I came back early because that guy took our picture. That's the guy who abducted me, right down the road from your apartment."

My stomach tightens. "Seth. I'm so sorry. I should have-"

"There's nothing you could have done, Lex."

My nails dig into my palms. He was so close, but I hadn't been able to protect him, and that hurt. "What happened after you came to see me, the night you helped me run away?"

"They caught up with me a few days after I left your place, but they were close several times before they actually caught me. I knew it was only a matter of time with these people; they are crazy trackers. Everywhere I went, they were either already there or right behind me. I hopped a train near your apartment and made it to Kitchener. I got off there because it seemed random enough, but I saw their car parked behind the train station. I hid in the bushes before running to the bus station, and again they had people there." He pauses, shaking his head. "I stole a car and drove to Peterborough, always choosing random places. I slept in the car for a few hours, too beat to keep going. I woke up, ditched the car, and got another one, driving north. Before long, I noticed their freaking car behind me. How did they do that? Honestly, I was just going to random places I'd never been, and yet there they were."

He stares at me, clearly distressed. His fists are balled and shoulders tense as he recounts his journey.

I don't know what to tell him, but I can't say I'm surprised. The Guardians seem to have extensive abilities, and even more extensive resources. I get the impression I'm only scratching the surface of understanding them.

We pause for a moment as Rose brings us some food, Seth's favorite: Mac and cheese with hotdogs. It's strange eating such simple food in this ostentatious place, but I'm not about to complain about comfort food.

"Wha bout yo?" he mumbles, mouth full of steaming noodles.

"I was caught in the forest right after we split up. I escaped once, but my runaway attempt wasn't nearly as successful as yours."

"Hold up, you ran away?" His brows rise in surprise.

"Of course I did," I say indignantly, punching his arm. I recount the tale of how I got here while he eats. He's pissed that Scott kept me sedated for most of the trip.

"They used drugs on you too," I remind him.

"Yeah, no offense, Lex, but you are like what? Fifty pounds? There was no need for them to use drugs on you."

"Hey, I'll have you know I'm pretty tough. I would have escaped if Drew hadn't been so freakishly fast. I even tripped Drew... before he tackled me."

"Drew?"

I bite my cheek. I'd left him out of my story. Hesitating, I'm not sure how to even begin to explain Drew. Luckily, Seth remembers something else, saving me from thoughts of that complex dilemma.

"Wait! Speaking of tackling, what were you saying about Erik?"

"Oh yeah! Well, when I got off the plane and saw him standing there, I realized that he had lied to me. Our whole relationship was basically fake, and somehow he thought that I would be *happy* to see him. Well, my anger got the better of me and I just... reacted. I tackled him before those two guards pulled me off and Scott almost drugged me again." The flash of memory brings anxiety and panic that twist my stomach. I'm surprised by a burst of tears freeing themselves from my eyes.

Seth pulls me into a hug, and I try to force my breathing to slow.

"Erik's been part of this the whole time. He knew you were taken, and when I told him you were missing, he assured me it was nothing. He knew everything and kept me in the dark. Erik let me stress about you for days, let me think I was going crazy and did nothing to help. He must have known I was going to be taken and still, nothing." Tears choke my words as everything floods from me, all of the things I couldn't tell anyone but Seth; only he could really understand Erik's betrayal.

"Lex," he sighs in a pained voice, arm around me as I cry on his shoulder like I used to do with Whitney. "That dick."

Sitting up, I wipe my face for the hundredth time and smile weakly at Seth.

"So, I guess you're ignoring him now? Oh, and can I punch him for you since Whitney isn't here? I know she would wreck him if she could."

"First, yes you can punch him, but make sure no guards are around. They won't let him get more than a scratch. And yeah, I'm trying to ignore him. I haven't seen him since my first night here actually, but everyone is against my plan. Apparently, I have been *matched* with Erik by the powers that be," I quote sarcastically.

Seth almost chokes on his water as he laughs. "You aren't serious, like *matched* matched? As in?"

"Yes, as in *happily ever after.* 'Over my dead body' is all I have to say."

"But, that's crazy." He meets my eyes, his laughter evaporating. He lets out a long breath. "So, what are we gonna do?"

"I don't know. Maybe-," I start, but we're interrupted by a knock on the door. "Crap, dinner." I just want to talk things out with Seth, but we don't have time right now.

Rose comes in with a man I don't recognize standing just behind her in the doorway. "Miss Alex, Mr. Seth, this is Mitchell; he will be Seth's help. We should show Seth his room now so you two can get ready." Rose steps back to the door. "We'll be right outside." She shuts the door, leaving us alone again.

"Mr. Seth, eh?" he imitates, straightening an imaginary tie at his throat.

I laugh, rolling my eyes. "Come on, we'll have to talk later. For now, we put on a brave face and get through until we can actually come up with a plan. We have a dinner to get ready for. Plus, I want to see your room!" I add with a smile as I pull him to his feet.

After confirming that his room is just as impressive as mine, I'm forced to spend the rest of the day much like I did my first day here. Rose tortures me with hair and makeup, zipping me into the perfectly fitted blue dress, far too happy about all she's doing.

This time it's easier though, because Seth is here, even if our conversation had been cut short. I'm confident we'll figure out a plan together, refusing to indulge the voice in my head that says with the Guardians, we're out of our depths.

I make my way down to dinner, sans Erik this time. He's been keeping his distance, but I'm not stupid enough to think I'm free of him. I'm proven correct when I'm seated beside him again in the dining room. The tables are just as elegantly adorned as during my arrival feast, except instead of red, the accents are blue. This time, there is also an empty seat to my right. Erik looks at me with a sheepish grin. I turn away without returning the gesture.

"You look beautiful," Erik mutters, reaching for my hand.

I sigh, focusing on the door.

"Alex, I need to apologize for the day you arrived." He gently lifts my wrist to examine the faded traces of bruising.

I pull my arm away.

"I thought... I pictured your arrival going differently. I assumed you would be relieved to see me, but you were just so angry; I couldn't get through to you and I acted rashly. I am so sorry. Please let me make it up to you."

I bite my cheek as his sincerity soaks through me. "It wasn't just the bruising, Erik. You lied to me."

"I know, you're right. I can't take that back. I'm sorry our relationship had to start off that way. It was misguided of my father to think our connection would make this place more welcoming. But please, Alex, can we try again?"

My heart aches as his deep blue eyes implore me to give him a chance. My insides pull, painfully polarized by the choice I have to make: let Erik back in, or shut him out for good.

Before I can decide, a man enters the room from the main doors and nods towards the head table.

Erik squeezes my hand gently. "We'll talk about this later."

Bryce gets to his feet, and everyone else follows suit, me a beat behind. The doors open again, and standing in the doorway is a nervous Seth. To be fair, I'm sure I'm the only one who picks up on the subtle cues that he's ill at ease. Seth covers it well by standing up straight and looking confidently straight ahead. His black suit fits him perfectly, and the blue tie he wears matches the decor, as well as my dress. I realize everyone is wearing blue dresses or accents. Had they been wearing red during my dinner? I'd been too nervous to notice.

"Everyone, I am pleased to introduce Seth Conry escorting Claudia Rickovich," Damian says from my left, giving me instant flashbacks to my arrival. Everyone claps as Seth walks into the room. His date subtly stops him part way down the table at her spot, and he finally makes his way to the chair beside me. The room fills with the sound of shifting chairs as everyone takes their seat.

"We are pleased that Seth had a safe journey and that we are able to hold this dinner in his honor," he recites as he smiles at Seth, offering him the greeting I had been given on my first night. "Seth, welcome. We are all so happy you are here."

Seth looks at me, I give him a sympathetic smile and squeeze his hand.

"Now, I know that you are all interested in greeting Seth and getting to know him better. As is our custom, we will share drinks after dinner. As for now, let's eat!" Bryce announces, and the food begins to appear from the kitchen just as it had on my arrival dinner. It's strange seeing all of this for the second time; it sort of lessens the impress.

Seth leans to whisper in my ear. "Why did they call me Seth *Conry*?"

I'm surprised, before remembering he wasn't even five when our families had moved. He was never told about the identity change. It's hard to get a four-year-old to keep secrets, so he was never part of the cover-up. "I'll explain later; it has to do with when we moved from Calgary. You were so young."

His brow furrows in confusion, eyes searching mine for a moment before nodding and looking back over the room.

This time we have a meal of seafood, which is a favorite of Seth's. He's suitably surprised when after salad and soup he's served lobster and crab legs with a baked potato on the side.

"Did you tell them to make this?" he asks, looking at me with shock bordering on hurt.

"What? No! Didn't you notice their freakish food knowledge on your way here? They had us followed for a while."

"I wasn't exactly conscious for most meals."

"Seth, I didn't tell them anything... I haven't...I'm not..." I say, struggling to explain.

He sighs, nodding with a small smile but looking utterly exhausted.

As we make our way to the lounge for drinks, I link arms with Seth and ignore Erik's attempts to get my attention. During one such effort, Erik's eyes widen as he approaches Seth and I. Confused, I look up and see Seth giving one hell of a death glare. Erik changes course, acting as though he was headed for another group.

After we've endured some introductions and the freakish drink knowledge of Bryce and Damian, we make our escape.

"Who was that guy?" Seth asks as we walk away from the lounge, stopping so I can peel off my painfully perfect shoes.

"What guy? Bryce? Yeah, I know he's off-putting-"

"No, the guy you were staring at who was intermittently staring at you."

I'm surprised he'd noticed with everything else vying for his attention tonight. Either he's more observant than I give him credit for, or Drew and I are being really obvious. I feel slightly vindicated that I wasn't crazy about feeling him staring at me throughout the evening, even if it is confusing as hell.

"Oh, Drew? Yeah, that's umm. Well, that's..."

Seth's yawn turns into a laugh. "Really? That bad, eh? And just after tackling Erik? You move fast."

"He's Erik's cousin," I say, biting my cheek.

"Well... Okay, that's kind of weird."

"Yeah, and he's hung up on the arranged marriage thing or whatever it is with Erik, so he won't even talk to me since we arrived here." I pause, taking a deep breath. "It's so weird, because he's been with me since they took me, but he was different. Like, he actually seemed to care if I was okay. But then, we had this fight... I don't know. He said he was only nice because of Erik... but then, why would he stop Erik from hurting me?" The realization just further confuses me. Not exactly what I need right now.

Seth stops to look at me, eyebrows raised.

"Nothing, I'm just tired. Anyway, I don't know what's up with Drew. He's a mystery, like everything else in this place. Enough about him. How are you feeling? Tired?"

Seth lets out a long breath as he opens the door to his room, already knowing the way perfectly; he certainly doesn't share my sense of direction. He flops back on the bed while I slide onto his couch. "Yeah, that was a bit intense. The favorite foods thing? What's up with that?"

"They did that for my intro dinner too...I think it's supposed to make us feel at home. Or maybe just assert their superior knowledge? Either way, it kind of just creeps me out," I reply as I suppress a yawn.

Seth grunts, sounding as tired as I feel.

CHAPTER THIRTEEN

At breakfast the next morning, I keep my eyes glued to the entrance, much to Erik's chagrin. Last night I'd shown weakness in my resolve to hate Erik forever. Now, he's doubled his efforts.

"How about I take you out today, show you around?"

"Pass," I say without looking at him, holding my breath as the door opens. A middle-aged couple enters, dashing my hopes. *Where the hell is Seth?* I'd stumbled back to my room last night after Seth fell asleep, but now I wish I'd just crashed on his couch. It's unnerving being away from him in this place.

"Rosalie wanted me to tell you *he* is still sleeping," a waiter mutters discreetly as he pours my tea.

Bless Rose for knowing me so well. I remember how tired I was the morning after I arrived, so I forcibly shake off my nervous scouring.

"How am I supposed to make things right between us if you never give me a chance?"

Biting my cheek, I decide stalling is the best option. Let future Alex deal with Erik. "I need more time. Plus, today I'm catching up with Seth."

After breakfast, I make a nuisance of myself, or so Mitchell's annoyed expression leads me to believe, by taking a book and sitting outside Seth's room. I'm not so much *reading* as deliberating, but the book provides a nice cover. Erik had taken pseudo-rejection better today, but I know full well that he isn't going to be patient for much longer.

Just as Mitchell starts recommending other areas of the estate with better reading light, we hear a door close from inside Seth's room. Mitchell glances at me with narrowed eyes before stepping inside. I want to follow, but I give Seth some privacy. A couple minutes later Seth comes out, pulling me to my feet.

"I was kind of worried when I woke up, and you were gone this morning," he chuckles. "I'm starving. Mitchell's bringing me food; keep me company while I eat and then you can show me around this monstrosity of a house."

It's mid-afternoon by the time Seth's ready, having slept until almost one. We spend our day wandering around the house and then out onto the grounds. We keep conversation light, seeming to have an unsaid agreement that it isn't necessarily safe to talk here. It feels like eyes are always on us, which to be fair, they are. Every hallway we tread seems to have a guard. I do however tell him what I've learned about our family's past and about the Guardians' search for the gifted. Like Whitney, he has a million questions that further highlight how little I know.

Mitchell finds us at the edge of the lake. "Mister and Miss Conry, will you be joining everyone for dinner?"

"It might sound like one, but that's not a question," I whisper as I get to my feet. Seth snorts, and we follow Mitchell through the house and to the dining room, which is only about half full. On less formal nights, dinner is served between 6:00 and 8:30, so people eat when it suits them, except us apparently. Damian watches us as we enter, giving me a half grin. I'm suddenly certain he had sent for us.

"Hey, after dinner I'll show you the library. It's ridiculous," I tell Seth as we're served prime rib, cooked how we like it without asking.

"Alex?"

I turn around, facing Erik for the first time since we sat down. "Not now."

"Come on. Enough of this," Erik says, sounding exasperated as he pulls on my shoulder, turning me back towards him.

"Watch it," Seth growls angrily.

Erik ignores him. "Listen I get it, you were mad, but we need to get past this."

"No, Erik, I *am* mad, and no I don't *need* to get past it." Standing, I add, "Come on Seth, let's check out the library."

"You are ridiculous. Don't do this."

Seth towers several inches over Erik, staring daggers. "Don't disrespect her like that."

Most of the diners have stopped eating and watch us with a mix of shock and intrigue.

"Okay, stop. We'll talk later." I hold a hand out towards Erik before pressing on Seth's chest.

Seth remains unmoving, glaring at Erik before finally letting me push him out. I change course, heading back outside. Erik's mood shifts quicker than Miles' when he loses to me in a first-person shooter. I have no idea how to let him down easily.

"We need to talk, *actually* talk," I say quietly as we sit beside the lake. Now that the sun has fully set, it's cold, but it's our best hope of privacy. "What's our plan? What're we gonna do?"

"I dunno." Seth pulls off his sweater and puts it over my shaking frame. "They're so intense. It's like we're always being followed."

"Yeah, I know the feeling." I bite my cheek, watching a pair of ducks lazily circling the lake, creating small ripples that glisten in the moonlight. After a few minutes of silence, my anger fades. "So maybe we just ride it out for a bit? Gain their trust and get the lay of the land?"

"I really don't like the Erik situation. He thinks he owns you."

"I know, but he'll get the hint... eventually," I say, but I'm not so sure. If nothing else, he's persistent. Truth be told his outward anger tonight scared me. It reminded me of the day I arrived. I rub my wrists, shivering at the thought. "Besides, aren't you kinda curious about this place?"

"Okay, we'll hang for a while, just to see what these people want," Seth concedes with a small smile.

We head back inside and to our respective rooms. Seth's pale with exhaustion, a feeling I remember well. We plan to meet up in the morning, hunt down Gabriella, and get as much information as we can. I'll have Rose bring me meals for a while so I can avoid Erik.

As I hug him goodnight, I can't shake the feeling this isn't going to be as easy as dodging Erik in the dining hall.

CHAPTER FOURTEEN

Loud voices rip me from sleep. My body is out of bed before I can even process where I am. Adrenaline surges through my shaking hands and shouts burst into my pitch-black room. I stumble towards the door, but it's thrown open before I get there, light from the hallway blinding me.

"Alexandra, sorry to awake you," announces a heavily accented male voice I don't recognize, a broad shadow filling the doorway.

"Who's there?" I ask groggily, hand shielding my eyes from the light.

"My name ees Frane. I was assign to your cousin's recon team."

"Okay, um, hi? What do you want?"

"I pologise for ze late hour, but I ave been asking to escort you to another part of ze estate."

"What? Why?" His eastern European or Russian accent is so thick it almost doesn't sound like English to my tired ears.

"Erik vishes to be speaking vis you."

"So? I don't *wish* to speak with him, and it's the middle of the night," I reply, more alert as anger starts to break through my fatigue.

"Unfortunately, Damian ees insisting." My eyes adjust to the light, and I see someone making their way past Frane into the room. I stumble back before realizing it's Rose.

"Miss Alex, I am so sorry. I tried, I really tried to stop them. I told them to give you time," she whispers, sounding near tears. Her panic does nothing to ease my own rising fear.

"Alexandra, I must eensist you come vis me. I am prepared to use forces eef necessary." As Frane says this, two more large shadows shift to become visible in the hallway.

I begin to shake as fear drowns out my anger. Looking around the room desperately, I try to think of some way to stall.

"Please tell Erik we can discuss whatever it is in the morning. I'll meet him for breakfast."

"I am fraid that ees no option, Alexandra. You must be coming, now. One vay or ze other." Frane steps away from the door, gesturing for me to exit.

My whole body trembles as I look desperately at Rose's now tear-streaked face. I turn to glare at Frane before pulling Rose into a hug.

"Please, tell Seth where I am. I need you to do this for me," I breathe into her ear before exiting into the hallway. Looking around, I see two familiar guards flanking the door, Frane watching me with a stony expression.

"Zis vay, Alexandra," he says, turning to walk down the hall, towards the main entrance.

I move slowly as one of the guards leads the way while the other follows directly behind me, matching my pace. My mind races, trying to think of a plan. My room is not near enough to Seth's for him to hear me scream, and would anyone else here care enough to help? As we near the hallway that leads to Seth's room, I have a lone, foolish idea.

I stop walking and glance down the hallway to my right, furrowing my brow. The bodyguard behind me stops to follow my gaze. Frane and the bodyguard ahead of me continue walking, unaware we've stopped. *Perfect!* I take my opportunity and run down the hallway to the left. Whipping around the corner, I head for Seth's room.

Too late it dawns on me that I really need to learn alternate routes around this place.

Stunned, I find myself on the ground after hitting something hard. A new bodyguard leans over me. I blink a few times, trying to shake off the dizziness flooding my thoughts. Jogging footsteps are followed by Frane looking down at me, expression casually curious.

"Could not be helping yourselv could you, Alexandra? Unfortunately, Scott tell me ov your tricks."

I scream, but Frane clamps a large hand over my mouth. The smell of dirt fills my nostrils as I feel my knees hit phantom damp earth. My body is ripped from the ground as my eyes flash between the Guardian hallway and a blinding light in a forest. The two scenes are so disorienting, I claw at the arms holding me, both real and phantom.

"Alexandra, calm yourselv," Frane growls, spinning into view.

I swing my arms, twist my body, kick my feet.

"Be careful vis her!" a voice shouts before something hard connects with the side of my head, and everything goes black.

I blink against harsh lights as consciousness returns. Groaning, I sit up, finding myself on a bed in a room similar to my own, only painted in cool silver with black and ice blue accents. I'm alone, but raised voices travel in from the hallway.

"Zis vas not ze deal, Erik."

"Nor was it part of the deal for my girlfriend to arrive here *unconscious!*"

"As I saying, zat vas accident. My men vere simply trying to be restraining her. But I vas under impression you and Alex vere jus meeting for ze discussing, not a guarded basement room. Perhaps I should be clarifying vis Damian. You are certain he sanction zis?"

"Look, Frane, you owe me, and as you know, I am not a man you want to be indebted to."

After a long pause, Frane continues. "Very vell. Jus... don' be doing anything reckless, Erik."

I stiffen as the doorknob clicks, and Erik enters the room. His surprise turns to a smile.

"Alex, how are you?" he asks, moving towards the bed. He takes my chin in his hand, looking at the side of my head. I pull away from him and get to my feet. Black spots fill my vision and Erik catches me as I begin to fall.

"Careful, you have a nasty bump on the head." He looks at me, concern narrowing his piercing blue eyes.

As my vision clears, I pull away again, making my way to the bathroom. In the mirror, redness surrounds my left temple, and my eye is beginning to swell shut. It burns uncomfortably.

"Are you feeling alright?" Erik tries again, leaning on the bathroom door frame.

"Peachy," I spit, pushing past him and pulling at the predictably locked door. "Seriously? You're locking me in here?"

"I tried talking to you in less abrasive circumstances, but you shut me down every time," Erik says calmly.

I clench my teeth, anger pushing away my fatigue. "And yet somehow you didn't get the hint. Erik, I'm not just going to get over this, you lost my trust. You pretended to have feelings for me to get information about my family. Do you have any idea how that makes me feel?"

"Alright, maybe it started off that way," Erik admits, looking down at his hands. I have never seen him nervous like this, and it gives me a small pang of guilt in my gut. As he continues, I clench my fists, nails digging into my palms as I mentally slap myself for feeling bad for Erik. "But you have to know that I truly developed feelings for you. Why does it matter the circumstances in which our love began? All I care about is that I love you and I want things to be right between us again."

My eyes dart up. Erik has never used the L word before. His eyes burn with sincerity as he pleads.

"Erik," I sigh sadly. My emotions feel completely twisted, and my head starts to pound. "Look, I can't do this right now. I'm exhausted, and my head is killing me."

"Of course, my apologies," he says, shrugging away from the wall he's leaning on. "Let me get you some aspirin and something to eat. I'll be right back." He walks to the door and knocks. The door opens a crack, someone peering in. After confirming it's Erik, he's let out, and the door is shut again, lock clicking into place.

Alison Haines

Wrapping my arms around myself, I drop onto the couch, exhausted. I close my eyes and rest my head on the back of the sofa. My mind fills with Erik's sincere expression as I try to make sense of this. His words echo; *All I care about is that I love you and I want things to be right between us again...*

What am I thinking? My eyes snap open as my thoughts clear. *Erik has me locked in here just so he can get what he wants. And how could I forget that he was about to pull out of the "mission" AKA break up with me when he was convinced that I wasn't gifted.*

My anger flares up again, further strengthening my resolve. *Damn Erik and his charm!* I'm so sick of my emotions being toyed with for this game. I get off the couch and walk toward the thick curtains on the north wall. Pulling them back, I'm startled to see a wall behind them. *Of course they would lock me somewhere with no windows; jerks.* I try to suppress the claustrophobia that's threatening to overtake the slight clarity I've gained.

I brush my teeth, wash my face, and pull my mess of hair into a ponytail; anything to distract from the panic. My mind searches for an escape but comes up blank. There's no clock in the room. I have no way to know how long I was unconscious. Is Seth up yet and looking for me? I desperately cling to the hope that Rose told him what happened. If she did, I can only imagine how frantically furious he is right now. Will he be able to find me?

I bite my cheek, trying to think of another way to get myself out of this mess. Maybe I can fake a medical emergency, a seizure or something? Knowing my luck, they probably have an onsite doctor and wouldn't need to take me out of the room at all. I really don't want to play nice with Erik, but I don't know what other option I have at this point.

Erik arrives a short time later carrying a tray of food for the two of us.

"Tea?" he asks holding up a teapot.

"Sure."

I remind myself there is no benefit in being rude while he is being decent, not that I forgive him. We eat in silence for the most part. I'm lost in thought, trying to figure out a plan. Should I play along? Act like I forgive him just to get out of here?

After we finish eating, someone comes to take the tray, asking if we need anything else. Neither finds it amusing when I ask for some freedom.

"So, am I forgiven?" Erik asks, sounding hopeful as he peers at me through dark lashes.

"Umm, no. What makes you think that?" I answer before thinking. *So much for playing along!*

Now it was his turn to be confused. "Come on, Alex! I've explained everything. I sent you roses to apologize-"

"Roses?" He hadn't sent roses.

Erik's eyes widen for a fraction of a second. "Flowers, whatever."

"What kind of flowers were they?"

"I'm not a botanist."

"What color?"

He squints. "Red."

"Are you serious! You didn't even send the flowers?"

"Fine. I had someone send them on my behalf. What do you want from me?"

"What do I want from you? I'm being held here like a prisoner, and you somehow think this is the way to foster trust and love in a relationship? This isn't going to work, Erik."

In a flash, his face transforms from apologetic to enraged, making me jump as he gets to his feet. "See, that's where you're wrong, Alex. You are *mine*. I will have you one way or another. So you better get over your anger and get happy, or it's going to be you who's miserable, not me. I always get what I want, and you will be no exception, I promise you."

Glaring down at me, Erik turns to the door. "Get some sleep Alex, and I suggest you wake up in a better mood. When I come back, we will see if you have, wisely, fixed your attitude." With that he knocks on the door, slamming it as he storms out.

I sit on the couch in shock. He has never yelled at me before. My hands tremble, fear at my current situation rising as I realize the power he has over me. I stay on the couch a long time trying to think of what to do. Tears fill my eyes as despair washes over me. Finally, I'm too tired to keep my eyes open, and I climb into bed, hoping I'll wake up back in Markham to find that this whole thing was just a dream.

*****

Feeling stiff, I sit up, realizing with a sense of dread that I'm still in the windowless cage Erik left me in. Movement catches my eye, and I let out a strangled shriek as a woman gets up from a chair near the door. She exits the room without a word, leaving me alone. There is no blissful forgetfulness upon waking; I remember everything that led to my imprisonment. My head pounds and my stomach is tight with fear.

The door opens, and I try to hide my dread as Erik returns. "So, I trust you've had time to think about our last discussion?" he asks, his face cold as chiseled marble. I stay silent, no idea how to respond.

"Nothing to say? Where's your renowned feistiness I hear so much about these days?" He walks towards the bed, looking me right in the eye, taunting me. "What? Not so tough without your audience?"

"Only tough because you have me locked in a room with a guard outside the door?" I spit, anger awakening my voice.

Erik reaches back, smacking me across the face so hard my teeth knock together.

My hand flies to my cheek protectively as a gasp escapes my lips. The only other time Erik had hurt me was when I first arrived here, and even then, part of me had thought it was an accident. This was no accident. I stare up at him, furious at the tears that slide down my burning cheek.

"You better start showing me more respect than that," he growls through gritted teeth. *Who is this man?*

"That's better. Now I will assume by your silence that we have come to an agreement. You will respect me, in public and in private. You will stop your childish avoidance of me. We will resume our relationship."

I glare at him, but he just smiles at me, not the smile I had fallen in love with. Nothing about this man was the Erik I had known. "No," I say, clenching my jaw tightly.

He lets out a sigh and shakes his head. Gripping the front of my pajama shirt, he drags me off the bed. I stumble, trying to gain my footing.

"What was that?" he whispers, pulling my face close to his.

I claw at his hands, breathing heavily and trying to steady myself. My toes are barely brushing the floor.

"Erik, let go of me." I cough as he tightens his grip, his fists digging into my throat. He throws me roughly to the floor, twisting me onto my back and straddling my hips before I can get up.

"Not so fun when it happens to you, is it, *Alex*? You might have them fooled, but I can see right through you. You are a *coward*," he hisses in my ear, pinning my wrists painfully to the floor. His hot breath on my neck makes my stomach roll.

"I'm a coward?" I counter, voice trembling. "Care to repeat that when you don't have me locked-"

He interrupts me with another backhand to my face; white spots flood my vision as I let out an involuntary cry. I push his chest away, but he's already getting up.

"Not quite the respect I was looking for. Let's try again."

Erik reaches down to grab me, but I roll away. Scrambling to my feet, I kick him while he's still crouching to reach for me. He stumbles to the floor as I race for the door.

"Open the door! Let me out!" I yell desperately, pounding my fists on the solid wood.

Two arms grab me from behind and throw me back to the ground. I scream, frustration fueling my rage and muting the pain.

"You bitch!" Erik growls, kicking me in the stomach repeatedly. Air rushes from my lungs. My vision constricts as I stare desperately up at the man I thought I knew.

He watches me struggle for a minute, breathing heavily before roughly pulling me from the ground and throwing me back on the bed. I gulp in air, trying to catch my breath. Erik stares at me, face impassive.

"Care to try that again, Alex? What did you want to say to me?"

"Go. To. Hell," I spit out between breaths.

THE SECRETS THEY KEEP

He yells, reaching his hand back and slamming into the side of my head.

My ears ring as a fierce wave of nausea crashes over me.

A loud bang and yelling voices flood the room from the hallway. Erik freezes and turns to the door, expression livid.

CHAPTER FIFTEEN

Erik's face blanches as the door bursts open. Seth's standing in the doorway, his eyes searching the room. Rage floods Seth's face when he meets my gaze. In three steps he's across the room, gripping Erik's shirt and throwing him off of me. Erik stumbles, barely managing to remain on his feet. A growl escapes Seth's clenched teeth as he twists his torso, his fist connecting with the side of Erik's head. Erik hits the ground with a thud. Seth spares his unmoving frame an infuriated glare, teeth bared, before turning to me.

"Alex?" His voice is full of concern as his face softens. Gripping my arms, he pulls me carefully to my feet. "Thank God! We have to go."

I don't ask questions. Gripping his hand tightly, we run from the room, down hallway after identical hallway. Blinking away the tears that flood my vision, I realize that someone else is leading the way.

"Drew?" I huff out, breathing heavily from exertion.

"Shhh!" is all I get in reply from both boys.

We climb a flight of stairs and as Drew pushes through a set of heavy doors, a cold burst of fall air meets us. Blinding sunlight reflects off the nearby lake. Drew curves to the right, heading for the forest. We finally stop in the thick cover of trees, just in time too; my legs are weak and shaking, and my lungs burn in desperate need of oxygen.

"Seth...you...saved...me!" I pant, hands on my knees as I try to catch my breath.

"Rose helped Drew and me find you. I can't believe Erik. I'll kill him." Seth looks at me, face shifting from rage to shock. "Did he hit you?" he asks, looking at my face with a furrowed brow. I try to turn away, knowing that Seth doesn't need any fuel for his anger right now, but he gently catches my chin. "Oh, he is so done!" Seth growls, jaw clenching as he turns back towards the house.

"Seth!" Drew steps in his path, putting a hand on Seth's shoulder. "I know, he's terrible, but we don't have time for him right now."

As adrenaline fades from my system, sharp pain surges through my right side, stealing my breath. Coughs force themselves from my struggling lungs. I can't catch my breath, which makes the sharp pain excruciating. I try to suppress a cough but holding it in is impossible. Clutching my side, I bend against a tree in desperation.

"What's wrong?" Drew asks, moving from Seth to me.

"My side, it's killing me!" I choke out, looking up at him through tear-filled eyes.

Drew gently moves my hand, gripping it firmly while lifting my shirt. He and Seth look at my ribs and then at one another. Drew swears under his breath.

"Alex, did Erik kick you or something?" he asks, tone strained. The coughing is making the pain so intense that I can hardly stand, white spots returning to claim my sight.

Drew curses Erik again. I want to tell him I'm fine, but I can't form words. My legs give out but Drew catches me before I can fall, hoisting me into his arms.

"What's...what's going..." I try to talk, but I can't catch my breath.

"I think Erik may have broken your ribs. Try to relax; I've got you," Drew says soothingly, turning to Seth. "We have to take her back to the house to see the doctor. We need to make sure she didn't puncture a lung or anything else."

I cling to the conversation, but the pain is so distracting I can hardly keep up.

"Seth, no. We need to leave," I try, but even to me, my voice sounds weak. Still struggling to breathe, panic pushes into my emotional whirlpool. Seth looks down at me, expression pained.

"If he comes anywhere near her-," he starts, looking back at Drew.

"I will personally help you kick his ass," Drew promises. "But Alex needs help."

I felt myself starting to shake. "It's cold out here..."

*****

In the weeks that follow, I remember very little about the rest of that day. Drew and Seth took me back inside. Seth settled me into an empty bedroom while Drew ran for the Guardian doctor. He confirmed I had three cracked ribs, two black eyes, and a body covered in bruises. I felt like I had been hit by a truck.

Despite everything, I couldn't bring myself to join Seth and Drew in their rage against Erik. I was too tired. Tired of all the crap that had happened over the last month since Seth was taken. I just wanted out of this crazy place. Everything in my world seemed completely out of my control. That, and Seth had more than enough anger for the two of us. Plus, if I was honest, I blamed myself. I should have been more up front with Erik. I should have stuck with ignoring him and shutting him down. I shouldn't have given him hope. Trying to let him down easy was a bad plan. Some part of my brain insisted that wouldn't have changed anything, he would have just imprisoned me earlier. I guess I'll never know.

The Guardian doctor came to see me frequently. He taped my ribs and helped me ice my swollen face. Drew tracked down Rose, who almost cried at the sight of me. Her apologies were profuse and unending, despite my reassurances that she wasn't to blame. Mitchell had blocked her attempts to wake up Seth, delaying my rescue. I reminded her the only person to blame was Erik... and maybe Frane.

Drew found out that apparently there was a miscommunication between Damian's orders and Erik's relay to Frane. The official word is that Damian said he would arrange for us to talk, but not in a locked bedroom, or in the middle of the night. Erik leveraged a favor to have me brought to his basement dungeon.

After two weeks, I've transitioned from exhausted and sore to bored and, okay, still pretty sore. I'm ready to leave the room we've taken over, but Seth is less than keen. He doesn't trust anyone here, and it's a hard point to argue against. He won't even discuss it, or Erik, so I've resorted to talking to Drew during our rare time alone.

I glance over to Seth, who's passed out on the couch, the light from the muted TV flickering across his relaxed face.

"What's gonna happen to him? To Erik?" I ask Drew quietly.

Drew bites his lip, shifting to check on Seth. "There's going to be a hearing."

My brow pulls together. "He was arrested?" Not that he doesn't deserve it, I'm just surprised the Guardians would actually turn him in.

"An internal hearing," Drew clarifies, searching my expression.

"Who presides over this *hearing*?"

"The Council of Head Members. Any Head Member can vote. People in line for a head seat can speak, and all Guardians can observe the proceedings."

I sit up straight. "So, I can vote on his punishment?"

"Actually, no. You haven't had your inauguration yet."

"What?" I yell. Seth shoots up from the couch to his feet. "Sorry, Seth, it's fine. Go back to sleep."

His eyes travel between mine and Drew's, narrowing as he takes in my likely red cheeks. "What now?"

"Nothing," Drew and I reply, too quickly.

Seth raises his eyebrows, crossing his arms across his chest.

Drew gives me a *"you brought this on yourself"* look. "Alex was asking about Erik's punishment."

"Death by firing squad? Or are you guys more partial to lethal injection?"

"There's going to be a hearing, and we don't get a say." I give up on trying not to anger Seth, selfishly needing him to join my rage.

"What the hell? Who, other than Alex, should have a say?"

"It's the head members society or something-"

"Council," Drew corrects.

"I thought we had head seats?"

"We haven't had our coronation-"

"Inauguration."

"Whatever." I wave Drew off. "It's bullshit. What do we need to do to get *inaugurated*?"

Drew and Seth share a wide-eyed glance.

"I thought you wanted to leave?"

"I do! But shouldn't we get to at least *vote* if we're stuck here? And why doesn't everyone get a vote?"

Drew closes his eyes, shaking his head with a small smile. "I can ask my father about you making a statement to the council if you want to do that, but Erik'll be there." His eyes soften as my posture stiffens. Pain shoots through my chest at the thought of seeing Erik.

"Lex, it's fine, forget about him. I'll keep you safe, regardless of the committee's decision." Seth sits on the bed, pulling me to his side.

"Council," Drew mutters again. "I'll call my father and get an update." He turns to me from the door. "I promise the Council won't take what he did lightly."

Seth's jaw and fists tighten as he paces, exactly what I was trying to avoid. "What the hell! How is it we're stuck here but have no power?"

"I mean, I think that's why we're still stuck here."

Seth lets out a breath as he drops into Drew's chair. "What're we gonna do?"

"I'm pretty much recovered. We should leave, right? That was our plan. Regardless of Erik's *sentencing*, do we feel safe here?"

Seth snorts. "Nothing about this place is safe." His brow furrows. "Who's actually in charge here?"

"You know when you ask a question too many times? And someone explains it, but you still don't get it, then you're too embarrassed to ask again?" I say. Seth's furrow deepens before he bursts out laughing.

"No, seriously! That's how I feel about the Guardian hierarchy." I laugh with him, but the sensation feels strained. I'm not sure if it's my broken ribs or just how long it's been since I laughed.

"Anyway, this head sewing circle or whoever the hell they are, Rose mentioned them. Most head members have a special role, plus I guess a seat on this committee. They get to vote on... things?"

"You should write a book on Guardian customs."

"Shut up! What do you know about it?"

Seth's saved by Drew's return. He bites his lip, eyes meeting mine. "My mom picked up. She says your inauguration can't be done before Erik's vote, which is scheduled for later this week."

Thinking about Erik makes my desperation to leave tangible. Seth and I need to get out of here before something worse happens to one of us.

"Drew, we can't stay here," I say as Seth nods supportively. "We don't expect you to help us, but we're leaving."

Drew sits on the bottom of the bed, his expression so sympathetic it's bordering pity. "There is something you guys should know before you decide."

I can't think of anything that would actually make me want to stay here, but I meet his teal eyes, curious.

"I know the methods were... horrible and there's been a lot of complications since you got here, but you should know that the Guardians of Enlightenment aren't the only like-minded organization that exists. They really were worried that someone else was going to get you when you ran away, Seth. And that is why I was so unwilling to let you escape."

"Other agencies watch our targets and try to recruit them. Some of their methods are unorthodox; they have actually killed recruits in the process of testing them or trying to get them to join up. They treat us like tools or weapons instead of people. I'm on their radar and have been for years. I don't go anywhere alone, which sucks, but it keeps me from being abducted. I can't say for sure if any have taken notice of you two, but I wouldn't be surprised if they have. They keep close tabs on our comings and goings; bringing two new people in likely wouldn't have gone unnoticed. Also, I have suspicions that there are moles within our organization. Basically, if you decide to leave, it won't just be the Guardians coming after you."

Seth lets out a humorless laugh, running a hand through his hair. "So, by abducting us, the Guardians put us in so much danger, they are now the safest place for us?"

"We found you first, but with your lineage, it's a miracle you stayed hidden as long as you did. Do you know that Alex's sister sent away for one of those DNA ancestry reports? You were on borrowed time."

Of course, she did. She had no idea we were targeted by a secret society... or several.

I exhale loudly, looking over at Seth; his wide-eyed expression mirrors mine.

"That does complicate things," I allow, looking back to Drew. "But, to be fair, the Guardians treat us like objects, too. They want to force me to marry Erik to make little super-babies or whatever."

He grimaces. "You were matched with Erik, that's true, but no one was going to force you to marry him. You and he hit it off, and Aunt Talia thought you seemed happy with him. Unarguably, Erik took it way too far, but that wasn't the Guardians' plan."

I bite my cheek, still not sure if I believe the *official* story, or if they were just covering their butts because it didn't work.

Drew watches me, compassion etched in the creases of his eyes. "What Erik did was inexcusable, no question, but not everyone here is so terrible. They won't force you to stay forever; once they feel you have a grasp on what we're all about, you'll be allowed to leave if that's your choice. They will even help you set up a different life. But, in truth, there will always be risk. You two will always be a target."

I can't argue that he is right: not everyone here has been terrible. In fact, many of the members have been welcoming and kind. But Erik's actions had been more than the casual controlling comments of Damian and Bryce.

"I don't like this. I can't let Alex get hurt again," Seth finally says after a long contemplative silence.

"Agreed," Drew nods.

I roll my eyes. "Thank you both for keeping me safe while I recovered, but please don't treat me like I'm made of glass."

"Lex, you're my cousin, and yes, you're older, but I am bigger." Seth glances at Drew before lowering his voice. "You've always been there for me, and I am going to protect you."

I smile. I couldn't resent him for wanting to keep me safe; it's exactly what I want for him.

"Now, you're always the brains, and I'm the brawn, so I'll let you decide," Seth says.

"Thanks so much," I snort. There are no good options here, so I lean towards the safest of the two precarious choices. Better the devil you know, right? "We'll stay for a while. We're new to this stuff anyway and getting some training and advice can't hurt. I have a feeling Damian and Bryce will both be on their best behavior, but one more incident involving either of us and we're out."

I turn to Drew. "You have been amazing, seriously. But I don't want to get you in any more trouble with your family. Now that I'm okay, you can go back to things as they were before we got here."

I want him to stay, more than I should, but it's not fair to ask that of him.

"I could never go back to the way things were before I met you." Drew smiles, getting to his feet and leaving me stunned. "If you're staying, I'm going to let Mom know. She's been trying to set up a meeting with you since the incident. She is appalled at Erik's actions and has been desperate to apologize. Would you be okay meeting with her?" he asks, looking at me.

"Um, yeah. Yes, sure," I stammer.

Drew offers a half smile. "Perfect. She wants to meet with Seth, too."

Seth shows great restraint, not teasing me about Drew while we wait for Gabriella, although his devilish grin says enough.

When Gabriella arrives, her concerned face rivals Rose's. "Oh, Alex, I am so very sorry about all of this." Flustered, she places a light hand on my shoulder.

"Gabriella," I say with a nod and a small smile. Not interested in rehashing the Erik situation, I lead the way to the couch. A slight wince escapes as I sit, my ribs still tender.

"I wanted to emphasize, to both of you actually, that Erik's actions were not approved by Damian or any Guardian. He has been reprimanded, and actions will be taken to ensure your safety in the future."

"Including Alex and I not being separated," Seth says with a defiant look.

"Understood," Gabriella replies easily, "and additional security guards have been assigned to your post by Bryce."

"Thank you," I cut in before Seth can say anything else. There's no reason to discuss this with her. "Now, I know you haven't had the opportunity to meet with Seth about his abilities," I prompt. Gabriella opens her mouth, brow furrowing as she attempts to further distance the Guardians from Erik's actions. After a moment, she lets out a sigh, closing her mouth before turning to Seth with a small smile.

"Before you arrived, I was able to meet with Alex about her gifts. We are still in the development stages of understanding exactly which areas the two of you will excel, but we strongly believe you both show great promise in a few areas." Pulling out a notebook, she glances at me nervously. "I, well, usually conduct these interviews in private, but I don't assume you will be willing to-"

"Not a chance," Seth interrupts.

"Very well, I'll leave that up to you, Seth," she nods as she opens her notebook, poised to take notes as she had during our meeting. "I assume Alexandra has filled you in on the history I told her about the Guardians?"

"Yeah." He subtly pulls on the neck of his t-shirt, a nervous habit he's had since he was a little boy. I squeeze his hand reassuringly as Gabriella continues.

"Okay, then we will get right into your profile. As Alexandra probably told you, my gift is to help sense gifts in others. You are both intriguing for me because you seem to have a few possible gifts. It's not abnormal for Guardians to have multiple strengths, as many overlap. My investigation has shown that you greatly take after your father and uncle. You are a prankster with a great sense of humor. Impressively, you were able to escape and evade our trackers quite well, even with minimal resources. Given a bit of training, I dare say they would have lost you." Gabriella tries to suppress a smile. "You remind me very much of them, actually," She watches Seth with inquisitive eyes.

He looks at me, eyes wide. I'd wondered the same thing about him when Gabriella had talked about our dads at my meeting. Gabriella continues, "Your athletic prowess cannot be ignored, either. You proved quite a runner when being chased by our team, and you did some damage to Erik. Off the top of my head, I believe you two could be part of a very successful recon team. Alex, with your intelligence and agility and Seth, your strength and speed... I wonder how you are with weapons?" she asks rhetorically as she jots down more notes.

"I would love to have you two enrolled in some training, that is, if you feel up for it?" She looks excitedly between the two of us. I glance at Seth, and he shrugs; getting some training lines up with our plan.

"Sure, we'll give it a try."

"Excellent! Well, Alex, I believe you need a bit more time to heal before you are cleared to do any physical training, but we can start you on intelligence training straight away. And Seth, I am dying to see you in combat classes." Gabriella scribbles enthusiastically in her notebook, her brown eyes sparkling. This kind of work is clearly her passion.

As she speaks, thoughts of Caleb and Whitney fill my mind. Recent events have made it clear that this is a totally unsafe place for Caleb. But hearing Gabriella speak of all the opportunities here, it's hard to deny that this place would open a lot of doors.

I jump at a knock on the door. Before I can move, Seth puts a hand on my shoulder as he gets up to answer it.

He greets Drew, moving to let him in. I can't help but smile.

"Ah, Andrew, I was just finishing up here. I'll be enrolling Seth in combat training this week. Would you mind showing him the gym?" Gabriella smiles affectionately at her son.

"Yeah, of course. You guys will love it." Drew unexpectedly reaches down for my hands, pulling me to my feet. A blush burns my cheeks.

"Alex, may I have a quick word?" Gabriella asks as we make our way to the door. Seth looks like he wants to protest, but I nod before he can say anything.

"I'll meet you guys in the hall."

Once they leave, Gabriella sits back on the couch, gesturing for me to do the same. "Firstly, I am sorry that you won't get a vote at Erik's hearing. If you and Seth decide you want to stay with us, I can arrange your inauguration at a later date. But I want you to take some time, consider if this is the life you want."

Her eyes are so intense I have to look away. She's quiet as I bite my cheek. I don't want to stay here, but I can't tell her that. Not yet.

"I don't mean to pry, but I can't help sensing something is bothering you. I noticed it last time we spoke as well, so I assume it isn't just concerning Erik."

Damn, she's too perceptive. "I'm fine. Well, maybe not fine. But I will be," I say, trying a convincing smile.

She raises an eyebrow, letting the silence ride for an uncomfortable moment. "Very well, but please remember I am here if you need to talk, or if you have questions, even hypothetical ones," she adds, giving me a knowing look.

I nod, eyes darting to the floor. I'm fairly sure she can't actually read minds, but I'm not confident enough to test the theory by staying any longer than necessary.

CHAPTER SIXTEEN

As we leave the room for the first time in weeks, I hesitate at the door, apprehensive despite my desire for freedom. The house feels so big compared to the room we took over: our safe place. In my defense, the house is massive. Seth drapes his arm over my shoulder, smiling reassuringly as we walk. Drew leads the way to the gym, kindly keeping pace with my slower than usual gait. We push through large glass doors to a bright reception area. White walls display clear-shelved rows of blue towels on either side. This, I'm sure, I had yet to see in my explorations of the house. A stretching birch table holds frosty glass drink dispensers filled with fruit-infused water. A precarious display of glasses is stacked beside the water, looking ready to shatter if the wrong cup is pulled.

"Mr. Jonasson, do you have a trainer booked?" the pretty young blonde behind the desk asks as she frantically types on her computer.

"No, just came to show the Conrys around the gym, if that's alright?" Drew smiles.

"Oh yes, yes of course," she says, still flustered.

"Thank you, Olivia."

Drew leads us through another set of towering glass doors, into a large room lined with mirrors and gym equipment.

Seth lets out a breath. "Nice," he mutters, darting around like Rose in a high-end boutique. He and Drew animatedly discuss weights, reps, sets, and other things I have no interest in. As they talk, I wander towards the doorway on the far side of the room, finding a massive gym. The floors are covered in mats that instantly give me flashbacks to my years spent training in gymnastics. Half of the gym reinforces my memories, containing a balance beam, parallel bars, a horse, and other gymnastics equipment.

I can't help myself. Excitement bubbles up inside me as I run towards the nostalgia. Like finding someone who speaks your language or cooks the food you grew up on when you're far from home, the familiarity calls to me. I waste no time hopping onto the closest apparatus: the balance beam. Feeling a slight protest from my ribs as I jump, I quickly push the sensation away in my elated state. It's been over a year since I've been on gymnastics equipment and I miss it more than I realized. I used to attend open gym nights at the local club to let off steam during high school and college, but I haven't done serious training since I was a kid. Extending my arms above my head, I pull off a simple cartwheel. Admittedly my ribs don't like it, but I still land gracefully.

"Alexandra, get down from there!" a stern voice echoes loudly through the gym. Startled, I barely manage to keep my balance, straining my tender muscles even more. Damian storms towards me from the far end of the vast space. Drew and Seth hurry in from the weight room.

"You are still recovering. What do you think you are doing? Gymnastics? Absolutely not. Not until you are cleared by the doctor," Damian fumes as he stops just short of the beam, glaring angrily up at me.

"Stay away from her!" Seth growls, jogging quickly to my side, fists clenched.

"Alex," Drew whispers. "Come on." He holds up his arms and lowers me back onto the ground gently as I sit on the beam.

Damian eyes Seth, looking like he wants to read him the riot act, but says nothing.

I take his wrist. "Let's go." I know he would love to take out his rage against Erik on Damian; their physical similarities are striking. Seth reluctantly lets me pull him towards the door, though his jaw is tight and fists are still clenched.

Seth swears, rolling his shoulders as we walk through the hallway and start up the stairs. "I really *really* want to punch him."

"Yeah, me too," I say, voice strained. Both boys pause, turning on me. *Crap.* "I'm fine," I press, but my voice still sounds tight. I can feel my nails digging into my palm as I try to breathe through the pain.

"What were you thinking, Alex?" Seth shifts his anger to me.

I look down at the carpeted stairs. "I'm sorry, I wasn't thinking. I just saw the equipment and reacted. It was stupid."

Seth lets out a sigh, pulling my pills from his pocket. "Take one." His expression dares me to argue with him. I'd resisted taking pain medication much to Drew and Seth's chagrin, but I'm in no position to argue right now; I can hardly stand upright. Drew jogs back towards the gym, returning with a glass of water. Both boys watch me with stern faces as I take the small white pill. Drew shakes his head but says nothing, a slight smile playing on his lips.

"Can we go now?" I gesture up the stairs, irritated. I hate having this kind of attention.

We arrive back at the room we've taken over to find Rose packing up our things.

"Hello, Miss Alex. How was the gym?" she asks. I sigh as I literally feel Seth's temper rising again.

"Fine, thanks. What's up?" I gesture at the set of suitcases.

"Gabriella asked me to move you both somewhere a bit more comfortable. The rooms are still being polished, but I want to get your things there so everything will be ready for this evening," Rose explains as she folds a pair of Seth's jeans and a sweatshirt, adding them to one of the bags.

"I thought we were clear. We aren't being separated again," Seth says in a near growl.

"Of course not, Mr. Seth. I apologize for the misunderstanding, my fault of course. We are having one of the family suites made up for you two, so you'll have a bit more space."

"That's a great idea," Drew says brightly. "You guys will love it. But I thought the Conry suite was at the England Manor?"

"It is. Gabriella arranged for another to be set up. There are a few vacant right now. The Graaf family has relocated, at least semi-permanently, to Prague, so we have use of that suite for the time being. I'll come get you both when it's ready." Rose closes both suitcases and wheels them from the room.

By dinner, the boys are sick of playing video games, which they have been binging on since lunch, and I'm up from my involuntary medication-induced nap. Rose offers to take us to our suite and bring dinner up there. I can't hide my excitement about having my own bedroom again. Seth snores.

Rose leads the way to another part of the house, a whole new wing for me to get lost in.

That's probably the Guardians' master plan: keep me too disoriented to leave.

As we walk, Drew points out landmarks—like the way to his family suite and the fastest paths to the gym and entrance hall. I retain nothing, but Seth seems to get it. When we arrive, Rose opens a set of intricately carved wood double doors, featuring the Guardian crest in the center. We step into a seating area, the furniture very ornate and beautiful, but uncomfortably formal.

"The Graafs are Dutch with French heritage, so their style is very French-vintage. We will, of course, redecorate to your tastes. I called for some of the Conry heirlooms to be sent here as well. Hopefully, this will suit for now," Rose explains as she pulls back the thick cream curtains, revealing a complete wall of windows. A set of French doors lead to a large balcony. It feels like we have stepped into a Parisian castle. The theme, although not my taste, is impeccably done with textured wallpaper and plush rugs covering the space. Rose leads us to a small kitchen, already stocked with my and Seth's favorite snacks and drinks. A large dining table fills the room next to the kitchen, lit with a sparkling chandelier, a miniature of the one in the dining hall several floors below.

"The suite has four bedrooms, so you can have your pick," Rose continues as we follow her through the space. I didn't think the Guardians could still surprise me with their wealth and grandeur, but they managed. The suite is as large as a house, yet it seems to be just one of many in this place.

"Dibs on the master!" Seth calls.

"Three of the rooms are set like a traditional master bedroom, with ensuites and walk-in closets. One is more of a nursery or office setup."

Seth and I exchange awed expressions, while Drew looks around with mild curiosity. "I've never been in this suite," he says conversationally.

"Is this like your place?" Seth asks him.

"More or less. Ours is a little more streamlined Swedish design." Drew shrugs, but he's not meeting our eyes. I catch Rose giving him a look and realize that his must be much bigger. His father and uncle do seem to be in charge here.

"More Ikea, less French revolution?"

"Ikea?" Drew's brow furrows.

Seth's eyes meet mine before laughing.

"I'm kidding. I know what *Ikea* is."

*****

Over the next couple of weeks, the three of us remained pretty much inseparable. Seth attended my first intelligence training class, but he found it painfully boring. I was intrigued by the strategy lectures and exercises in problem-solving. Seth just fidgeted like he was trapped back in high school math class. I felt like a total nerd, but I loved it. We decided after that that it would be okay to split up for classes.

I did go with him to combat training, since I was eager to start as soon as I was cleared. The guys luckily did weights while I was in intel, so I didn't have to endure that, but combat training was fascinating. Seth was thrilled when he found out that Damian is the main instructor, but his bubble burst when Drew informed him that he didn't spar with the students. Seth was also hoping for a go at Erik, though we still hadn't seen him since the incident.

After talking it over, Seth and I decided to skip Erik's sentencing hearing. The thought of seeing him again outside of my already punishing nightmares was more than I could handle. Gabriella delivered a statement on my behalf, and Erik was sentenced to house arrest on one of the other Guardian estates and removed from some political mission he'd been eyeing. I'm not sure house arrest was an adequate punishment; Seth and I were pretty much on house arrest, and this place wasn't exactly a prison. I got some comfort when Drew told me that Erik had been working towards the assignment for years. I couldn't let myself think about it too much. Every time I saw his face in my mind's eye, I felt sick. My whole body hurt as a wave of fear crushed me, leaving me powerless and anxious.

I neglected to tell Seth about the nightmares that had me waking drenched in panicked sweat. Seth would just worry, and I didn't need him hovering again. The dreams left me exhausted, but my days with the Guardians were surprisingly fulfilling.

I couldn't participate in combat classes, but it didn't mean I couldn't watch. I was a visual learner anyway, so I gained a lot by studying the more experienced fighters. I was amazed by how they were able to react so quickly to a punch, avoiding or blocking even the fastest fists. I soon realized they weren't reacting to the punch, they were reacting to the positioning before the punch. This gave them more time to respond. They could tell from the shoulder position. No, wait, even before that, a shift in the foot position. I watched, amazed by the intricacy of something I had once just considered flying fists with lucky blows.

Admittedly, during warm-ups, my eyes would slide to Drew. Watching the tight cords of muscle twist as he did effortless pushups was mesmerizing. I reminded myself that Drew was off limits, but my eyes ignored the reprimands. I couldn't let myself actively pursue a relationship right now; I had serious Erik issues to get over before anything could happen romantically. Plus, Drew is a Guardian, through and through. I can't tie myself to this place.

Unsurprisingly, Seth was doing really well in combat. He occasionally sparred with Drew, but the two of them always ended up laughing by the end. I've never understood that about boys; they could be intensely fighting one minute and joking the next.

At the end of the second week, the doctor meets me at the gym to check my progress. My ribs have healed enough that I can start gentle physical activity and stretching. I instantly look towards the gymnastics equipment that I have been dying to try again. "No running, no gymnastics, right?" he adds, effectively deflating my balloon. His Australian accent is way less charming when he's telling me news I don't want to hear.

"Fine," I grumble.

"Alexandra, you're heaps better. I just don't want a secondary injury to set you back. You understand that, don't you?"

I sigh, irritated that he's right. "Yeah, I do. Thanks."

He nods as I turn to rejoin Drew and Seth in the weight room.

Drew glistens with a sheen of sweat, highlighting his chiseled jaw and toned shoulders. Looking up, he smiles, leaving me momentarily dazzled. He wipes a towel over his face, pulling off his sweat-drenched t-shirt and exposing his impossibly perfect abs. Doing combat class and weight training five days a week left him in fantastic shape.

"Hey, how did it go?" Drew asks.

"Wh-what?"

"The doctor appointment?" Seth clarifies, sitting up on his weight bench.

"Oh, that, right. It went great," I say, turning around to get a glass of water to hide my blush. *Lay off the Guardian boys, Alex!*

"My ribs are healing well. He said I can do light physical activity and he'll reassess again next week."

"So that means... you aren't so breakable anymore?" Seth smiles wickedly, glancing at Drew with eyebrows raised.

"Oh no." I back towards the door to the gym; I know that look. Ever since Seth got bigger than me, he's been paying me back for the years I used to beat him in wrestling matches. My uncle had warned me he would outgrow me, but short-sighted 10-year-old Alex thought that would never happen.

Seth follows me out of the door with Drew right behind him.

"Guys...no!" I squeal, but I can't help letting out a laugh. Turning to run, I get about halfway across the floor before I'm lifted off my feet, Seth laughing in my ear. "Put me down, you big oaf," I demand, though my laughter makes it less convincing.

"Your wish is my command, Pixie." He gently throws me onto the mat, crouching over me with a smile. I lean onto my side and push him to the mat. Laughing, I get up to run, but Drew blocks my path. I try to dart around him, but he grabs me, picking me up easily, and tossing me over his shoulder.

"You okay man?" Drew asks Seth with a laugh, his arm wrapped tightly around my thighs. "She did the SAME thing to me once, little brat."

"Hey, I can hear you!" I say, punching his back playfully. "You guys are bullies."

Drew chuckles, setting me on the mat before he plunks down beside me. It feels so good to just laugh with Seth again. All the stress of the last month hadn't left much time for horsing around.

"So... Pixie?" Drew asks, looking at me with raised eyebrows.

"Shove it," I glare, but can't help smiling through my blush. Why do the worst childhood nicknames have to stick?

Drew's playful expression quickly hardens, turning into the more guarded Drew I'm used to as a shadow falls over us.

"Andrew, Seth," Damian barks, staring down at us. *killjoy.* "If you have so much energy, I would love to see it channeled into sparring... if you can fit combat into your evidently busy schedule."

I roll my eyes as I get to my feet.

"Alexandra, you have been cleared to use the gym, I assume?" He raises an eyebrow doubtfully.

"Yes," I reply, crossing my arms.

"For light exercise," Drew clarifies, which earns him a glare. *Traitor.*

"Very well, I suggest you go and see Mary-Anne. She is teaching a yoga class in the small gym." He points to a set of glass doors past the gymnastics equipment.

Eager to do anything active, as well as to get away from Damian, I go for it.

I push through the smooth-gliding glass doors into a wood-floored, mirrored room that smells like a spa, an essential oil diffuser misting in the corner. Scanning the room, my entire body stills, paralyzed as my eyes meet Erik's.

CHAPTER SEVENTEEN

Fear freezes my thoughts before flooding them with panicked flashes: Erik on top of me, laughing as I screamed. His hand connecting with my face. The split second it takes my mind to register the rest of the person standing in front of me lasts an eternity. *That's not Erik.* My mind finally frees me, showing me reality.

"Oh, hi," a shy voice murmurs, eyes shifting to the ground and cheeks burning red.

"Chloe," I breathe. *Erik's sister.*

"Umm, I can go." She reaches down to grab the yoga mat she's standing on.

"No, no stay." I force a smile, voice shaking. *She didn't do anything, Alex. It's not her fault her brother is a jerk. Drew is Erik's cousin and they couldn't be more different.*

I take a deep breath, trying to calm my erratically racing heart. Erik's disappearance had let me believe my anxiety resided only in nightmares. Seeing Chloe proves that I'm nowhere near over what happened.

Alison Haines

I focus on the differences between Chloe and Erik. I haven't seen her since my *welcome* feast, and I was a bit distracted that night. She looks about twelve or thirteen, and it's already clear she's going to be stunning, like her mother. Her face is thinning into a woman's; prominent high cheekbones are already evident, but her cheeks still maintain their youthful glow. Her eyes are exactly Erik's, almond shaped and deep blue. She has tan skin and long chestnut brown hair, like Talia. Chloe's shy smile is nothing like her brother's. It's unassuming and kind, not confident and dominating.

A woman in her forties watches the exchange while sitting cross-legged on her yoga mat, her thin eyebrows raised. She introduces herself as Mary-Anne, the in-house yoga and Pilates instructor; because of course the Guardians employ a full-time yoga and Pilates instructor. "We're about to start our yoga session. Would you like to join?" She gestures towards a tall set of shelves. Yoga mats are rolled in organized tubes beside blocks, straps, and other yoga accessories. I'm not exactly prepared in my t-shirt and loose-fitting jeans. Well, it could be worse.

Grabbing a mat, I sit cross-legged a few feet behind Chloe with a growing sense that this class isn't going to go well. It's been a long time since I've done any flexibility training.

Forty-five minutes later, I'm so done. Mary-Anne didn't go easy on me and my shaky legs are having a hard time walking. It didn't help that Chloe had perfect form, and kept stealing glances at me in the mirror.

I hobble outside to the gym where Seth and Drew are just finishing combat class. It's completely unfair; why does Drew look so hot when he works out and I look like a sweaty cherry tomato that's about to burst?

Leaning against a nearby pillar, I catch the tail end of Seth's last face off with some poor guy in his class. I've learned that Seth's skill is half psychological. Although he's a good fighter, more than that he knows how to get in his opponent's mind and make them prematurely feel like they've lost. Seeing the hopeless look in his opponent's eyes, I know Seth has already won. He makes it look effortless as he takes him down. Once Damian calls the match and ends class, I make my way onto the mat and collapse dramatically at Seth's feet. "Kill me now."

Seth chuckles and drops beside me on the mat. "That good, eh?" he asks, wiping sweat from his face with a towel.

"I wish I could be in combat class with you," I pout, not sure Mary-Anne's yoga should really be classed as *light* exercise.

"I would crush you, little cousin."

My fatigue evaporates as I take in his confident expression. "Oh yeah?" I shift into a crouch. "You think so, *baby* cousin?"

He hesitates, which is all I need. I lunge at him, easily knocking him down in his unprepared stance. Unfortunately, this is where his strength and my lack of weight comes into play. I pin him, but he lifts my body off of his chest using just his arms, tossing me onto the mat beside him. I get to my feet quickly, and he makes the mistake of leaning up on one elbow, looking satisfied with his assumed victory. Darting forward, I roll him onto his stomach and sit on his back. Seth starts laughing at the turn of events, only making my job easier. I'm just in the process of moving his arm above his head when Mr. Killjoy strikes again.

"Alexandra! Get off of Seth. That is not considered light exercise," Damian yells. I pause for a second, annoyed to leave the fight unfinished.

"My mistake," I say, getting off of Seth and giving Damian my innocent smile. Drew is standing beside him, lips pressed firmly together as he tries to suppress a laugh. Damian's face slacks in confusion as Drew turns away with shaking shoulders, unable to contain himself. I hurry out of the large gym before Damian can reprimand me further, Seth following close behind.

Walking to the exit, Drew gives me an appreciative smile. "That innocent look is a dangerous weapon."

I smile and shrug, cheeks warming. The weight room is crowded with young Guardians, as always after combat class. Although Seth and I have been here for several weeks, we haven't exactly made friends. Perhaps it's because we stick together so tightly that we don't seem approachable, which is a fair assessment. We're both pretty leery of Guardians and haven't put out any effort, other than civil *hellos* to people we pass in the halls or share gym equipment with. Drew is an exception, but only because he'd helped us in a severe time of need, earning our trust. I doubt Seth would have opened up to him otherwise.

Drew greets a few people as we exit, but his tight posture and stiff smile make me wonder if he was naturally an outsider. Did his tight alliance with us push others away? Or had the Erik situation alienated him?

"You're lucky Damian saved you, Pixie," Seth teases, trying his psychological game again. I don't think he even knows he's doing it. I give him a light shove and hiss as a shooting pain runs up my side. *Okay, so maybe I overdid it a little bit.*

As we leave the gym, we run into a group in the lobby.

Seth stops, face slackening. "Mayumi?"

A tall, heavy-set Asian girl turns with raised eyebrows, smiling as she sees Seth.

"I heard they brought you in! Sorry I wasn't here for your feast; I got pulled into another mission. You know how it is."

My brow pulls together. *How could Seth know someone here?*

"You... but..." Seth sputters, face pale.

The girl reaches out and squeezes Seth's arm. "Look, I really have to go. The Junior Combat class is starting soon, and I have to do a report on one of them. No hard feelings, right? We'll catch up later." Mayumi shifts her bag over her shoulder, eyes darting curiously between Drew and me before following the rest of the group into the gym.

"Who is that?"

"Mayumi... but... she worked with me back home."

"She was your Sensor," Drew says quietly, nodding towards the door as he starts walking again.

"No, she was a waitress. We were friends."

Drew and I share a sympathetic look. I know the feeling of betrayal too well. *How have I never wondered who shadowed Seth?*

"She's very good at what she does," Drew explains.

Seth shakes his head after a long moment, forcing a smile. "I call first shower," he shouts, jogging away from us towards the room. Even though we have our own showers, this has been a running joke of ours since we were kids at the cottage. Of course, at the cottage, the *first shower* means a lot if you actually want warm water. He turns to face me before rounding a corner. "We *will* finish that fight later, Lex." Laughing maniacally, he disappears out of sight.

I turn to Drew, opening my mouth to ask more about Mayumi, but he speaks first.

"Even though Damian yelled at you, he was impressed."

"Really?" I ask skeptically as he nods. "Well, Seth would have gotten me. I had the element of surprise but he has a huge strength advantage."

"Yeah he does, but you are quicker and more agile. You're both smart, but you were able to use your speed to augment your strategy, and I'm not so sure he'd have been able to stop you pinning him. After a bit of training, you'll be tough competition."

I'm unable to repress a wide smile as I look up at him, my heart soaring. It's amazing how different he is from Erik. He actually encourages me instead of making himself feel bigger at my expense. Something my grandmother used to say comes to mind: *Find a man who compliments you, not flatters you.* I always thought it was a silly distinction, but maybe now I understand what she meant.

*****

I ask about Mayumi later that afternoon, when Drew's gone, but Seth shrugs it off. He assures me it's fine, but I can sense it bugs him. I don't get why he doesn't want to talk about it, but I leave it alone, even though I'm itching to make him open up about his feelings.

For the next week, I continue with light exercises, which consists of various forms of flexibility torture, along with daily reminders from Damian to stay away from combat and gymnastics. I don't see Chloe in Yoga again. It's usually just Mary-Anne and me. Watching Seth have more fun in combat is annoying, but it pays off.

"Everything looks aces," the doctor says with a smile during my weekly assessment. "I want you to keep the tapes on when at the gym, but I'd say you're ready for full gym privileges."

"Seriously?" I squeal, jumping up from the crinkly-papered exam table and giving the man a hug. He freezes before patting my back with a chuckle.

"Just listen to your body, Alexandra. If something is causing you pain, ease up; I'll give you a note and you can take a sickie," he adds with a wink.

"I'll try to take it easy," I reply with a noncommittally. I know myself better than to promise that.

"Come and see me if you are experiencing any trouble breathing or increased pain," he adds as he packs his supplies, handing me a roll of support tape.

"Oh, one more thing?" I ask at the door. "Can you send something to Damian in writing about this? He definitely won't believe me when I tell him."

*****

The next morning, I make my way to the gym feeling lighter than air. I'm so excited to try some real combat training and maybe even get that rematch with Seth. Damian's narrowed eyes track me as I sit on the mats beside the boys, but he doesn't say anything. After a brief warm-up, Damian starts calling names, one pair at a time, for one on one combat demonstrations. I'm surprised; most Fridays another instructor teaches a Krav Maga or Taekwondo group class. I watch as pairs of Guardians face off. They all seem way more skilled as the reality of going head to head with them sinks in. Nervous energy fills me as they tackle, kick, and evade one another. Damian watches me closely, probably looking for fear. I try not to show him any, but I can't help jumping as body after body hit the mat with a resounding thud. I'm not sure if he's trying to scare me by making me go last or whether he's just gauging my reaction to combat; my bet goes for the former. Finally, after Drew and Seth finish a long drawn out match, it's my turn.

"Alexandra, you'll spar with..." He pauses for a moment, scanning the group. Everyone has already sparred once since we have uneven numbers today. "Marcy."

I get to my feet, as does a woman who looks about six feet tall and easily double my weight. She saunters to the mat with a confident smile.

A grin lifts the corner of Damian's lips as he watches us. I stumble to the center of the mat to face my Amazon of an opponent, her sneer menacing.

Perfect, underestimate me. I help encourage her by looking up with wide, scared eyes, acting like I have no idea about starting positions. Damian blows his whistle and Marcy comes barreling for me. I step out of the way and use her momentum against her by stretching my leg towards her stampeding feet. She stumbles, landing on all fours. I kick her elbow, and she falls flat on her stomach. Taking advantage of this surprising luck, I quickly straddle her back and pin her arms.

As Damian blows his whistle, everyone in the class is silent, eyes wide and lips parted. Seth laughs and I smile as he starts the group clapping. I climb off Marcy and offer her my hand, which she ignores, pushing to her feet.

"Well done, Alexandra. Good use of the element of surprise. Marcy, this is a lesson for you in not misjudging your opponent. You are strong, but you can't forget that the little ones are often fast, and in Alexandra's case, also clever. Now that that lesson is learned, let's see you two go again."

Damian's right; I had relied on my opponent going for the easy pick, but that won't work the second time around. Plus, instead of being overly confident, Marcy's just pissed. She glares at me as we face each other again. This time when Damian's whistle sounds, she doesn't go straight for me; she waits, patiently circling the mat. I match her pace; a sense of dread tightens my stomach. This is where my lack of combat training will show.

Finally, Marcy steps towards me, going for my right side. I mirror the act but use my speed to get behind her, locking her right arm and going for her left. She tries to spin around to grab me, but I manage to secure her left arm as she twists. She drops to her knees, taking me awkwardly with her, and slams onto her back, crushing me. My side explodes in burning agony. She twists easily from my loosened grip, and I roll out from under her, slow to get to my feet as I blink rapidly to clear my sight.

"Alright, Alexandra?" Damian calls.

I nod, focusing on Marcy as I try to ignore the pain ripping through my chest. Marcy circles again, a delighted smirk playing on her lips as she glances at my ribs. She'd noticed my response to the drop, but will she stoop that low? Answering my question, she charges my right side. I move to dodge her, but her reach is too long. She pulls me into a headlock. Before I can wriggle from her grasp, she punches my right side. Everything goes white; my knees hit the mat before I fall heavily on my side.

"Marcy, enough," Damian shouts after his whistle doesn't stop her dropping onto my stomach with her full weight. She sneers, taking her time getting off my chest. My eyes clear but I'm close to tears. I clench my teeth, refusing to let her see me cry. Before I can sit up, Drew and Seth are staring down at me, eyes tight with concern; Damian joins them a moment later.

"Alexandra, are you alright? Do I need to call the doctor?" Damian asks, his voice flat but eyes betraying concern. His expression reminds me of one I used to see on Erik when he was worried: just the hint of a crinkle in the eyes, mouth tight.

"I'm fine," I spit, repressing tears and forcing myself to stand. Marcy glares at me with disgust and turns away, no remorse in her expression.

"That's enough for today," Damian says, addressing the class. "Well done, Marcy. You were able to sense your opponent's weakness and use it to your advantage."

"One weakness of many, I'm sure."

"Yeah? Too bad you needed to use my broken ribs to beat me. And on my very first day of combat? Yikes."

Marcy scoffs, "Big talk from a weak little princess."

Cursing, I stomp towards her. "I'll show you what a *little princess* can do."

"Whoa there." Seth grabs my waist, pulling me back as the class draws in a collective breath.

"I said enough," Damian barks, stepping in Marcy's path as she advances on me.

Breathing heavily, I pull against Seth's grip, but he's unwavering. I stare Marcy down, itching to smack the vexing grin from her sweaty face. She rolls her eyes and turns to the weight room.

"Don't let that ogress get to you," Seth says supportively, shifting his grip to my shoulders. "She's like two of you, and you still beat her easily the first time."

"I need to be able to beat people even when they don't underestimate me. I can't rely on the element of surprise all the time," I seethe, my mood sour. I never have been a good loser.

"That's true," Damian adds, inserting himself into our conversation. "But do remember that it is your first day. Give it some time."

The boys look just as stunned as I feel, watching Damian walk away. "Was Damian just... supportive?" I ask, unsure if I imagined his encouragement through my dizzying pain.

"I believe so," Drew laughs. "Don't get used to it. It's a rarity, I promise you."

"I won't; it kind of freaks me out." My bruised ribs ache, but it's nothing compared to the pain when I broke them. I take a deep breath trying to clear my head, but it still hurts like hell.

Seth places his hands on my shoulders. "Enough of the gym for today. You'll get her next time." I walk out of the gym at a normal pace but as soon as we're in the hallway, I slow down. I don't want anyone to see how hurt I am, especially Marcy.

When we finally get back to our suite, a handwritten note is waiting for Seth on the front table. His jaw tightens as he reaches for it. We both know who it's from. Barely glancing at the words, he crumples the thick paper, tossing it back to the table.

"Seth, maybe-"

"Going to shower." Seth storms down the hall. I jump as he slams his heavy wood door. Biting my lip, I reach for the crumpled note.

Mr. Seth Conry,

Alison Haines

> Your father phoned again,
> requesting you return his call.
> At your service,
> Mitchell

Letting out a sigh, I toss the note in the garbage as I walk to my room. Seth called his dad the day after he arrived. I'd pushed him to do it. Maybe I shouldn't have. I thought my conversation had been rough with my dad, but it was way worse for Seth. My dad has always been a closed book, but Seth and Uncle Jack, they were close. Seth thought they talked about everything, so this lie stung him worse. He'd been pissed and confused, but truthfully, he was hurt. Since then, Uncle Jack has called a few times a week, but Seth won't call him back. He also refuses to talk about it. I can see he's hurting, but the only thing I've been able to do to ease the pain is distract him, changing the subject to that day's combat class, or starting up a video game.

As I pass Seth's room, the sound of the shower running is drowned out by his blaring music. Shutting my door, I grab the phone, calling the number I've dialed most since arriving.

"Hello?" Uncle Jack's voice cracks, exhaustion palpable in that one word.

"He's not ready. I'm trying, but he's not ready."

"Lexie, please get him to call. I need to apologize."

"I know. *He* knows." I bite my cheek.

"How can I fix this?"

"You understand what you did to him, right? Seth trusted you, and you betrayed that."

"It wasn't my choice. Your father-"

"Uncle Jack, stop. I know it was his idea. I get that, but you can't hide behind him. You still had a choice. It was a crappy choice, but you made it."

I close my eyes as he takes in a sharp breath. He's stuck in a loop, hashing out the same conversation every time I call. I've tried reassuring him, but it's time to change the script: call him on his role in all of this. After a long pause, he finally speaks.

"I tried to tell you, you know. When you came over, the day after Seth disappeared. I tried to... I should have told you."

I can't bring myself to berate him anymore. He's in agony, but I'm not in a position to make him feel better. I'm team Seth, all the way. "Yeah, you should have told me, but it is what it is. We're both safe. I promise I'm keeping an eye on him. He's actually doing pretty amazing here."

"I can believe it," he says, the first hint of a smile I've heard from him in weeks. "No doubt you're shining, too. I've always known you were gifted. Your father would've too, if he'd let himself."

I roll my eyes, skeptically. My father loves me and knows I'm smart, but I can't imagine him ranking me more skilled at anything when compared to Whit. "We had some bumps at the beginning, but we've kind of settled in here. Why did you and dad try so hard to keep this from us? What were you so afraid of?"

"That's... It's complicated."

I groan. "I guess secrecy is a hard habit to break, eh Uncle Jack? I better go before Seth's out of the shower."

Hanging up before he can answer, I toss the phone onto my bed. I try to ease the angry tension knotting my shoulders and my still burning ribs by cranking up the heat in the shower. Why the hell were they still keeping secrets from Seth and me? Sometimes my anger at my dad spills onto Uncle Jack, but he has a choice. He could tell me, tell Seth, why they hid this world. If it's so awful, shouldn't they warn us? Shouldn't we know what to watch out for?

CHAPTER EIGHTEEN

There's no combat class over the weekend, but I go to the gym with Drew and Seth in hopes of picking up some tips before Monday's class. Unfortunately, although Seth and Drew are both great fighters, their skills lie in strength and, in Seth's case, manipulation. I need help with agility.

"You need Andrea," Drew muses, seeming to read my mind, or perhaps my discontented expression. "She's not huge on combat class, but she's a good fighter, smart like you. You can usually find her in the gymnastics area." We both look towards the bars and beams, finding them empty. "Well, I don't see her right now, but when I do, I'll introduce you," he offers.

I nod vaguely as I walk to the equipment. My desire ignites as I move around each piece slowly, examining them. I thought I'd been fine with my switch to dance, but being here, I have a near-tears level of lament for lost time in my training. Maybe it's just how much agility would help in my new life.

Alison Haines

I let my hand run over the smooth wooden balance beam. Stepping on the springboard for the horse, I jump a few times, feeling a slight protest from my still aching ribs. I ignore the throbbing and move towards the uneven bars. They've always been my favorite. I fell in love when I was taught my first leap transition; it's like flying. I loved the skill and timing required to launch yourself from one bar and catch yourself gracefully on the next.

Moving to the chalking area, I cover my hands before jumping onto the lower bar. I swing back and forth gently a few times, getting my bearings. Picking up momentum, I do a smooth transition to the high bar. I pick up a bit more speed and circle smoothly, stretching my legs to each side, so my feet touch the bar. I extend my legs as I rotate around again before tucking them into my stomach for a dismount. My landing is a little shaky, but it's a satisfying first try.

Before I can hop back up on the lower bar, I hear a slow clap from behind me. A beautiful girl around my age is standing at the edge of the mats. She has smooth mocha skin and thick black hair pulled into a braided updo. The proper leotard she's wearing immediately makes me feel self-conscious in my shorts, t-shirt, and sloppy ponytail.

"Hi, you're Alex, right?" she asks, walking towards me with a wide smile. "Drew pointed you out. I'm Andrea."

"Oh, hi!"

"Not bad," she comments, gesturing towards the bars I've just left.

"It's been a long time; I was just playing around," I mutter, feeling a blush spread across my cheeks.

"Well, your landing was a little sloppy," she allows with a chuckle, "but you've got moves."

I smile, appreciating her honesty. "So you're a gymnast?" I ask unnecessarily, the answer obvious.

"Yeah, among other things. I also enjoy combat training from time to time, but, between you and me, I much prefer gymnastics." She frowns, gently picking up my right hand. "You don't have grips?"

"No, I just wanted to try-"

"Come with me." Her unusually dark eyes widen with excitement. She grabs my wrist, towing me to the exit.

I follow her as she hurries out of the gym, yelling a quick "I'll be back!" to Seth and Drew. I'm nervous to go with her alone, but Drew seems to trust her, so I try to push down my apprehension. As we jog upstairs, I surreptitiously watch my back for a sneak attack by some guards... or Scott. She ushers me into a bedroom much like my original room but decorated with a lot more personal accents: posters, pictures, and trinkets. I close the door, but only after turning the interior knob, ensuring it's not locked.

"Here, sit." She nods towards an overstuffed sofa, loaded with purple pillows. While I perch on the edge of the couch, taking in the purple overload, she darts into her closet. Loud proclamations of "Yes!" and "OMG yes!" only increase my sense of fear. Finally, she returns with the promised hand grips as well as an unexpected stack of colorful leotards.

"You look about my size, and I can't have you practicing on *my* equipment like that," she says with an easy laugh, taking in my casual gym gear. I can't help but think how well she would get along with Rose, who barely holds in a groan when she sees me after the gym.

We spend the next half hour trying on leotards and talking all things gymnastics. Andrea's quick whit eases my frayed nerves, not a common occurrence with the Guardians. It's refreshing to have a bit of girl time; it reminds me of my sister. As much as I love hanging with the boys, it's really nice to have a break. Andrea's excitable personality is contagious. I can't help laughing as she darts between the couch and her closet, clothes flying in her wake.

Once we've tried on all the leotards, and she's insisted on giving me some until I can go shopping for my own, conversation shifts.

"So, how do you know Drew?"

"He's my cousin, on his mother's side."

I'm irrationally relieved. Andrea is beautiful, and I found myself jealous of her potential relationship with Drew. Despite my internal protests that I have no claim over him, I like Andrea even more now.

"I, um, heard about what happened with you and Erik. I'm so sorry. I can't believe he would do that. He's kind of my cousin, too. Truth be told, I was never as close with him as I am with Drew, but still, I wouldn't have thought he would… go that far," Andrea says, tracing the seams of the pillow on her lap.

"Thanks," I mumble, biting my cheek. I haven't talked to anyone other than Drew and Seth about what happened, and even that had been weeks ago. I take a deep breath, pushing down the flutter of panic that presses into my chest. I had a particularly nightmarish sleep last night. I didn't want Erik darkening my waking hours when he already had so much power over my nights. Scouring the room, I desperately try to find a change of subject. Andrea saves me from having to ask about the movie poster on her wall.

"Oh! And Drew said you were interested in help with combat? He told me you faced off with Marcy," Andrea says, wrinkling her nose. "She is a lot bigger than us but easy enough to beat with a bit of training." She gets to her feet, walking to the door. I stumble to follow the ball of energy that is Andrea. Leading me back to the gym, she chats happily about Guardian gossip. I don't know most of the people she mentions, but it's nice to have someone talking to me casually, not staring at me like I'm the new kid in school. I do get confirmation that Talia is miffed with me. I'd noticed her cold-shoulder the few times Seth and I had dinner in the dining hall. Andrea fills me in that, according to Talia, I'd ruined her son's reputation. After all the deceit I'd experienced here, I can't say I'm surprised. Mostly, I just hate that my mom was right about her.

"There you two are. We were just coming to find you," Drew says as we enter the gym lobby. Relief softens the worry on Seth's face as he sees me. Some of the elation from my girl time fades as I realize I'd stressed him. "Seth, this is Andrea. I didn't get a chance to introduce you before."

"Hi." She smiles widely, her perfect white teeth gleaming.

"H-hi." A matching grin pushes away any remaining worry lines on Seth's face.

Drew gives me a knowing smile.

"I'll see you tomorrow, Alex. Nice to meet you, Seth." Andrea winks her mascara-clad lashes at Seth before retreating to the gym.

Seth's grin sticks as we walk to our room.

"So, Drew, Andrea seems really nice," I manage as Drew and I struggle to contain our laughter.

"Yeah, she's great. She'll definitely help you with combat. And, interestingly, she's single."

"Really? That *is* interesting."

Seth looks at us with a furrowed brow, rolling his eyes as he takes in our Cheshire grins. "What are you getting at?"

"Oh, come on! We totally saw the way you were looking at her." I shove Seth lightly.

"What? I don't know what you're talking about," Seth insists, his beet red cheeks betraying his lie.

I don't tease Seth anymore about Andrea; after all, he has shown uncharacteristic restraint when it comes to Drew. I do notice that he watches her while we're training, distracted enough to let Drew get more than his usual share of pins. It's so cute; I've never seen this side of Seth before. Andrea is less subtle. Our combat practice and gymnastics conditioning is peppered with frequent comments of, "My god, your cousin is stupid hot." I bite my tongue, wanting to say, "Right back at you" as I struggle to keep my eyes off of Drew.

Even aside from Seth's adorable crush, it's great training with Andrea. She's pretty good, and I learn a lot from her. Mostly how to get my ass kicked, but I'm starting to see how agility fighters move differently than strength fighters.

When we meet the following weekend, we pick up where we left off. I know I'm going to need more practice to catch up to the Guardians with their years of training, but I can already feel my body moving more instinctively. Maybe they weren't entirely wrong about this gift thing?

After sparring, we shift gears, moving to the gymnastics area. Andrea is exceptional, which makes sense; she's had 24/7 access to equipment and coaching her whole life. The grips Andrea lent me help a lot, and she's full of advice about my form.

"Why do I never see you in combat class?" I pant, reaching gratefully for my water bottle after completing an intense combination.

"Oh, I go every once in a while, but that isn't my *gift*, so Damian doesn't get on my case if I don't go. He doesn't encourage me to go at all, actually." She shrugs, moving to the chalking station for her turn on the bars.

"That's crazy! You're really good."

"Thanks." Her smile doesn't reach her eyes. "But I'm a sensor. I sense talents in others, so combat isn't very important for that. And trust me, give yourself a couple weeks, and you'll be whipping my butt. I can already tell, you're a more natural fighter than me. I grew up with older brothers, so being able to fight was a required skill. Beyond that, I'm below average around here."

"I can relate to the older sibling thing," I say with a chuckle. "Trust me, it's not just brothers; sisters throw down, too."

Andrea jumps onto the lower bar, but my mind stays trapped in thoughts of Whitney. I miss her, and spending so much time in the gym makes it impossible not to wonder about her Guardian potential. She's always been undeniably more athletic, excelling at every sport she touches. She left gymnastics to me, but she would have owned in combat training, I'm sure of it. Biting my cheek, I try to suppress my fear that one look at Whitney and the Guardians would forget I exist. More troubling is how much the thought of that happening scares me. Does that mean I actually *want* to be here?

As Andrea twists and leaps, my thoughts shift inevitably to Caleb. I still agonize over his potential feelings of abandonment. I've talked to Whitney a couple of times since telling her about the Guardians. She, of course, got the full story from Dad, or as close to it as anyone could get from him. Dad must have told her to keep Caleb out of things, but I did ask her if she was taking care of Dad's puppy, which after a pause, she seemed to understand. She assured me she was picking up the slack, but I couldn't help being skeptical. I was probably just being over-protective. I talked with Seth about it during our evening walks around the lake. He always reminded me that Caleb is tenacious enough to get what he needs.

Andrea dismounts with a thud. I pull my thoughts away from sweet little Caleb and give her a smile. "Do you like being a sensor?" I ask, trying to distract myself.

She pauses for a moment, toying with the top of her purple water bottle. "Yes and no. I enjoy being able to help others with their talents, but Aunt Gabriella gets most of that work. I don't really like the recruiting part, and that's usually what I'm sent to do: spy on people to confirm their abilities. Taking people by force wasn't our ancestors' intention at all! The original outsiders were courted by Guardians." Her fists ball as she speaks, but her expression softens suddenly. "Oh god, I don't mean like Erik did to you; that was twisted. No, they were told about the organization and all they could gain from joining, then allowed to make the choice for themselves. There weren't kidnappings."

"Uh-oh," Drew says, making me jump. I hadn't noticed him walk up behind me. "You didn't get her started on the old ways, did you?"

"Shut it, Drew." Andrea shoves him playfully. "I'm still your older cousin. Show some respect."

"Yeah, I try that one on Seth all the time. Never works with him, either."

As we're leaving the gym, Olivia hurries after us from behind her desk. "Mr. and Ms. Conry? I have a message for you. Gabriella will be waiting in the lounge for a meeting before lunch."

I turn to Seth with a furrowed brow.

"Thanks, Olivia." Drew offers when Seth and I don't say anything.

I like Gabriella, she's always been nice, but meeting with her is never casual.

We get to the lounge half an hour before lunch, and Gabriella is waiting for us, as promised.

"Seth, Alex, wonderful. Please come in. I had them bring us some tea."

Seth tugs at his collar as we take a seat across from her on the stiff couch. Gabriella fills the china cups. It's impossible to ignore that her warm smile isn't joining us this morning.

"So, let's get right to it. We spoke several weeks ago about the idea of Guardian inauguration. You two were not in the right space to make the decision then, but circumstances have changed." Gabriella twists a large ring on her right hand.

Seth and I exchange a wide-eyed look, neither of us missing the apprehension in Gabriella's usually confident tone. We hadn't even talked about the inauguration since we decided to skip Erik's trial. "Circumstances?" I urge.

"The Conry seats have been vacant for many years. This happens from time to time, usually without incidence. There is, however, an old law that allows another family to appeal the empty spots. To make a long story short, that is what we are dealing with: another family has laid claim to your seats."

"Okay. And?" Seth shrugs.

Gabriella's mouth opens as she looks between the two of us, seeming surprised by our lack of reaction. "You have sixty days to be inaugurated, or you will lose them. Once the seats are forfeit to another family, the change will be permanent. You won't be able to get them back."

"So, we won't be Guardians?" I ask.

"You'll always be Guardians. You will just lack voting rights, and it could change your long-term career prospects."

"I think we can deal with that," Seth says with a humorless laugh.

Gabriella looks to the floor, her shoulders slumping. "It's not that simple." Her eyes meet mine, and the pain in them twists my stomach. "If you take the seats, it'll be sure to bring more attention your way, both within the organization and... within other societies. That being said, Damian and Bryce are not interested in your seats being given to the other family. They are allowing you thirty days to take your places. If you don't, they will have Miles and Whitney brought here to take the seats."

I gasp, and Seth gets to his feet.

"No. That's not happening. Who is trying to steal the seats?"

"I'm afraid that's confidential. I don't even know which family it is. I'm very sorry. This situation isn't ideal but-"

"Not ideal? Damian promised my father Whitney wouldn't be taken!"

Gabriella purses her lips. "I will leave you both to discuss your options. I'm available if you have questions." Getting to her feet, Gabriella walks briskly to the door. She turns before she leaves, and her eyes meet mine again, tears pooling in the lids. "I'm so sorry."

"What the hell?" Seth growls, pacing the lounge as I press my face into my hands.

"This can't be happening."

"Apparently it can." Seth curses as he paces back towards me.

"So, I guess we have to-"

"Nope."

I lift my head, rolling my eyes. "Seth, we can't just *nope* this away."

"watch me." He storms from the room, leaving my ringing ears in silence.

*****

Combat training runs three times a week, and I practice with Andrea on the off days, which brings me to the gym every day. I need the practice, but I also need the distraction. Seth and I still don't know what to do about the inauguration, and I don't even want to think about it. If we do it, we keep Miles and Whitney out of this, but we put ourselves at risk by making our presence here known by Guardians across the globe. Plus, there was no denying the inauguration would tie us to this place. But saying no seemed like a non-option. Seth has taken to completely avoiding the issue since his outburst with Gabriella. Every time I bring it up, he turns to stone. The most I get out of him is a muttered *whatever*. He needs time, so I let myself dive into training.

After a couple of weeks, my muscles stop protesting and begin craving the workouts. It feels good to be back in shape after neglecting the gym during university. I've been Erik-nightmare free all week, leaving me better rested than I've been in years. The increased energy from exercise and several nights of uninterrupted sleep also improves my focus during intel classes.

During my early weeks here, I just observed lectures and seminars. Since I've found my footing, my inner-nerd has flourished, and I'm finally confident enough to participate. I was so conditioned to stay in the shadows it was hard to step back into the spotlight. I don't have to worry about that with the Guardians. I don't stand out when I share ideas. If anything, it helps me fit in; it's incredibly freeing.

I take my seat in the intel seminar, tea in hand. Another Guardian perk: hot coffee and tea available everywhere, all day, with baked goods. It's ridiculous. Our seminars take place in a large boardroom. There are about fifteen of us in each group, but we rotate to different groups based on assignments and areas of expertise. As the new kid, I get floated around a lot. At the head of the table, one of the intel coordinators, Nylah, is chatting with Peter, a frequent guest speaker. He's a genius and the father of probably the smartest person in my intel class, Fredrick. Fredrick is a computer whiz, and his father is the Guardians' top security expert. He knows every system, every trick, every tool. His lectures go way over my head, but they're still fascinating.

"Alright group, put your laptops away and give your full attention to Dr. Walter," Nylah announces to a few groans. Not everyone can see the beauty in Peter's genius. He can be a little dry when he does a deep dive into a topic. Peter also insists we go screen-free while he's lecturing. He says he finds them distracting.

"Please, please call me Peter. Happy to be here sp-speaking with you, all of you, this morning." Peter says, wringing his hands.

"Today we will discuss a recent Guardian excursion that d-didn't go well." He chuckles, turning to the large whiteboard.

"The assignment seemed s-s-simple enough. Our t-team was to p-procure a sample from a lab. One of our researchers had been employed there for eight months and was w-well respected. She learned of the s-s-sample's location without much trouble. She had access to the l-lab in q-question," Peter continues, writing point form on the board in shaky green lettering.

"So, what went wrong?" Peter asks, turning to the group. All our eyes slide to Frederick, who looks down at the table, his blond hair shielding his face.

"The sample was moved?" I try, hoping to pull the attention away from Fredrick. I haven't known him long, but his hyper-introverted nature is obvious.

"G-good guess, Ms. Conry, but no; the sample was there."

A few murmurs spread through the group but no one else says anything.

"The s-sample was locked in a fridge-safe that the employee did not have access to. How should we have solved this?"

"Break open the lock?" someone offers.

"That was what the inside team thought as well. Unfortunately, most lab safes are set up with reinforced security measures. When the lock is broken, and the fridge opens, not only does the system alarm, alerting s-s-security and administration, but a chemical compound releases, destroying the sample and burning the attempted thief."

I gasp, drawing the attention of everyone in the group. "Sorry, but what happened to the lab tech?"

Peter looks perplexed for a moment. "She's quite alright, of course. Sh-she was detained, but the Guardians sorted out her r-release, as they always do. The burns may scar, but they will heal."

I blush uncontrollably as everyone finally looks away, returning their attention to Peter, who was now explaining the mechanism of action of the safe. I guess they had all heard enough of these cases to focus on the facts instead of the people.

"So, your task today: divide into pairs, look over the schematics, and come up with a better plan," Nylah interjects before Peter can continue his overly detailed review of the swiveling cameras they had in the lab.

"Partners?" Frederick asks, pulling me from my examination of the task file. Everyone in intel had been friendly enough, but I usually worked alone. Most of the group had well-established pairs.

"Really? I mean, yeah for sure."

"Cool." Frederick nods, pulling his chair closer to mine and opening his laptop.

"Your dad's pretty great," I say, spreading the blueprints in front of us.

"He's very good at what he does." Frederick's fingers blaze across the keys. Turning to me, his dark eyes don't meet mine, staring instead at the papers spread in front of us. "Any initial ideas?"

I let out a breath. "I'll be honest, security systems are new to me."

"That's alright; I know more about them than I should." His mouth twitches in a faint smile. "Pass the blueprints."

We examine the sheets together for a while. Frederick suggests a few ideas before quickly refuting his own thoughts. The other groups seem to be just as stuck as we are. A few have already given up, pulling out their phones or discussing other assignments. The lock is unpickable; any manipulation of the pins results in lockdown of the fridge and surrounding lab.

Frederick searches the web for ideas while my attention shifts to the lab blueprint. The fridge is in a secured room, near the elevator, two stories below ground.

"What kind of backup battery does the fridge have?"

Frederick looks up, startled. "I'm not sure; it would be at least 30 minutes. It would need to activate in case of a power outage while the lab's generators activate."

I bite my cheek, tracing the route to the nearest exit.

"What are you thinking?"

"It's probably too basic to work."

"Let's try it," Frederick prods.

"Well, we have access to the lab, right? So we use one of the lab technician transport carts. They are plenty big enough for a battery and the fridge safe. We cause a power outage while the lab tech is inside the lab. Once the power is out, she switches the safe for a replica, plugging the safe fridge into a battery on the cart. The cameras will go down for a moment before the generator kicks in. Security will be scrambling. When the power returns and the labs unlock, the lab tech can roll the cart with the real safe fridge to the elevator. We'll have a diversion ready for security so she can roll it out the rear service door." I trace my finger on the blueprint, marking the exit path. "We'll need someone to get that door open, but that should be easy enough with our resources. Once we have the fridge, we can open it in a controlled setting with whatever tools we need at a Guardian lab."

Frederick's eyes dart from side to side as he processes. "You're right. We're confining ourselves to solutions we can subtly perform. If that's not a barrier, we open up several other options." He drums his fingers on the desk. "But there will be some sort of security measure to prevent even accidental unplugging."

"That's why we cut the power. There will be at least a few seconds of lost power, and the alarm will likely be deactivated, or if it goes off, it'll be buried in the chaos. Even if security comes to check, they'll find our replacement fridge plugged in. They aren't likely to know the difference."

Fredrick nods several times, fingers still drumming rhythmically.

We call Peter and Nylah over to discuss our idea. They like the start we've made, so we rejoin the rest of the group to smooth out the edges, getting feedback on other aspects of the job until, as a group, we've made a pretty awesome plan.

I'm always left exhilarated after an intel seminar. I love the collaboration; everyone encourages the sharing of ideas. It's such a contrast to the competitive spirit fostered in combat training.

Most days, it's hard to choose which I like better between intel and combat. The next morning, Damian threatens to tip the scales in intel's favor when he calls me to the mat.

CHAPTER NINETEEN

"Alexandra, Marcy, you're up," Damian says, leaning against one of the thick pillars to face center mat.

Marcy and I had a rematch a couple weeks after our first head to head, and she destroyed me both rounds. I was less than keen to repeat the experience. To make things worse, we have an audience. Once a week, Sensors watch our combat class. It's supposed to help them tune their abilities or whatever, but they usually use it as an excuse to check out hot combats and gossip. Either way, they know this rivalry and their hushed voices silence. Andrea gives me an encouraging smile as Marcy swaggers to the mat.

Marcy glances at the Sensors before giving me a half grin. I smile inwardly, but keep my face neutral. I can't use the tactic of being underestimated during every fight, but I'm not going to turn down the opportunity when it's practically gift-wrapped. Marcy clearly needed a refresher, and what can I say? I'm a giver.

Damian's whistle sounds and Marcy begins to circle. I take hesitant steps to match hers, glancing at my feet nervously. She smiles and charges. Eyes wide, I watch her barrel towards me until she's too close to change course. I dart to the side and easily dodge her, extending my foot to trip her. She stumbles, and I use her momentum to bring her to the ground, sitting on her back just below her shoulders. It's a complete rerun of our first face off as I pull her arms above her head. Damian blows his whistle, and I get off her back, extending my hand to help her up. She glares at me and ignores my gesture as I knew she would; it just makes her more infuriated.

"Good, Alexandra. Marcy, I thought we learned that lesson about misjudging our opponents?"

"Again," Marcy growls.

Damian gives me a half smile and raises his eyebrows. I nod. "Very well." He gestures for us to take our places on the mat.

His whistle sounds, and I lock eyes with Marcy. Her cheeks burn red as she charges towards me again. I duck below her extended arms, putting my new agility skills to good use. She stumbles, recovering quickly to turn on me again. Her teeth clench as her rage increases, which I've learned never helps Marcy. She plows towards me, this time getting lower. I dive over her extended arms, tucking to land in a roll. I get to my feet in time to see her spinning, her mouth slacking in confusion. The class laughs, causing Marcy to turn a deeper crimson, anger reignited. She's irate as she faces me again, circling me.

"Enough dancing, ladies," Damian calls.

I take a step towards her, and she mirrors my movements. Marcy never mirrors, always setting the pace of her matches. I charge, too fast for her to react. I try to sweep her legs from under her, but size plays to her advantage, and I realize too late that I should have spent more time practicing against Drew or Seth and not just Andrea. Marcy only stumbles slightly and easily regains her balance, reaching out to grab me. I dodge her, sacrificing my footing in the process and landing in a crouched position. She drops to get on top of me as I jump to my feet, turning to see her do the same. Marcy glares, running towards me with teeth bared. This time I don't dodge her. As she reaches me, I put my hands on her shoulders, arms extended, and raise my right leg, my foot connecting with her hip. I roll backwards, using Marcy's momentum to flip her over my body. She hits the mats hard, and I pin her before she can recover. Damian's whistle echoes through the gym, and I can't hide my satisfied smile.

"Alexandra takes the set. You were able to take down your opponent without relying on being underestimated. Your practice is paying off, but you still have a long way to go. Your defensive skills are nearly satisfactory, but your offense remains weak. Work on that," Damian says. He spares a sharp glance at Marcy, who's still lying on the mat in wide-eyed surprise.

"Andrew, you're up next. You will face off with Misha."

I make my way back to the side of the mat and sit beside Seth. He nudges my shoulder with a smile. "Nicely done, Lex! Nearly satisfactory defensive skills! Damian will be writing you love sonnets in a week. Although, I think Marcy may want to kill you, so watch out for that," he whispers, tilting his head to the right. I follow his gaze to see Marcy shooting daggers my way. Her cheeks burn red as she sits up stock straight, fists balled. I smile, giving her a wink before turning to watch Drew. I'm not going to let her rage dampen my elation at beating her in a hard-fought match. Plus, I don't want to miss Drew sparring. Damn, he's sexy when he spars.

Marcy corners me in the changeroom after class. "So I guess you think you're top of the class now that you got a lucky pin?"

"That would imply that you were top of the class," I say calmly, washing my hands and only sparing her a glance in the mirror, enough to see her already pinched face tighten further. Thin blonde tendrils cling to her sweaty neck.

She lets out a snort "Whatever, you're just a new toy. Damian will tire of you like I already have."

I turn with a smile. "Ahh, I wondered why you hate me so much. I thought it was because I so thoroughly embarrassed you, but it's more than that. Don't like sharing the spotlight, eh? Well, let me enlighten you. Damian is all yours, and you can have his asshole of a son in the deal. I'm not here to impress him; I guess it just comes naturally to some of us."

"You couldn't handle a real man like Erik, but he sure as hell *handled* you, didn't he? I should send him a congratulatory card for ridding himself of you. Now he's free to pick someone worthy of his position."

My jaw clenches. It's my own fault for bringing him up, but hearing Marcy talk about Erik turns my contained hatred into rage quicker than I can suppress.

"OMG Marcy! How are you?" Andrea smiles as she pushes through the change room door, moving to one of the sinks and repositioning her already perfect bobby pins. "Look, I want to apologize again, you know, for last time I was in combat class and put you in that hold. You remember? The one that made your pants rip in front of the whole class. I admit the pom-pom underwear was a bold choice for gym wear. God, that was so humiliating. Anyway, what are you ladies talking about?" Andrea's eyebrows raise as she turns, her dark eyes locking onto Marcy.

"Whatever," Marcy mutters, turning to stomp out of the change room.

"Nuh-uh, no way does that troll get to try and embarrass you. Trust me, I have lots of dirt on her," Andrea says, glaring at the door. "If she knows what's good for her, she'll back down."

I smile, letting out a shaky breath as I try to shake off my anger. Andrea is quickly becoming one of my favorite people here, the older sister I so desperately need. She takes a minute to make sure the change room is empty before turning back to me.

"Hey, can I ask you something?"

"Sure."

Andrea picks at her thumbnail, avoiding my eyes. I've never seen her nervous. "God, this is so rude, but I'm desperate. Don't hate me for asking, but how did you and Erik meet?"

Blood drains from my face as I pull in a deep breath. I look up at the bright lights, blinking away the sting of tears at the sudden mention of my so-called *relationship* with Erik.

"I swear, I would never bring him up if I wasn't totally desperate. I have to go on a mission. I leave in two days actually, so I am really pushing it. I need to assess a target, which means I have to get close."

"What?" I glare in surprise.

"I know, it's so bad. I wasn't really given a choice in the matter. But I have a plan! If I'm part of the mission, I can prevent a kidnapping. I'm going to give the target a choice, and I'll do everything I can to keep him safe."

I let out a breath, shoulders relaxing. I knew this was part of the organization, but for Andrea to actually take part in the deception? It hurts. I do appreciate her efforts in preventing another kidnapping though.

"Never mind. I'm sorry I asked; it was insensitive."

"Grocery store."

"What?"

"We met at a grocery store. Someone tried to steal my purse. Erik chased them down and got it back. He actually got punched in the process. I was so grateful that I insisted he let me help him get cleaned up. We just hit it off after that," I recount flatly. I hadn't thought back on this since arriving here. A wave of humiliation crashes into me as I realize it wasn't a random criminal that took my purse. It was a setup.

"That's..."

"It was a dick move. Don't do that to someone. Seth's sensor was better. Erik isn't even a sensor! Why did I get landed with him?"

"I think Damian wanted to skip a step, build the relationship with your match early."

I sigh. "Seth had Mayumi. She worked with him and became his friend to get close. That's a better idea." I look at Andrea, jaw tight. "You're beautiful, Andrea. Any guy would fall in love with you, but please don't do that. It's cruel." My nails dig into my palm as Andrea rests a hand on my shoulder, face sincere.

"I won't, I promise. Plus, I have my eye on someone already," she adds, smiling as she raises her eyebrows.

Andrea hurries to meet with her intel group, and I try to shake off the tight grip anxiety has on my stomach. Every time I think I'm past the Erik situation, something catches me off guard, and I'm pulled right back into my fear and insecurity. I rationalize that Erik is gone. It doesn't matter how we met, he's out of my life now. *He's just living at a different Guardian house;* my cruel inner voice reminds me. *He could show up again.*

After a long walk around the cold lake, my anxiety eases, and I drag myself back upstairs to shower. It's then I realize I left my gym bag in the change room. I have a not-so-irrational fear of what Marcy would do to it if she were to find it. Seth tells me to leave it until the morning, but he's playing video games anyway, so I go back on my way to the library.

"That was better, Pratyush." A familiar voice catches my ear. "You're still doubting yourself, though. Remember to take control of the fight. Let's try again, you and me."

I lean on the doorframe between the weight room and the gym. Chloe's stretching in the gymnastics area, but my attention is quickly captured by the owner of the voice I'd heard. Drew and three young teenagers are on the combat mat. Pratyush, a lanky boy who looks about fourteen, squares off across from Drew. He's blinking rapidly as he wipes sweat from his brow. He and Drew rotate a few times before he charges Drew, getting a good grip on his waist. Drew stumbles, but easily twists the younger boy to the mat.

"Really good," Drew says with a chuckle, reaching down to pull Pratyush to his feet. "That was much faster, much more assertive. Alright, I want you to try that again wi-" His eyes meet mine, and he smiles.

"Pair up with Sylvia. Be right back." Drew jogs towards me. "Can't get enough of this place?"

"Nah, forgot my gym bag this morning. What are you up to?"

"I teach the Junior combat class sometimes."

"That's the whole Junior combat class? Are the Guardians in some sort of population crisis?" I ask with a laugh. There are at least twenty-five regulars in our combat class level.

"Most are away at school. Ever notice the lack of rambunctious kids and surly teenagers around here?"

I bite my cheek, trying to picture the dining hall during busy nights. There's always a few kids, but not near as many as there should be, I guess. "What about Chloe?"

"She goes to a Swedish boarding school, technically, but prefers to do most of her classes online. She's a real homebody and a daddy's girl. Damian can't say no to her." Drew smiles indulgently. "Some kids do stay around if they're interning with someone, or already selected for missions, like these three."

I try to picture lanky, baby-faced Pratyush breaking into a mansion, or infiltrating a government agency. I still don't really get what everyone *does* here.

"Did you go to boarding school?"

"Yep, in America. Started there at eight years old. Would have been five if my dad had his way, thirty if my mom did," he laughs.

"Ah, that explains the mystery of your mild accent."

He nods. "That's a big reason for boarding schools around here. My dad had other ambitions for me, and an American accent is helpful. Being fluent in English is essential."

"Ow! Did you just pull my hair?" Sylvia yells. Drew and I jump, lost in our own conversation.

"No! Well, even if I did, what're you gonna do?"

I laugh as Sylvia pushes Pratyush to the mat with a growl.

"I better get back there. See you at dinner." Drew says, jogging back to the group but keeping his eyes on me.

I blush as I retrieve my gym bag. It shouldn't surprise me that Drew spends his free time helping others, but that doesn't make it any less adorable.

I've tried to be patient with Seth, but our thirty-day window is almost up. So, when I get back to our suite, I step in front of the TV before he can load up a new round.

"We're talking about it now. We're making a decision today."

"Totally agree. Dead Zone or Killing Code? Which should we play first?"

I roll my eyes. "I'm not playing the distracting game anymore. Are we taking the seats?"

Seth tosses his controller onto the couch as he pulls on his collar.

"I know. It's a garbage choice. But if we don't choose, that's still a choice."

He finally meets my eyes. "We're taking the seats."

I nod, biting my cheek, "We're taking the seats."

Decision made, I leave Seth to his distractions and head to my bedroom. I pull out my laptop from its hiding place: a hollow in the back of my dresser. Rose had brought Seth and me laptops shortly after we moved into our suite. I hadn't trusted it for anything other than basic Google searches, that is until I met Frederick. Something about his blunt nature led me to confide in him. I'd stopped him after intel earlier this week, asking him to beef up my security. I was a bit embarrassed at first, but as always, he was gracious with my ignorance, explaining things that were way over my head and setting me up with a more secure computer. He found some spyware, which didn't surprise me. Why would the Guardians stop watching me just because they had me trapped here? Luckily, the Guardians had ignored Peter's security recommendations, sticking with weaker firewalls. He set me up with a VPN, assuring me the encryption would be more than strong enough.

Now, Seth and I trusted the computer enough to skype Miles and Whit. I still wasn't willing to ask Whit to put Caleb on screen. I told myself it was because I wanted to keep him safe, but truthfully, I don't think I could handle seeing him. My resolve would crumble at sight of his crocodile tears. I also haven't told Whit about the head seat drama. I guess secrets are contagious, and I've been here too long.

Whitney's beaming face fills my screen, and my heart lifts. I miss her so painfully.

"Finally! Did you have to wait for someone to get off the phone to use the dial-up connection?"

I roll my eyes "Yeah, I'm basically living in a cave." I stretch to let her see my ornate headboard, the door to my ensuite open revealing enough of my massive soaker tub to send my message.

"Whatever." She scrunches her nose before laughing.

"Let's see the new place."

"Well, now I'm self-conscious!"

"What? You mean you don't live in a mansion that's centuries old?"

"No, but I do have a secure phone line," Whit fires back.

"Too soon!" I pout as she gets off her couch, walking me through a detailed tour of her new house. She and Sam had just moved in a couple weeks ago. It was so weird not being a part of this huge milestone. I hate thinking about all of the things I'm missing. But she seems happy, and I do my best to hide my dejection, excitedly pointing out my favorite features.

When she's done, she interrogates me about intel and combat. I have a feeling the Guardians wouldn't be thrilled with me sharing this with her, but if they aren't going to respect my privacy, they can't expect me to keep their secrets. At least, not from my sister.

I tell her about my recent intel work and the current Marcy situation. I leave out my lingering irritation with Andrea, but I can't help sneaking in a bit about Drew.

Whit's smile stretches as she shakes her head. "My god, Alex. I can't believe it. You actually did it."

"What? Beat Marcy? Why are you so surprised?"

"Not that. I mean, good job, she sounds awful. But you actually got a life."

"Hey!"

"Seriously. You really fit there, don't you?"

I furrowed my brow. "What? No. This is temporary. I'm going to find a way home."

Whit just smiles, shaking her head. "I'm not sure you should, Alex. I love you, and I miss you like crazy, but I've never seen you like this. You are so... I dunno. Alive? Maybe that place isn't all bad."

That comment from Whitney clings to me long after we hang up. I want to say she's wrong, that I'm only pretending to fit in here so I can gather the information I need to escape. But when was the last time Seth and I had even talked about running away? And my excitement when I'm in combat class is genuine, as is the satisfaction I get from working through a case in intel.

And then there's Drew.

It dawns on me that, before the Guardians, this was not my reality. I'd liked teaching, but in hindsight, I didn't have the passion for it. When I'd watched my preceptor, Kelly, or even Drew teaching combat, they lit up with enthusiasm. I'd never felt that for teaching. I was doing it as a means to an end, a path to make a stable life for Caleb. This epiphany makes me nervous. It wasn't my plan to fall in love with this place. Somewhere between the gym, the massive library with every book I've ever wanted to read, and adults who actually took an interest in teaching me, I'd found a home. I know I can't tell Seth; I can't admit out loud that I'm happy here.

So instead, I convince myself it's just new and shiny, the luster will fade over time and become mundane. Knowing this, I'm content to enjoy it while it lasts. For once in my life, I don't have a boulder of responsibility crushing my chest; even with the impending inauguration, I feel lighter. Although I'd been captured to get here, I finally feel free.

CHAPTER TWENTY

Later that day, I take one for the team and offer to tell Gabriella our decision. Seth doesn't argue as he turns back to killing zombies.

Gabriella is visibly relieved and tries to reassure me that the inauguration will be small and quick. I'm not interested in her placations. I'm pissed that Damian and Bryce forced us into this decision, and Gabriella is the unfortunate messenger. The ceremony is scheduled for Saturday; Seth and I have an unspoken agreement to totally ignore it's happening until absolutely necessary.

When I get to combat class on Friday, I take my usual seat between Drew and Seth. I'm distracted by Seth's hilarious retelling of a dream he had about running around the Guardian house completely naked, but only finding socks in every closet.

"Alright, let's get into this."

My eyes snap to the front mats, praying that this, too, is some twisted dream. Scott leans on the pillar Damian usually occupies, wearing track pants and a t-shirt. His hands rest idly in his pockets as he looks around the gym with indifference.

Eyes wide, I turn to Drew with a questioning look. He furrows his brow in unhelpful reply.

"What is Scott doing here?" I whisper, crouching to try and hide behind Drew's shoulder. I glance back at the door, wondering if I can sneak out before he sees me.

"I guess it has been a while. Scott teaches combat a fair bit, but he's been away on back-to-back assignments." Drew gets to his feet with the rest of the class.

"Oh, how cute! Alexandra, in combat," Scott says, smiling at me; that *antagonizing* smile.

A snort of laughter further vexes me; I don't need to turn around to know it's Marcy.

I glare at Scott. "I'm not sure why you're here. Are we learning how to use sedatives to incapacitate our targets? I didn't realize that was a combat skill, but you certainly would be the expert."

It's Drew's turn to laugh, which he quickly tries to mask with a cough.

Scott's smile widens, but a hint of pink satisfyingly colors his cheeks. "I had no need to fight you before. Care to experience my true skills?"

"Oh, I have seen your sarcasm and inflated self-perception already. No need to show me again. I'm still in awe." A wave of laughter echoes through the class.

"Front and center, Conry. No, Seth, not you," he adds flatly as Seth eagerly steps forward. Everyone laughs, except me. I let my face fall, eyes growing wide.

Scott's mouth twitches, tempted to smile.

I swallow thickly, eyeing Scott nervously.

"Come on, Alexandra, I'll go easy on you."

I know you will. I make my way slowly to center mat. Looking back at the class, I catch Marcy's eye. She's practically salivating.

Scott can't suppress his eager smile as I get into an awkward crouched stance. He darts forward with surprising speed.

I dodge him. Twisting, I land a kick on the back of his knee as his momentum pushes him past me.

He stumbles, recovering quickly. Turning back to me, his brow furrows for a moment, before a smile returns and he shakes his head.

"Well played," he allows, almost laughing.

Before I can shift my casual position, he darts again, easily lifting me off my feet. Scott throws me over his shoulder and onto the mat. I let out an involuntary grunt as air rushes from my lungs on impact.

I struggle to catch my breath for a minute before Scott reaches down, easily lifting me to stand.

"Lace-up peons, we're doing boxing conditioning today," he calls, keeping his eyes on me with a grin. The group groans, moving to the end of the gym where the boxing gear is stored. I turn to join them, but Scott catches my arm. "I'll lace your wrists," he offers.

I look at him skeptically, finally shrugging when his expression remains condescending-smile free. Admittedly, I don't have the skill to lace my own wrists, but I'm not sure I want him doing it. I usually use my ignorance as an excuse to have Drew do it for me. Scott grabs a roll of thin woven fabric sitting at the side of the mats and stands in front of me, taking my small wrist in his large hands.

"That was impressive, Alexandra." He's surprisingly gentle as he twists the fabric. I don't like the intimacy of him holding my hand, but for once he's not being a creeper about it. I try to focus on what he's saying.

"You beat me."

"Yeah, of course I beat you." *There's the Scott I know.* "But you tricked me, again. I bought that doe-eyed act of yours. If I bought it, it's pretty convincing. What is Gabriella saying about your gift profile?"

I shrug. "Still unknown, I guess." I haven't spoken to her since agreeing to the inauguration.

"Well, I'll tell her to add deceit to the list. I already sensed it, but that was a lovely confirmation. I'm looking forward to your inauguration tomorrow, but, rather surprised. I thought you would have fought it," he mutters.

"I wasn't in a position to fight it. It wasn't my ass on the line."

His deep brown eyes meet mine for a moment before beginning on my other wrist. "So, not getting on with the Cirkovic girl? Margret, is it?"

"Marcy? Yeah, she's not a fan. Careful, she's coming for your brand."

He looks up, surprise widening his eyes. "See, now I don't know if you're kidding. I don't dislike you, Alexandra. Truth be told, I rarely think of you, but when I do, it's with intrigue, not distaste."

I snort. "Now who's the liar. *Rarely think of me?* Sure, sure."

Scott turns out to be a passionate teacher when he gets warmed up, but an intense one. By the end of the hour, I'm soaked in sweat and have an unsettling appreciation for him. Apparently, he's the only one who's allowed to tease and abuse me and teaches Marcy that lesson by making an example of her the entire class. "No, Miss Cirkovic, do it again. Still wrong. Somehow even worse, which is admittedly impressive. You know what? Just stop. Five laps." Scott repeatedly stopped Marcy, which only flustered her further. It was satisfying after she made jabs about how ridiculous I looked flying over Scott's head. She's a bully, and sometimes it feels good for the bully to get squished by the bigger bully.

Even with that satisfying smackdown, I'm totally drained after class. I hate my past self for agreeing to gymnastics conditioning after combat. I only have time to choke down a granola bar and some water before my training session with Andrea and one of the Guardians' in-house coaches. I worry things will be awkward with Andrea after yesterday's discussion about Erik, but she's her usual bubbly self, so I roll with it.

"Damn, I knew I should have come to combat today," Andrea pouts, as the stragglers leave the gym. "Scott is *so* hot."

Eyes wide, I follow her gaze. I guess, objectively speaking, Scott is pretty attractive. He has short, gelled hair that's always perfect, firm muscles he's not shy about displaying, and a clean-shaven chiseled jawline. Maybe if I had never actually spoken to him, I'd see him that way too. As it stands, I give Andrea a *"you're crazy"* look. She shrugs, watching him walk out of the gym with a wistful expression.

I struggle through the hour, but Andrea's consistent berating drives me to push through the exhaustion.

"I'm so done," I exclaim, collapsing to the mat when the coach finally calls it.

Andrea laughs, sitting beside me. "You are *weak!*"

"Shut it." I slap her leg lightly.

"You two just about done here?" Seth asks, standing at the edge of the gymnastic mats. For some reason, he can't bring himself to actually enter the gymnastics area. I think the equipment intimidates him.

"I am!" I scramble to my feet before Andrea can guilt me into a boot camp class.

"Andrea?" Seth asks, looking hopeful.

"Nah, I'm gonna stay for a bit. Working on a new layout Jaeger and haven't nailed it yet."

"Okay well, um, later," Seth mutters, cheeks turning pink.

Andrea smiles, fussing with her already perfect ponytail. "See ya." She winks.

It's a true testament to my love for Seth that I suppress my laughter as I walk with him towards the gym door, Drew waiting for us there.

"I call first shower," Seth shouts, running down the hall, laughing.

Letting out a tired sigh, I stretch my arms as I fall into step with Drew.

Drew chuckles. "Good workout?"

"Yeah. Andrea's a tyrant, though."

"I thought you'd like that."

"I do," I admit. I like being pushed, and Andrea definitely does that. It seems to be mutual; I've noticed her clocking a lot more gym time since we started training together.

When Drew and I arrive at the temporary Conry suite, I'm about to invite him in when he stops me with a light hand on my wrist.

"Hey, If I promise there will be no discussion about tomorrow's ceremony, d'you want to have dinner with me tonight?" he asks, rubbing the back of his neck as he peers at me through his unfairly long eyelashes. "We could go for a walk by the lake first. I mean, if you want," he adds, more to the floor than me.

If my stomach wasn't so full of butterflies, I might be able to enjoy how cute he looks. A grin lights my face against my will, my brain screaming so many things at once it's hard to focus. Maybe the workout will hide my blush? "Okay. That'd be great."

"Yeah? Alright! Um, I'll go get ready. Pick you up in an hour? Well I mean, I'll come here, and we'll go."

"Sure, sounds grood- I mean good." I close my eyes as I push through the door into the sitting room. *Smooth, Alex.*

I brush off my embarrassment as excitement takes its place, flooding through me. *Oh-my-gosh-oh-my-gosh-oh-my-gosh! Is this really happening?*

My mind tries to remind me that relationships are out of bounds right now. Reciting that we're trying not to tie ourselves to this place, but I drown it out with my irrepressible excited squeal. I've been sensible for too long. I really want this, and I'm not going to talk myself out of having dinner with Drew.

I run straight into Seth as I bolt for my room.

"Woah there," he says, catching my shoulders to stop me falling to the marble floor. He takes in my expression, confused.

"I need to get ready, now!"

"Ready? What?" Seth asks, clinging to my shoulders as I try to pull away.

"Drew, me, dinner! He asked me. I mean, we're going..." I try to explain as I successfully break free, running down the hall.

Seth laughs, yelling as I dart into my room. "It's about time! Plus, I actually like this one."

Alison Haines

I roll my eyes, but my smile returns. I wasn't sure how Seth would react. *So far, so good*. Relief combines with the elation rushing through me.

Forty minutes later I'm showered, my hair's somewhat tamed, and I'm tearing through my closet, trying to decide what to wear. I should just text Rose, but I can't handle her entirely predictable expression when I tell her about dinner. She'll find out soon, that is, if she doesn't already know. Remembering Drew mentioned a walk, I grab a pair of jeans, a long sleeve T-shirt, and a zip-up sweater. Casual is better; I don't want him to think *I think* it's a date. Is it a date?

As I leave my room, the distinct music and shooting sounds of Seth's favorite video game fill the suite. I find him sitting on the couch, staring at the large TV in our converted living room. I'd accepted Seth's suggestion of soft leather couches and obscenely large TV when redecorating. No reason he shouldn't enjoy some of the wealth thrown at us while we're here. The only traditional element in the room is a large portrait of our grandparents that Rose ordered from the England estate. It hangs over the fireplace we had yet to use. I kind of love having it. My dad's parents died before I was born. Even though I had never met them, I had grown up seeing their pictures. It's comforting having some small recognizable tie to my past here. In the portrait, Grandfather is wearing a large medallion of the Guardian crest around his neck. I wonder if he'd been wearing it in any of our old photos.

Taking my eyes off my grandfather's blue, ever-following gaze, I turn to Seth. He has that blank expression all guys get when they're playing video games. I'm actually glad, though. He hasn't had much alone time since the mess with Erik happened. Well, really, since he was taken. It'll also help keep his mind off of tomorrow. Seth hates being forced to do anything, and joining a secret society he wanted to escape was a pretty big breach. I can tell he wants to run but knows he can't. Miles and Whit are depending on us.

"You gonna be okay for dinner?" I have to repeat the question louder when he doesn't answer.

"Huh? Yeah, go have fun. Mitchell's bringing pizza. I have zombies to kill."

A knock startles me, and the butterflies resume their fluttering. "Come in," Seth yells, eyes glued to the TV and fingers mashing the controller impossibly fast.

Drew opens the door, looking between Seth and the TV before noticing me in the dimly lit room. I smile, relief relaxing my tight shoulders; he's wearing jeans and a hoodie, too.

"You look great," he says, taking a step towards me. My cheeks heat up, and I bite my lip.

"Dude, TV!" Seth yells, trying to see around Drew. He steps back, and I run past the TV to meet him on the other side.

"Goodnight, Seth."

"Don't keep her out too late, young man," Seth calls as I shut the door.

As we walk to the lake, our conversation is strained. We comment on the light layer of snow that had fallen throughout the day—the first snow of the season—but the pressure to say something interesting traps my thoughts in self-doubt.

We round a small patch of trees blocking our view of the lake, and the glistening gazebo comes into view. Hundreds of tea lights line the railings, flames flickering in the gentle breeze and casting a warm glow on the blanket of snow.

Drew smiles nervously, his eyes searching my awed expression.

"You did all this? For me?" I manage, stunned.

"I had some help," he admits, reaching down to lace his fingers through mine. The warmth of his touch spreads through me, reigniting my smile as he leads me to the gazebo. A welcoming warmth breaks the chill in the evening air, thanks to the well-placed heat lamps.

"This is amazing."

Drew wipes his palms on his jeans as he darts to pull out my chair. It's impossible to miss that he's as nervous as I am. *Okay, this might be a date.* He opens a compartment under the table, and the smell of garlic bread emerges as he pulls out a steaming selection of Italian foods. I shouldn't be surprised that they are all favorites of mine.

"Bon appétit," he says, his smile illuminated by the flickering flames that surround us.

A giggle escapes at his cheesy sincerity. I'm not used to being treated like this by anyone, let alone Drew.

The awkwardness evaporates as we eat. We slide back into our usual ease and conversation flows freely as time slips away. Being with Drew is easy. It's like taking a hot bath at the end of a stressful day. I don't catch myself constantly analyzing his mood or facial expressions. I don't have to play back our conversations a hundred times, agonizing over what I said, or didn't say. I'm just me. And it's undeniable: this is the best date ever. Despite the feelings I've been trying to suppress, I have only grown more attached to Drew. With all of the drama surrounding Erik, I worried we would never get a chance. Perhaps too much water under that bridge. Kidnappings, family betrayal, secret societies; it's a lot to overcome. Against all odds, we are standing together in companionable silence, sipping wine and watching the candlelight dance on the smooth surface of the lake.

"Name an unfulfilled ambition or dream," Drew poses.

I blanch, mind going right to Caleb's adoption. Stalling, I take a sip of wine. The whole date, we'd both avoided questions about family. I wonder if, for him, it's a sensitive subject; I'd sure as hell be touchy if my family consisted mainly of Damian, Bryce, and Erik. I certainly wasn't going to bring it up. I haven't told him about Caleb. I don't want to lie to Drew. I want to trust him. I do trust him, but Caleb isn't something I can gamble with, however low the risk.

"Law school," I blurt.

Drew looks at me intently for a minute, a smile stretching across his gorgeous full lips. "Yeah, I could see that for you. But why didn't you pursue it? You're brilliant, there's no way you didn't get accepted."

Blushing, I run a hand through my curls. "I did get in actually, to a great school in British Columbia." *Well done, you circled right back to Caleb!* I realize too late. I'd skipped on law school because it meant moving thousands of kilometers from Caleb, not being part of his life for years. I picked teaching instead; it only required one year of school after my undergrad; then I could start building a future.

"It was really far from my family. Who knew I'd be moving a whole continent away! BC would have been practically neighbors compared to Europe." I nudge his shoulder that's pressed against mine, diverting the question back to him; something he's made very difficult tonight. He has so many questions about me, about my passions.

"I mean, I was just going to say eat an entire lasagna in one sitting, but now I'm gonna have to dig a bit deeper." I laugh as he pauses to think. His eyes meet mine again, and

I blush at the attention. He treats me like there's nowhere he would rather be. I'm not even sure he brought his phone.

"Well, I love teaching actually. My goal is to take over running combat. My father wants me to work *in the field* before *settling* for teaching." He shrugs; it's clear he is not keen on Bryce's plan.

"That's awesome. You'd be way better than Damian."

Drew smiles, but his expression falls as he bites his lip. "I need to apologize. The way I spoke to you at the café..." He shakes his head like he's trying to erase the memory of the argument we had months ago. "When I said I only cared about you because I was on a mission, it was cruel. I was trying to distance myself from you so I didn't get in the way of your relationship with Erik, but I shouldn't have hurt you like that."

Taking his tense hand in mine, I try to meet his downcast eyes. "Yeah, I kind of pieced that together, what with you threatening Erik when I first arrived then saving me from his basement dungeon. It didn't really scream *I'm just doing my job*. Sorry to say it, but you're not as sneaky as you think."

"Hey, I'll have you know I'm a literal spy."

"Yikes. You should probably work on that."

He laughs as I lean between two candles, watching an otter scurry under the gazebo from the water's edge. Drew turns to face me as I straighten, his strong arms bracing on the white rail. His eyes dart between mine. Licking his lips, he tilts his head, so close his warm, sweet breath caresses my cheek. He gently wraps his arm around my waist to pull me against his chest. I close my eyes as his lips near mine. My thoughts ignite with a long-held desire to kiss the lips I've spent months imagining.

"Andrew?" Bryce's voice fractures my fairytale, his anger cutting through the cold night air.

Drew's body stiffens, his arm releasing me as he twists to face Bryce. "Father, I-"

"What is the meaning of this?" Bryce asks, incensed. I inexplicably feel like a kid getting caught with her hand in the cookie jar. The shame is short-lived, rapidly replaced with my own rage.

I step towards Bryce, but Drew catches my wrist thanks to his lightning-fast reflexes. He pulls me to his side, holding me firm. "I thought you and Mother were out for the evening."

"Andrew, this is unacceptable. Erik is your cousin. I can't believe you would even think of-"

"Hi, I'm Alex!" I shout, causing Bryce to pause and turn to me, brow furrowed and mouth agape. "I'm not sure if you know this, but I'm actually a real person. A sentient being in fact, with my own will; not your pawn. I'm not here to be matched for *ideal breeding*."

"Not now," Drew whispers.

"You are ungrateful. You're completely ignorant of our customs and yet you parade around like you're above it all." Bryce's face grows red as his eyes narrow.

"Father, enough! Don't talk to Alex like that. *You* are the one who's ignorant, you know nothing about her," Drew snaps. His dad is struck silent, and so am I. I have never seen Drew even disagree with his dad, and based on Bryce's face, it was a rare occurrence. Drew grabs my hand, taking advantage of his father's shock to escape. I follow, unsure of what to say. My anger thaws with every step away from Bryce, like the snow melting off our boots. What's left is a painful lament for what could have been. What had been so close I could literally taste it. The perfect kiss that had been stolen.

We walk in silence all the way to my door. I can tell Drew is still mad; his hand trembles in mine as he stomps through the twisting halls. "Drew... thanks for standing up for me," I say, wishing I could calm him.

"I'm sorry," he says, shaking his head. I'm not sure if he even heard me. "My dad can't seem to let the idea of you and Erik go." His eyes are so full of pain like I've never seen in him before.

"You know there is *no* way anything is gonna happen with Erik and me, right?" I clarify, my voice trembling. The change in his expression makes my stomach tighten. Something has shifted in Drew since his father's date crash. It's unsettling.

"Yes, I know. Sorry, it's..." Drew pauses, pulling his hand from mine to run it through his hair, looking away. "I know this all sounds ridiculous to you, but this is how I was raised. What Erik did was terrible, but he's still family. He's like a brother, Alex."

"What are you trying to say?" I whisper, chest tight like I've been punched in the stomach. Is he seriously saying anything even remotely nice about the sleaze-ball formally known as Erik? And to me, of all people?

"No, nothing. It's... I just..." Unlike this afternoon, Drew stumbling on his words is far from sweet. It cuts through me, shredding any remaining warmth from our almost perfect date.

"You need some time to think? Take it," I finish for him, opening my door. "Thanks for dinner," I add flatly, closing the door before he has a chance to answer. After everything Drew's done for me, I don't want to be mad at him. I know he must be having a hard time, but this is something I can't talk about. I'm far from objective; any thought of Erik brings bile surging to my throat. I'm in no position to discuss how us dating will affect his relationship with the man who abused me.

I move to the couch and drop down beside Seth. Biting my cheek, I try to hold in the tears already pooling in my eyes.

"You're back early," Seth says, eyes fixed on the TV until I don't answer. He looks at me and pauses his game. Hot tears stream down my cold cheeks. "Lex, what happened?" He puts his hands on my shoulders, looking me up and down, probably for injuries.

I shake my head. "I'm fine. Things just didn't go as planned."

Through irrepressible sobs, I recount the story, leaving out most of my conversation with Drew. I don't want Seth pissed at him; he's pretty much our only friend here.

Seth swears, shaking his head "Bryce is a total ass-hat. That whole family sucks. I mean, except Drew."

A new wave of tears burst through at the mention of Drew. I'm so miserable it's hard to imagine how happy I was an hour ago, how perfect everything seemed. Seth pulls me into a tight hug, and I sob on his shoulder, too wrecked to fight the flood.

CHAPTER TWENTY-ONE

A loud knock on the door pulls me from the movie world I was absorbed in. Seth always knows how to pull me out of a downward spiral: blood and car chases. Gunfire and screeching tires blast from the surround sound as another urgent knock echoes through our suite.

Seth and I both get to our feet, rushing to the door. I throw it open.

"Rose? What's going on? You're shaking!" I grip her trembling shoulders and pull her into the room.

Rose wrings her hands, looking between Seth and me with wide eyes, light from the TV flashing across her face. "You need to leave, now!" My eyes dart to Seth as his expression hardens. His eyes mirror my anxiety. I nod, and we run to our large hall closet, throwing lights on in our pitch-black suite. Rose turns off the TV as we both pull out a backpack. We had packed some essentials, with Rose's help, shortly after the Erik incident. As much as I had let my guard down, I'm no fool. I trust this place as much as I trust

Caleb to brush his teeth before bed. In the back of my mind, I knew there was a reasonably good chance we'd need to make a quick get-away.

We dump everything in front of the couch and sit to pull on our boots, Rose still talking so fast it's almost incomprehensible. It does nothing for my growing panic. I silently thank my past self for being so prepared. It's been too easy to get comfortable in this place.

While Seth and I gather our things, Rose hastily explains herself. Another housekeeper overheard Bryce ranting to a guard about how "ungratefully" I'd behaved this evening. He had decided to take me to Erik again, who is hiding out at another Guardian estate. Bryce decided that if I were in an unfamiliar house with just Erik and some guards, I would be less likely to escape, be more pliable. Seth's face is red with anger as Rose speaks, but he keeps his cool well enough to keep moving. Having something to do with his hands seems to help; not so much for me. My trembling fingers can barely tie my laces. *How in the hell can this be happening?* Thoughts of being locked in a room with Erik again threaten to paralyze me.

Once we have everything together, I pull Rose into a tight hug. Thanking her for saving me again, I add a hasty request for her to tell Drew that we had to leave. He knows our escape plan and has the number to our secret phone, which I run to my room to grab. I've kept it plugged in, hidden under my mattress for months. After our rushed goodbye, Rose leads the way out of the suite and through hidden hallways used by the staff. She's certain Bryce will wait until later tonight when he thinks Seth and I are asleep, but it's safer to go unseen.

She opens a door at the bottom of the narrow staircase we descend, peeking out into what I see is a hall near the main foyer. Closing the door, she turns back to face us. "Marcella is just finishing her polish; she'll be gone in a minute or two." Her eyes shift from mine to Seth's. "Take a right out of this door and head straight to the end of the hall. Make a left, then go through the last door on your right. That's the garage."

Rose offered to take us all the way to the gates, or even into the city, but I don't want her anywhere near us if we get caught. She quickly assures us that the front gates will be open when we get there. I have to trust her connections. What other choice do we have?

We make it to the garage unseen, pushing open the heavy steel door that stands out from the wooden ones on the opposing wall. Unsurprisingly the *garage* is the size of a large car dealership. I quickly fashion a makeshift lock with a crowbar and a few other miscellaneous supplies from the nearby mechanic's bench. It won't hold for long, but it'll make a ton of noise if someone tries to enter, giving us some warning. I scan the room, yet another location not included in my grand, heavily-censored tour. Paneled steel doors make up the entire far wall, and dozens of cars litter the concrete floor. There are standard black SUVs and sedans that security use, then there are the *toys* of the overly privileged Guardians. Sports cars and jeeps in every color gleam in the bright overhead lights. I start peering through windows of the vehicles closest to the exit while Seth slides the large horizontal doors open.

"Crap," I mutter. "All of these have activated alarms. Guess I can try to rewire the system around the alarm; put my intel training to the test. It's risky, and it'll take a few minutes. What year do you think this car is?" My attention is ripped from thoughts of colored wires by the revving of an engine.

"Umm, do you even know how to drive that thing?"

Seth just shrugs and pulls on a helmet, which seems wise, seeing as he's straddling a two-wheeled death rocket. I have to admit, the motorcycle looks fast; an appealing attribute right now. His black and yellow helmet matches the bike perfectly.

"This one should fit you," he adds, tossing me a green one. Hardly the time to pull out a color-wheel.

I put the helmet on and walk around the bike. "You didn't answer my question!"

"Lexie, we don't have time for this; you're just gonna have to trust me." As if to highlight his point, the crashing of my make-shift lock echoes through the concrete space. No time to second-guess him, I hoist myself on the back of the bike, wrapping my arms around Seth as he kicks into gear. We shoot out of the garage, the cold night air stinging my exposed hands. For a minute, I'm too scared to notice my eyes are closed. When I finally open them, we're fast approaching the main gates. I say a silent prayer thanking Rose when we find them uncharacteristically open. The exhilarating rush of freedom surges through me. Riding on the back of a motorcycle feels like flying. After being locked up in the Guardian's grounds for so long, I forgot what it felt like to just be free. Laughter echoes in my helmet. *We actually got out*! I had let myself get too comfortable, let myself forget how trapped I really was.

We speed past darkened forests, the landscape quickly shifting to much busier and brighter streets. Seth weaves expertly through the city, dodging traffic like he's been riding this bike for years. Making several turns that seem random, he finally slows to a stop in an alley not too far off the main strip of downtown Gavleborg. I climb off the bike, removing my helmet to find Seth's expression just as elated as mine.

"Seth, that was AMAZING! I had no idea you could drive like that."

"Neither did I!" he says with an exhilarated laugh. "I've only ever ridden dirt bikes, but somehow I just knew I could do it."

"Well, you nailed it." I nudge him with my shoulder, too euphoric to scold him for the reckless decision.

Looking around the dark alleyway, the excitement of our escape seeps from the air like the mysterious water trickling towards the nearby drain. "Okay so," Seth starts, tone flattening.

"Step one, complete, I guess. We managed to escape, any idea how to get to the ferry in Norrtalje?"

"No clue." Seth looks around like there might be a handy arrow to point our way hidden in the colorful graffiti.

"Our emergency phone does have GPS. Is it worth the risk that it's been somehow compromised?"

"I'd rather chance that than start asking for directions. Who knows who the Guardians have in their pockets around here."

"True." I pull the phone out of my backpack. As I turn it on, a text from Drew pops up. My stomach twists; I swipe away the notification, reading only *"I'm sorry"* before opening the GPS app. I'll deal with Drew later. My fingers itch to open the text, but my first priority has to be finding a safe place to lay low. I don't trust myself to read his message and not break down in tears again. The phone finds our current location quickly, and I enter in the harbor.

"We have about three and a half hours of driving ahead of us. You up for it on that bike?"

"Oh yeah! And I guarantee you, on this beast, it's not gonna take anywhere near that long." He pats the seat of the motorcycle fondly.

I roll my eyes, shifting to his side so we can both see the map. Once we've found the most direct route, we pop our helmets back on and hit the road. Seth winds through city traffic before pulling onto highway E4.

The exhilaration of being on the bike fades less than an hour in. I'm tired of sitting in one position, and as pretty as this bike is, the seats aren't meant for comfort. My back screams as I try futilely to adjust my aching hips. I notice something is wrong, more serious than my sore butt, when Seth turns off the highway before our scheduled exit. I tap him on the shoulder, but he shakes his head, the movement exaggerated by his helmet. It's infuriating not being able to talk to him. Seth makes a few tight turns, then speeds up again. He takes a turn so sharp I actually scream, our legs nearly brushing the road. The bike stops abruptly and my body slams into Seth's back.

Cutting the engine, Seth scrambles off the bike, pulling me into a tight, darkened alley, out of the pool of light igniting the bike. He takes my hand and leads the way into an adjacent wider laneway. As we pull off our helmets, Seth's wide eyes dart around the dimly lit, high-bricked space. His breath comes heavily as he leans against the wall. "We're being followed," he whispers, pulling me beside him so he can see past me.

"How?"

He shakes his head "Maybe the phone? Not sure, but I noticed the same car following us for too long on the highway. When I would change lanes, it was always right there. That's why I got off the highway, to see if the car would follow. It tailed me the whole way-" Seth stops abruptly as squeaking brakes echo from the neighboring alley. Two doors slam, and he takes my hand, leading me deeper into the shadows. His rapid breathing persists as his head twists, looking for escape. I pull him into a recessed doorway, straining to hear footsteps on the wet cobblestones.

CHAPTER TWENTY-TWO

A deep voice breaks the silence. "Sir, bike's here. No sign of any Guardians. We'll look around and call if we see anyone." My heart races as two sets of measured footsteps get louder, nearing our alley.

A chilling wave of realization floods over me, but I push it aside so I can focus. My frantically searching hands close around a door handle. Turning the cold knob, I find luck on our side: it's unlocked. My eyes dart to the mouth of the alley as my ears pound, desperate to pick up the sound of our pursuers. Seeing no one, I gently nudge Seth forward and step off the narrow door frame so I can pull the door open. Loud music erupts through the narrow laneway, reverberating off of the brick walls that tower over us. Seth and I rush inside, and the door snaps shut behind us. The loud, smoke-filled bar is a sharp contrast from the silent chill of the dark alley, but there's no time to adjust. I grab Seth's hand, moving away from the stage and into the crowd. The place is blissfully packed. Bodies jostle me as we head for the bar, deafening music blaring, only increasing my tension. As we get to the bar, two guys are just getting up. I quickly snag one of their stools and pull Seth into the other. I stuff my backpack, jacket, and helmet against the bar at our feet, nudging him to do the same. Running my hands through my hair, I pray for an intentionally windswept look instead of unmistakable helmet head. It's lucky I'd been on a date tonight, so I'm actually wearing makeup. It'll help me blend in. I wipe under my eyes, wondering if my earlier crying gave me raccoon eyes. Hoping for the best, I turn my attention to Seth. His short hair is perfectly unfussed, but his face is tight, eyes still darting around the room.

Two beers, not quite finished, sit on the bar in front of us. Picking up the plastic cups, I force one into Seth's hand and grip the other.

"I'm not drinking this, Alex!" He looks at me in disgust. "And shouldn't we be running now? They must've heard the music; it won't take them long to find where it came from."

I glance at Seth briefly before returning my gaze to the door we came through. Seth starts to turn, but I grab his shoulder to stop him.

"No, keep your eyes on me. Don't drink the beer. Just hold it. And fix your face; you look terrified."

My ears ring as the band stops playing. The crowd fills the silence, talking and laughing as another group sets up on stage.

"What's going on?"

"The bike," I mutter. He's silent for a minute before swearing under his breath. "Yeah, they must have had a GPS tracker on it."

"How did we not think to switch vehicles?" Seth asks rhetorically, his face tight as he thinks. "But still, we need to move. They'll see us sitting here."

"Not necessarily..." I scan the room quickly to see if we look out of place. People dressed in every type of clothing surround the bar, flooding onto the small dance floor. Some are clad in leather with piercings and chains, while others, like us, are wearing jeans and casual shirts. No one is watching us. Even the bartender is too busy to take notice of us, a large line of customers at the end of the bar keeping him occupied. *Perfect*. I return my gaze to the door. "If it's not them following us..." I start, but I don't have time to explain. It's time to test my theory.

"What are you talking about?" he asks with a hint of hysterical laughter.

I shift my eyes to Seth with a wide smile, leaning towards him. Nodding once as if listening to a story, I let out a laugh and playfully slap his knee. He looks at me like I've lost my mind, head tilted to the side and eyes wide, mouth agape. I ignore him for a moment to scan the dance floor. The two men I had just seen enter through the stage door pick their way through the crowd as a new band begins their set. They're dressed casually, one in a brown leather coat, the other in a green sweater. Leather Coat is wearing a stern expression; anyone who happens to meet his eyes moves hastily out of his way. He's on a mission, and no one seems eager to interfere. Green Sweater's expression is more desperate than intimidating as his eyes dart frantically around the crowded space. Whenever they look at the bar, I focus on the stage and move with the music for a moment before searching the dancing crowd again. Seth's expression is so confused it's almost comical.

I force a smile as I whisper in Seth's ear, "Trust me for a minute. Turn towards the stage and move to the music, keep that beer visible in your hand and act like you're having fun." I lean away, raising my eyebrows expectantly.

He smiles, uncertainty still tightening his eyes. A moment later the two men saunter past the bar. I hold my breath as they scan right past us, heading for the front entrance.

Letting out a long breath as they leave, my shoulders relax. I shift my attention to the band for another minute, just in case they look back in. When I'm satisfied they're gone, I turn to Seth. He's still smiling like a tool, which actually makes me laugh. His eyes narrow, giving me a well-deserved glare. Pursing my lips, I stop laughing and reach into my backpack for my wallet. A second bartender, carrying a large bin of used cups, returns to the bar. When she deposits them on a back counter, I get her attention and order two Cokes, totally parched.

"So, good news is it's not the Guardians following us," I tell Seth after a grateful sip.

"What the hell was all of that?" Seth demands, enraged.

"I'm getting to that, calm yourself. Two guys came in the back door shortly after us and scanned the room. They aren't Guardian guards. We had to blend, and I think it worked. They left without any sign they recognized us."

"How is that possible? Who are they?"

"First, I think what you meant to say is thank you, so you're welcome." He looks at me, deadpan as I carry on. "I can't be sure, but something isn't sitting right," I admit, irritated at my own ignorance.

"Then how are you so sure they weren't Guardians?"

"I wasn't, but I had a strong feeling that they weren't. The phone call we overheard outside, the guy referred to the Guardians as a group, like he didn't belong. When they didn't recognize us, it just proved it. But I can't figure out who else would have a tracker on Guardian vehicles..." I can feel I'm missing something, like a word on the tip of my tongue that I can't quite grasp.

Seth takes a drink, looking pensive. "So, what now?"

"It's too loud in here," I comment. We've been talking into each other's ears for the last several minutes. "We'll leave in a few minutes, find somewhere to plan." I don't want to be the first people leaving the bar, in case they're still out front.

Seth nods, and we both finish our drinks. For the first time, I realize the music isn't bad. The screaming band who was playing when we arrived had been replaced by a punk-rock group with a pop sound. Of course, the lyrics are all in what I assume to be Swedish, so I have no clue what they're saying, but it sounds catchy, and the crowd's really into it.

I keep an eye on the door. Once a few other groups leave, I figure it's as safe as it's going to get. We retrieve our backpacks and coats, leaving the helmets behind. We're already going to stand out with backpacks; helmets would be a nice red flag to whoever's looking for us. Since I have no idea where we are, I follow another group, hoping they're at least heading towards a main road. Seth and I don't talk. I think we are both of the same mind that it isn't the best time to show off that we don't speak the language or have an accent to match any neighboring countries.

The street that we exit onto is dark, except for a swath of light escaping the bar. As we walk, light from the adjacent street floods onto ours. The men are nowhere in sight. Luck is on our side again, but I can't help wondering when it will run out.

The group we're following takes a right, but I steer Seth left, seeing a neon sign that looks like a restaurant. It turns out to be a laundromat, but next to that is a 24-hour diner. It's mostly deserted, only a tattered-looking man in one booth drinking coffee and a college-aged group, dressed like they'd come from a bar. We slide into a red vinyl booth in an empty corner. The restaurant's theme seems to be "very cheesy American diner." A girl saunters over, dressed in a pink poodle skirt. I almost laugh, her black makeup and sour expression in complete contrast to her baby blue fuzzy sweater and high ponytail.

"Vad kan jag fa dig?"

"Ummm," I stare at her blankly for a moment, and she rolls her eyes with a sigh.

"Drink? Boisson?"

"Oh, right. Water for me and a coffee for him," I say with a smile.

As she walks away, unsurprisingly not returning my smile, I grab the phone. Opening the GPS, I set it on the table between Seth and I. "We're in Os... tha... I can't pronounce that, but somewhere in Sweden."

Seth takes it for a minute, his fingers swiping and pinching as he gets his bearings. He is unarguably the better navigator, so I let him sort that out while I scan the restaurant. I don't sense anyone paying us particular attention. The scruffy older man is focused on his coffee, and the other group is chatting and laughing animatedly, totally absorbed.

The waitress comes over with our drinks. I turn hurriedly to put the phone away, but Seth's already slipped it out of sight.

"Food?" the waitress asks. Her English mustn't be great, she brought me a dark soft drink of some kind instead of water.

"Two hamburgers," Seth says pointing to a picture on the front of one of the menus.

"Well done," I compliment as she saunters away again.

He shrugs with a smile before his face tightens. "We are a bit off course, but not too bad. There is a ferry about thirty to forty-five minutes from here. If we take that one instead, we'll have to take a second ferry, because it'll take us to some island off Finland. It gets us out of Sweden and into Finland quicker. What d'you think?"

The truth is, I have no idea at this point. My adrenaline has evaporated, leaving me near exhaustion. But exhausted or not, a decision has to be made. We clearly aren't safe here. "Let's do it," I say with more certainty than I feel. We'd discussed taking a ferry when originally planning our escape. You don't need ID to buy a ticket, and we saw it as a pretty random choice, so we'd kept it as a possible option. Seems safest to stick with that plan.

Seth nods, his hand moving reflexively to his collar and tugging it as he asks, "So, I don't know if this is a bad thing to bring up right now, but are you...how are you doing about leaving Drew?"

I bite my straw, eyes on the speckled laminate table. "I don't know. I haven't let myself think about it. Just have to keep telling myself it doesn't matter, there's no choice. We can't stay, and we can't exactly keep dragging him into our mess." Looking up into Seth's sympathetic gaze, I shoot him a forced smile as the food arrives and try to reign in my thoughts that are galloping towards Drew. Seth doesn't know about the date-ending argument I had with Drew this evening. I can't even begin to sort out if that changes my feelings.

While we pick at our food, I distract myself with more important matters: figuring out who's following us. It scares me that I don't know who it is, but I find some comfort in the fact that they don't seem to know who we are, either. Who could they be? Are they hunting Guardians in general? If so, then surely if we keep a low profile, we'll be fine. Technically, we know more about them than they do about us; at least I've seen them.

"Should we call Drew?" I ask, startling Seth, who was either lost in thought or half asleep.

"Umm, I don't know." He looks at me apprehensively. I realize he wasn't privy to the debate going on in my head, so my question came out of nowhere.

"I was thinking we could ask him about who might be tracking us. It'll help us avoid them if we know who they are and if they're a threat."

"True," Seth says, thinking for a moment as he catches up to the conversation. "What's the risk?"

"Well, I'm guessing by now someone's realized we're missing. Bryce and Damian know we're friends with Drew, so they'll be watching him pretty closely. I don't know that he would be able to take a phone call without being overheard."

Seth nods, and we are both quiet for a minute. "Let's do it," I decide, the analysis paralysis more draining than our actual predicament. I dial his number before I have time to come up with a reason not to.

"Hello?"

"Drew? It's Alex. Sorry to call you so late. Seth and I had to leave, and now I need your help. I think we are being followed."

"Where are you? I don't know of any Guardians following you, but I can look into it." The robotic note to his voice tells me that I was right, he's being watched closely. I have to assume the call is being overheard. I also got a pretty clear signal that the Guardians are out hunting us; no surprises there.

"No, Drew, it's not the Guardians, it's someone else. I don't know who it is. They didn't recognize us, but they had a tracking device on the motorcycle we... borrowed." Seth tries to suppress a laugh, a snort slipping out.

Drew pauses, the silence stretching out so long I almost ask if he's still there. "Alex, where are you? You aren't safe. Let me come and get you," Drew's tone completely shifts, sounding panicked.

"I can't. I don't feel safe with the Guardians either. I was hoping maybe you could at least give me a bit more information on who's after us."

"Alex, I'm serious. If it's who I think it is... those people are very dangerous."

"Who are they?" I ask again, anxiety causing my tired muscles to constrict. Drew is pretty laid back; if he's worried, it's no joke.

"If I tell you, will you come back?" Drew asks. I can almost see him biting his lip.

"I can't promise that."

He mutters something in a language I don't understand, sounding angry. "Fine. Look, do you remember I told you that the Guardians of Enlightenment aren't the only secret society out there?" He pauses for a moment, and I shut my eyes. *Idiot! How could I forget that?* I'd been so focused on escaping the Guardians, I'd totally forgotten one of the main reasons we didn't leave sooner. "There are organizations that," Drew pauses, seeming to search for a way to explain, "dislike what we do. There are extremists who hunt us. Some kidnap and torture Guardians for information and ransom, or to convert us to their *cause*. They've been known to kill Guardians. This isn't a joke. If we... if I don't know where you are, I can't protect you."

"Thank you, Drew. I'll try not to bother you again. We will watch out for ourselves, I promise. Please don't worry about us."

"Wait. Alex, please!"

"Goodbye."

Nausea twists my stomach. I take a deep breath, trying to keep my burger down. It physically hurts to know I'm causing Drew pain. On top of that, my concern over Seth and my safety rekindles. I quickly fill Seth in on Drew's side of the conversation.

He swears under his breath. "What're we gonna do?"

I bite my cheek, shaking my head. "There's nothing we can do. We keep going, try our best to be invisible. We can't go back. Well, you could. I don't think you're Erik's type."

He snorts, getting to his feet and pulling me to mine. Next stop, a steal-worthy car.

CHAPTER TWENTY-THREE

In the back of my mind, it strikes me as funny that my life now involves so much casual crime. *Desperate times.* Drew's words about our pursuers spin around my head as we walk through the streets, flowing with the crowds of late-night bar-hoppers. The idea of being abducted by another organization terrifies me, but the Guardians seem far from a safe haven. In the busy streets of urban Europe, at least we stand a chance.

I hold onto that hope as we scout out the area, finally finding a paid parking lot. The security guard is watching a tiny tube TV in a small windowed booth, letting us slip past unnoticed. Seth heads straight for a shiny blue BMW, but I catch his hand and shake my head. That kind of car will have a complicated alarm and GPS tracking, even remote vehicle deactivation. I pick an older model sedan, much to Seth's dismay. After opening the door with our slim jim, I set to hotwiring it, a skill I've practiced several times during intel class. The engine starts quickly, and I hop into the driver's seat so Seth can focus on navigating. We are learning a bit about playing to each other's strengths, thanks to the Guardians. Their lessons have certainly increased our likelihood of escape. Part of me mourns for the training we're missing out on by leaving, but safety is a stronger pull. Stronger than being with Drew, but secretly, I know that it's a close call; I really fell for him and the Guardian life.

After driving for about forty minutes, I notice a car shadowing our moves.

"Are we almost at the marina?" I ask.

"About two kilometers out, why?"

I take a couple of sharp turns, pulling onto a side street of a residential area. "We're being followed." I pull to the side of the road, cutting the engine and lights before our shadow can follow.

"Grab your bag and get out now!"

Seth reacts without questioning me. Obedient as he is, when we get out of the car he takes my hand and leads the way to a deserted park behind the nearby houses. Since we're playing to our strengths, getting out of hot water is Seth's forte. It's pitch black in the field, the lights from the neighboring street unable to penetrate the darkness of the large, open space curtained by trees. Another vehicle pulls to a stop somewhere in front of the houses, brakes screeching in their haste. The sounds of the engine idling to a stop and slamming doors pierce the quiet night air. Seth squeezes my hand, pulling me deeper into the field. We take off at a run. I try not to panic, but the similarities to the alleyway are too stark. *How did they track us? We ditched the bike!* Seth keeps us on the frosted grass as long as possible, preventing foot noise. Once we reach the edge of the field, he moves to the right, darting behind the shadow of a closed convenience store. Seth pulls me to his right side against the building, leaving himself room to look around the corner. I strain my ears to listen for following footsteps, every small shift of my trembling body against the metal siding is impossibly loud.

Seth nudges my shoulder as he silently shrugs away from the wall, on the move again. We change streets often but generally head in a northeastern direction, according to Seth's internal compass. He stops every couple of blocks to check if we're being followed, but we lost sight of the shadowed figures shortly after the field. This is both good and unsettling. If we can't see them, it could mean that we lost them, or that they have the jump on us this time. With trembling hands I turn off our phone, just in case it's somehow informing our pursuers. Seth keeps focused on our route, but his rigid posture and clenched fists show me he's just as scared as I am. I keep envisioning someone jumping out from a building or alleyway at any moment; I tense as we near each corner. I'm so grateful for Seth's intuitive evasion skills. I'd be completely lost without him.

We finally make it to the harbor, and I move to the ticket window, which is discouragingly dark. I groan and drop on the ground beside Seth, leaning on the wall of the ticket wicket. "No ferries leaving until 10 AM. It's around 3 AM now," I say, recalling the time before I shut off the phone. "Any sign we're being followed?"

"No, but waiting around here for seven hours is a bad idea. They're bound to check this area eventually, and we don't exactly blend in. We should've checked the ferry times before making our plans," he adds in frustration.

"We're new to this; just make a mental note for the next time we're trying to escape multiple secret societies on very little sleep." I smile, nudging his shoulder. He lets out a humorless laugh, and I continue. "So, other options. I think driving is out. They seem to track us every time we do. We could steal a boat. I can pilot one, but I don't think it would be the safest idea in the middle of the night in unknown waters."

Seth yawns and my body copies. "Maybe we should find somewhere to sleep?"

"I didn't see any hotels on our run here, and this town seems small. I doubt they even have one open at this hour."

"Well, this was one way for us to dodge the inauguration," Seth says with a half smile.

"I guess so."

I want to laugh, or cry, but I can't. My tank feels empty. Fatigue hits me hard, and my body begs for a warm bed. We both sit, sulking, until something resembling hope floats by. Blindingly bright fog lights flood the boardwalk as a tugboat pulls towards the dock. One of the crew members jumps off, tugging the boat ropes, as I dig deep for the strength to get my feet. Someone on board shouts at the man on land as I walk slowly down the dock. He's not speaking English, so I have no idea what they're saying.

"What do you think?" Seth asks, catching up to me.

I'm too tired to consider pros and cons at this point, so I shrug, and we walk over to the kneeling sailor making a series of fancy knots.

"Um, hi. English?" I ask awkwardly. He jumps, looking up at me, then Seth, then back to me.

"The harbor closed to visitor at the night time," he says in heavily accented but comprehensible English.

"I know, but we're kind of in a bind. We really need to get to Finland ASAP," I explain. He looks at me with a blank expression.

"We, Finland. Money," Seth reiterates, using gestures and pulling out some cash. This, the man seems to understand. He turns to what I assume to be his captain, yelling incomprehensibly again. They argue for a minute before he turns back to us.

"Okay, come on boat. We leave one or two... timme." He says pointing to his watch. I'm not sure if he means hours or minutes, but either is better than plan A. He leads us below deck, eyes scanning the dock frequently. It's probably frowned upon for

tugboats to take foreign stowaways across the border. We enter what looks like a dining room/living room area. "You stay for here until we getting there." He looks at Seth expectedly.

Seth hands the man a hundred euros. "More once we get there," Seth says, using more hand gestures. It's humorous but effective.

The man pockets the cash and leaves us alone. We're both so exhausted we beeline straight for the two couches. Seth puts his backpack under his head, laying down as I pull my knees to my chest to rest my chin. We have no reason to trust these guys, but at this point, we're too desperate to discriminate.

"Seth?"

"Hmm?" he responds sleepily.

"I'm sorry for all of this. I mean, I know it was the Guardians who took us, but I keep complicating things."

"Lexie, none of this is your fault," he says. Before I can argue he adds, "And even if it was, I would still do it in a heartbeat."

"Thanks. I'd do the same for you."

"I know," he says through another yawn.

Alison Haines

Seth's snores quickly fill the cabin, but the rocking boat isn't enough to soothe me to sleep. I sit, lost in a thought spiral. Drew and Rose, the life I'm leaving behind, Erik and Bryce, the danger I'm fleeing from. Everything shifts as we leave the port. Seth doesn't even stir. The boat tosses gently, and black nothingness is all I can see through the port windows.

I naw on my already raw cheek. It's only a handful of hours until the inauguration. The one Seth and I only agreed to to keep our siblings safe. What will happen if we don't show? Can I get a hold of Whit and Miles somehow? Warn them? Would that even help?

I'm shaking with exhaustion, and my cheeks are wet with tears I don't remember shedding as the sun lightens the horizon hours later, the passed time a complete blur.

"Getting ups now," someone calls, startling me out of my daze.

Seth is quick to wake, on his feet and pulling on his bag before I can even untangle my numb legs. The now bright sunlight filling the cabin stings my tired eyes.

"We here almost now," the man who let us on the tugboat says, standing in the doorway. His skin gleams with a layer of sweat, eyes darting between the two of us before hurrying back above deck. His nerves send a shiver down my spine, and the look on Seth's face tells me he didn't miss the change in our new friend. I sigh with a shrug, grabbing my backpack. Nothing we can do about whatever's coming, we just have to keep moving.

"Here is," our tugboat friend says, looking at us before looking nervously around the dock. It's deserted, save for a few fishermen checking nets by their nearby boats.

"Thank you," Seth says, handing him another wad of cash as we hurry off the boat.

THE SECRETS THEY KEEP

We have to clear customs before we can leave the harbor, but we're prepared with fake passports, different identities we both have well memorized.

"You look pale, Lex. You okay?"

"Yeah, just tired. I'll be okay once we get some breakfast." I try to smile, nausea pushing any thoughts of hunger from my mind. I'm exhausted and nervous, but I don't have time to dwell; we need to focus.

The customs officer's bushy white eyebrows pull together, looking at the clock as we reach his booth. We're the only ones there, and the ferry isn't due for several hours, assuming we're at the right marina. Luckily, he seems too tired to be curious and processes us anyway.

"Amanda Green and Jack Green?" the man asks, eyes flashing between us and our passports. Another Guardian luxury: flawless forgeries.

"Yes," we reply in unison.

"What is your business in Finland?"

"Just traveling around Europe," I say with a smile.

"Are you two married?"

"Brother and sister," Seth corrects.

He looks at us and our photos for another long moment. I cling to the small table ledge at the customs office, starting to feel light-headed. Running away is no day at the beach. My mind can't stop *what if-ing* every possible outcome. What if our fake passports are flagged? What if we're arrested? Can we make a run for it here? Do those doors lock automatically?

Finally, he stamps our passports through a long yawn. "how long are you staying?"

"A week or so," I answer vaguely. We won't be using these passports after today anyway, I have several more sewn into the lining of my backpack.

The man hands us our passports and we exit the port into a large parking area.

"Any idea where we are?" I ask Seth, taking in the deserted lot.

"You're in Turku, Finland, little Guardian." A suit-clad man with a faint accent startles me, leaning against the marina wall. He's not alone. Leather Coat from the bar is standing beside him, casually smoking.

"I'm sorry? What did you call me?" I say after regaining my composure.

"Let's not play games," he says with a smile, raking his dark eyes over me in a way that sends a shiver down my spine. "We just want to have a little

chat." The man is not very tall, much shorter than Leather Coat, but he maintains a calm sense of authority.

Movement in my periphery catches my attention. Green Sweater from the bar walks towards us through the parking lot, stopping just beside Seth.

"I think you have us confused with someone else."

I grip Seth's wrist, lifting my fingers one at a time as a countdown: a trick we'd developed as kids. As I raise my last finger, we both take off at a run, Seth pushing Green Sweater to the pavement. I'm reasonably confident that these men aren't going to shoot us. I'm sure they want more than a couple of Guardian bodies, but that isn't enough to slow my thundering pulse. We bolt through the parking lot and take a left onto the roadway.

The early morning sun is unseasonably warm, relentlessly beating down on us as we search for safety. Seth groans as we scan the nearly deserted industrial area just beyond the port. Taking his hand, I run towards the rising sun. A tan SUV blows past us and turns to cut off our path. Seth spins me, making to run the other way as three men jump out of the vehicle. Leather Coat and Green Sweater come jogging out of the lot, blocking the road and any possible return to the marina. My eyes dart, looking

for another exit. Both sides of the road are fenced, leaving us surrounded. *Yep, we definitely left our luck behind in Sweden.*

Seth and I exchange a glance; he nods at Leather Coat and Green Sweater. We run at them, and they step back in surprise. Just what we need. I dive low, sweeping Green Sweater's legs and knocking him to the hard pavement. Leather Coat hits the ground beside him with blood pouring from his nose, courtesy of Seth.

We turn just in time for the three men from the SUV to catch up with us. One of them swings for a temple shot, but I duck, kicking his ankle. He's fast and jumps to avoid the hit, dropping to land on top of me. He presses his weight to force me onto my stomach. I hear Seth grunt, but I can't see him. A

surge of adrenaline hits me. Clenching my jaw, I swing my head back as hard as I can, connecting with the man on top of me. He curses, leaning up enough to allow me to turn my body. I swing my legs to wrap around his torso as blood drips down his face. Pulling him backward, I sit up, landing an elbow to his throat. He goes limp, gasping loudly for breath.

I untangle myself and get to my feet. Seth is circling one of the men, the other unmoving on the ground. Before I can help him, another car stops in front of us, and four more people get out. Two quickly grab me, the other two going for Seth. I struggle against their grip, but I'm already out of breath; my eyes are having a hard time focusing as the pain I'd been ignoring demands attention. The back of my head throbs, my arms sting and I notice blood oozing from my elbows.

"You were able to evade us last night, but not this time. That would hardly be fair," Fancy Suit says with a saccharine smile. I hadn't even noticed him leaning on the fence surrounding the harbors parking lot.

"Who are you? What do you want?" Seth demands. He pulls against the woman and man gripping his arms, his head bleeding just above his eyebrow.

"Like I said, we just want to have a little chat. My name is Felix; my friends and I occasionally meet with Guardians to keep up with inside information."

"We aren't who you think we are," I insist.

"I know you are Guardians, so you can stop embarrassing yourself," Felix says, his smile holding firm, dark eyes shifting eagerly between Seth and me.

"We aren't! Not by choice anyway. We're trying to get away from them," I say, pivoting tactics.

Felix raises an eyebrow, rubbing a hand along his jawline. "Really, that so? And why's that?"

I have no interest in explaining anything to him, but our only hope is to stall while we try to come up with another plan. "It's... complicated." My throbbing headache makes it hard to think as my heart pounds uncomfortably fast.

"We don't believe in what they stand for. How did you find us here?" Seth asks.

"Tugboat crews are notoriously chatty; you should take note of that for the future. I have friends in the shipping and receiving industry. Put the word out I was looking for someone. You leaving from Grisslehamn, I admit, was a surprise, but alas, I have famously good instincts. When a friend heard a tugboat crew boarding a couple of stowaways, I decided to come see for myself."

My brow furrows. How could Felix be surprised about Grisslehamn? They'd tracked us there, hadn't they? I was certain a van had been following us.

"Now, back to you kids wanting to leave the Guardians."

Seth's gaze meets mine, looking me over with concern. His eyes dart, calculating.

Before I can form an answer for Felix, screeching tires echo through the open road as a black car hurtles towards us. *Oh great, like they need more back up.* The vehicle stops close behind us, just as two sedans come into view from the other direction. I turn to Felix to comment on his heavy-handed response, but he looks just as surprised. He blanches, cursing as

doors slam behind us. I spin, the cause of his panic making my jaw drop. Scott, flanked by three bodyguards I recognize from the house, saunter towards us. I wonder momentarily if I've passed out and am having some twisted dream, but Seth looks just as stunned, and my head is pounding. *If I were unconscious, I wouldn't still be in pain, right?* The

other cars pull to a stop near Felix but remain idling. Based on Scott's confident smile, I assume it's another Guardian team.

"Felix, what a delightful surprise," Scott says with a smile. *Of course they know each other.*

"Always a pleasure, Scott." Felix returns pleasantries, but his narrowed eyes make his smile look more like bearing teeth.

This would have been an entertaining exchange if Seth and I weren't stuck in the middle. As it is, I feel like a mouse stuck between a cat and a hawk.

"It seems you have found something that belongs to us. We appreciate that, but we'll take it from here."

"The way I hear it, they aren't interested in coming back with you. Maybe they should try our world for a while. Let them decide for themselves," Felix counters, voice calm but fists balled.

The Guardian security step closer to us slowly. My captors let me go, shoving me forward toward Seth. The five left standing from Felix's crew form a loose circle around us as Seth grips my shoulders and pulls me tightly to his side.

"We need to run," I whisper.

"I don't think that's an option right now."

Scott glances at us for a moment, his expression doesn't falter. "Well, as fun as that sounds, I believe Seth is going to need some medical attention before he bleeds out on the pavement. Unfortunately, those two are kind of a package deal; I really hate to break up a matched set. Perhaps another time."

He's not wrong about Seth. His head is bleeding pretty heavily now, dripping off his jaw to the ground.

Felix's eyes shift, appearing to notice Seth's head wound for the first time. He turns, his expression calculating as he looks at the other vehicle, then hungrily at Seth and I.

"I may just take you up on that offer. These two are clearly more important than I thought. Seth. Seth's... sister, is it? I'll be seeing you two again soon, I'm sure."

The Guardian guards push past Felix's crew and escort us, rather roughly, towards the sedan they arrived in. I catch a glimpse of Felix. He gives me a mocking bow as the car door is slammed in my face.

THE SECRETS THEY KEEP

Seth's fists tighten as he tries to open the backseat door, but fails. I get the feeling his mind can't help but search for an exit. It's totally against his nature to surrender like this, but we have no choice. A pang of guilt twists my already tight stomach. I blame myself for necessitating this rushed escape. I've become an anchor, dragging Seth deeper into the world he's desperate to escape.

CHAPTER TWENTY-FOUR

I sit on the edge of a car's open trunk, Seth right beside me.

"Sorry, Mate. That's gonna need stitches," the doctor says, crouching in front of Seth with a pen-light in his hand. "And as for you, Miss Conry, I'm watching you for a concussion. The blood on the back of your head seems from your attacker."

"Nice one," Seth smiles.

"Stay put. I'm gonna grab more supplies and get a feed for youse."

After speeding away from Felix, our caravan stopped a few kilometers from the marina in one of the industrial lots. We arrived in time to see a Guardian helicopter land, carrying the doctor and a few additional guards.

"Well, you two sure know how to keep things interesting." Scott laughs, sauntering towards us from the group of guards he'd been talking to.

"That's the plan," Seth mutters, pressing gauze to his forehead.

"So, do I get to hear what spurred the great Conry team into this abrupt departure? I know you're talented, Alexandra, but I thought you and Seth were settling in. If you two were just biding your time, you did a hell of a job playing the part. Is this because of the inauguration?"

My breath catches. I'd actually forgotten all about the ceremony in my haste to escape. "No, this has nothing to do with that. Why not ask Bryce. He's the reason we left."

Scott's eyebrows pull together. "What are you talking about? He was as surprised as I was to hear you had run away."

"I'm sure he was. He didn't know I heard about his plan. I'm not going to let myself be taken to Erik again." I cross my arms over my chest, trying to suppress the anxiety forcing it's way past my exhaustion.

"Erik?" Scott's confused expression deepens. "Give me a minute. You, watch them." He turns, pulling out a phone and snapping his fingers at a guard who promptly moves to stand in front of us.

"Lay a hand on Alex, and I'll lay you out on this pavement."

"Not just yet, Mate. Lemme get you stitched up first." The doctor chuckles, laying his bag on the road and unfolding a stool. He hands each of us a protein bar. "We'll get you proper brekkie when we're home. You both look knackered." Sitting in front of Seth, he sets up his supplies and gets to work. Seth's clenched jaw is the only indication he's in pain.

"Alexandra?" Scott calls, beckoning to me a short distance from the car.

"I'll be right back," I say to Seth, struggling to pull my aching frame from the trunk.

"I spoke to Bryce. There has been a misunderstanding; he wasn't going to take you to Erik. He was upset when he saw you and Andrew... together, that's all."

"Right, I'm sure he was just joking around."

"Alexandra!" Scott grabs my wrist as I turn back to Seth. "What Erik did was horrible. No one wants that to happen to you again. I won't let him get anywhere near you."

There's a disarming level of sincerity in Scott's words, but I can't trust him.

"Thanks." I pull my wrist from his hand, moving back to Seth.

I fill him in on my chat with Scott as the doctor leaves us to talk to the helicopter pilot, arranging our ride home. "Scott assured me that he'll make sure we're safe when we get back."

"And you believe him?"

"Hell no. Scott has no authority over Damian and Bryce, but right now, we're not exactly flooded with options." I bite my cheek as I take in Seth's stitches. "Are you going to be okay?"

"I'll be good as new in no time. How did they find us?"

I'd been mulling this over since Scott arrived. "I think Drew was really worried when I told him someone was following us. I'd wager he told that we were headed to Finland. I overheard Scott telling one of his men that the Guardians have an inside man at border control. They were watching for scanned passports matching our descriptions." I take a breath, watching the Guardian crew hurriedly packing up. "We're in way deeper than we thought."

"So it seems." Seth agrees, closing his eyes.

The doctor takes Seth and me, along with a couple of guards, back to the estate in the helicopter. I want to be excited about my first time in a helicopter, but I'm too exhausted. I'm surprisingly grateful when we land on the well-manicured lawns of the Guardian estate.

Being in the infirmary causes a stress-inducing flashback to my post-Erik injuries. I'm in much less pain, but if possible, we're more trapped. Our escape attempt had gone very poorly. Sure, we learned a few things, but we still know next to nothing about who else is out there watching our every move. The Guardians' connections in border control also add a layer of difficulty to any future escapes.

"Let's make a pact to stay as far from this room as possible from now on." Seth says through a yawn, strolling back into the infirmary.

"Agreed! What did you find out?"

Seth had gone on a little spying mission when we got back to the Guardian's estate. I'd distracted the doctor, claiming I was feeling dizzy. He started assessing me, and Seth snuck out. The doctor wasn't happy that Seth left the infirmary; we were both supposed to stay there until the following day. I promised he'd be back soon. He was irritated but did me the favor of not alerting security.

"Well, when you came back with a concussion, I think it defused any potential anger from Bryce or Damian."

"But, I don't have a-"

"I may have embellished your injuries slightly," he adds with a half grin. "Apparently, Drew freaked on his dad for putting us in that risky situation. I confronted Bryce, but he's sticking to the story that he wasn't taking you to Erik. So now Bryce's pissed that what he said was *'taken out of context.'*"

Seth rolls his eyes, and I agree with his skepticism. That's easy to say, now that he got caught.

"He and Damian seem keen to apologize for any misunderstanding, but we've seen that before. We'll just have to stay alert... more alert this time." He squeezes my hand as he drops into the chair beside my bed. "Drew's kind of a wreck after hearing about your injuries. He tried to visit you when he ran into me, but the doctor ordered the guards to keep everyone out. I think he's afraid you're pissed, maybe because he told everyone where we were?" Seth shrugs, but I have a feeling it has more to do with the fight before I left.

"And Rose?"

"Haven't seen her. Drew didn't mention her, so I think she's probably fine."

I let out a breath, hopeful she hadn't been implicated in our escape. I owe her so much.

"And the ceremony?"

Seth rolls his eyes. "It's been postponed a couple of weeks due to *extenuating circumstances.* They don't want it getting out that we ran away. I guess it would give the other family leverage or something. Either way, we're still going to have to deal with it, but not today."

*****

We try to convince the doctor to let us go back to our suite, but he's unwavering. He insists that he needs to be sure I'm not concussed after my (fake) dizzy spell. I have a feeling he's just punishing us for tricking him earlier. Rose finally comes to check on us early the next morning, and I'm so relieved she's safe. In *typical Rose* fashion, she brings us a massive stash of food, all our favorites, before hurrying off to talk to the doctor.

While we're eating, both starved, Drew sheepishly sticks his head in the door. Seth has the sudden urge to take a walk, leaving the two of us alone. Part of me wants to make Seth stay. I'm nervous about how this conversation is going to go. I don't want to fight with Drew, but we left things on such an awkward note, and that was *before* he told his dad our escape plan.

Drew shifts awkwardly at the door, brow furrowed as he bites his lower lip. "I'm really sorry."

"Come, sit." I gesture to Seth's abandoned chair. "You don't have to apologize. You seriously saved our asses by sending help. I should have listened when you warned us." Shaking my head and looking away, I mutter, "I thought we could handle them."

"If anyone could, it would be you guys." He drops into the seat, dark circles under his eyes showing how worried he must have been. "I just don't get why you ran away. Seth told me about the rumor you heard. Why didn't you come to me? You do realize that my dad would not have you moved against your will, right?" he adds, his tone bordering on anger.

"How could I know that? He had me brought here against my will. I was locked up with Erik against my will. Is it really unreasonable for me to think it could happen again?"

Drew's expression softens. "That's fair. But next time, please, come to me. I'll always protect you. I have my own share of connections here. Plus, you're in line for a head seat, and with that comes your own authority; you just need to learn how to assert it."

"I guess I do. Know any tutors?"

Drew smiles, but it doesn't reach his eyes. "I didn't just come to apologize for ratting you out. I need to set straight what I said the other night. I actually thought that's why you guys ran away. I wasn't thinking... the things I said... I didn't mean them."

"Drew, stop. It's fine. I'm not mad. You were just being honest about your feelings. I love that you were so open-"

"Those aren't my feelings!" he interrupts, gripping my hand. "Alex, you are amazing. You disarm me, and I'm not used to that. I guess... I just got scared. You running away *killed* me. I was terrified I wouldn't get the chance to tell you how I really feel. I've wanted to be with you since... well, for too long."

I can't stop the smile lighting my face as his teal eyes search mine. "I want to be with you too."

Getting to his feet, Drew puts his hands on either side of my pillow, his lips diving to meet mine. This isn't at all how I pictured our first kiss, me in a hospital bed. But, to be fair, nothing about my relationship with Drew has been normal. Drew's lips brush mine softly. As I wrap my arms around his neck, the kiss deepens. My hands tangle into his soft curls as if drawn there. Like they were meant to be there. For the first time, I'm my true self to a boy. Not the repressed student, or Whit's little sister. Drew picked me for perhaps the most authentic version of myself I've ever been. The kiss deepens and my mind loosens, releasing the anger towards Drew's defense of Erik and my anxiety about the Guardians. My lips tingle as he pulls away. Sitting on the side of my bed, Drew smiles shyly, searching for a reaction.

My mind feels bubbly like I've had champagne as I try to force myself to believe this is real. Drew really kissed me. *Finally!* He squeezes my hand, his elated expression warming me like sunshine.

"So, I hear you had a run in with your dad?" I ask, eyebrows raised as I try to shift the focus away from my rising blush. "I think I might be a bad influence on you."

It's Drew's turn to blush. "Oh, that. After you two were reported missing, my father came straight to me, demanding to know where you went. I told them nothing, of course, until you called. Once I realized that you guys weren't safe, I lost it on him. He's the reason you two ran away, and it was more than I could take, thinking of you being seriously hurt because of his ignorance. Well, you *were* seriously hurt." He points to my head. I wave him off, and he continues. "I told my dad where you two were headed, and we scrambled to find out who was tailing you. Then I gave him a piece of my mind," he says, trying to sound nonchalantly tough.

I purse my lips to suppress a giggle at his facade. "I'm surprised you guys were able to find us so fast. I mean, I know the Guardians are good, but how did the trackers find us in Grisslehamn? I thought they didn't have a location until we cleared customs."

His brow pulls together again. "No, they didn't have anything on you until your passports hit the system in Turku. What happened in Grisslehamn? Is that where you guys got a boat?"

"Yeah. That's where we got a ride from a tugboat, but before that, someone was tailing us. Felix said it wasn't his guys, and he has no reason to lie about that."

"We had nothing on you except that you were headed to Finland."

I let out a breath, the small wall of hope holding back my intuition breaks down. "I swear someone was following us on the highway." Fear surges as I try not to jump to the conclusion my gut has been shouting since our chat with Felix.

Drew presses his lips together. "Alex, that was a pretty high-stress situation, maybe it was just... I mean, it's possible another organization... but that would be one hell of a coincidence."

"Maybe we just imagined it," I allow, but it's more for his benefit than mine. I know we hadn't. I make a mental note to talk to Seth about it later.

"I'll talk to my father, just to be sure." Drew squeezes my hand.

"Speaking of your father, what's he going to do now? Is he still planning to take me to be Erik's prisoner?"

"I don't even know how you guys heard that rumor. My dad sometimes lets his anger get the best of him and says things he doesn't mean. He's a bit hard headed, not that you would be able to relate to that," Drew adds with a wink. "Actually, he and Damian realized that they were missing something. I'm almost as eligible to be 'matched' with you as Erik."

I can't help laughing. "What do you mean *almost*?"

Drew shrugs with a forced smile. "It's complicated, and not worth discussing. My dad and uncle are actually supporting our relationship. I mean, if you want a relationship with me."

"Well, now I don't know. If Bryce and Damian are on board, it's kind of counter to my whole image."

"I can go try to convince them that we're horribly matched, if that would help?" Drew gets to his feet, expression daring. I catch his hand, pulling him back to the bed.

"On second thought, I guess we can agree on a few things."

EPILOGUE

Bryce and Damian

"Well, that was eventful, but I suppose that's what we should expect with Seth and Alexandra. I can't help but question the timing," Bryce says, leaning forward in his green leather armchair.

Damian's eyes narrow, not looking up from the folder he'd been reviewing on his mahogany desk "I agree, it was a terrible time to let your temper run away with you. Trust that I know she can be taxing, but right now, she's important. They both are. If those seats go to-"

"I know! But, that's not what I meant. How many times have we complained about those kids, about any number of people, in this very office? It's one of the few places in the house we know to be secure."

This catches Damian's attention. He supervised the daily bug sweeping, and the staff allowed in this area of the estate were scrutinized extensively. "That... is certainly something we need to investigate. But not tonight. For the moment, our only priority is moving forward with the inauguration."

"True. How are we going to ensure they don't escape again?"

"I believe Andrew provides fairly good assurance of that. Conceding to their relationship should pacify Alexandra," Damian says as he moves to the fully stocked bar in their office. Grabbing a crystal bottle of whiskey, he pours himself a drink and refills his brother's glass.

"Andrew, indeed. No hard feelings I trust, brother. I did try to dissuade him for the sake of Erik."

Damian drains his glass, pouring a second before joining Bryce in front of the fire crackling in the large hearth. "Erik ruined that opportunity for himself; nothing could be done to recover from that." The orange firelight illuminates Damian's tight smile, casting doubt on his casual acceptance of his son's change in fate.

Nodding, Bryce swirls his drink distractedly. "That may be true, but Erik was... a sure thing. Focused. I'm not so sure the same can be said of Andrew. I've seen a change in him. You spend more time with him than I do these days. Do his loyalties lie stronger now with her than us? We both know the pull of young love."

Damian offers a knowing half-smile. "Perhaps, but he's aware of the risks if they leave, and he will protect Alexandra above all else." He pauses, taking a drink. "That girl really is a glass cannon. She has shown immense improvement and promise in combat training. However, her habit of landing in the infirmary is undeniable. That, and when she's taken out, Andrew and Seth are brought to their knees."

"True. But we can't have that information getting out. She's an easy target, and I fear the Cupitor Verus discovered that. Scott believes Felix got a read on how important she and Seth are. If we can get Alexandra working for us though,

Seth will follow. That is a team that we could really use. Add Andrew into the mix, and they will do great things."

"Undoubtedly they will. Let's just focus on making sure it's for us and not against us," Damian replies, raising his glass to his brother.

Loud voices in the hallway pull the brothers' attention from their drinks.

"Ma'am please-"

"Don't you sass me."

Bryce lets out an audible groan as a woman with silver hair pushes her way into their office, an assistant trying futilely to slow her progress.

"It's fine." Damian waves the assistant off, and she hastily retreats, pulling the door shut. "Clarissa, to what do we owe the pleasure?"

"Ah good, I get Tweedle-dee and Tweedle-dum together; saves me some time."

"It's late, let's skip the pleasantries." Bryce gets to his feet, crossing his arms over his broad chest.

"Fine by me. Now, I'm sure there must be some tanglin' in the wires, but the way I hear it, you ain't been treatin' my niece and nephew right."

"There was a misunderstanding, but it's been resolved," Damian says calmly, gesturing for Clarissa to sit on the green couch adjacent to the fire. She raises her eyebrows, ignoring his offer.

"A misunderstanding? Now that *is* good to hear. I'll just see myself out then. Before I do, I'm sure it was just a misunderstanding that my Lexie was *locked* in a room with your son?" Clarissa's glare locks on Damian.

"Everything does seem to find its way back to you, doesn't it, Clarissa?"

Alison Haines

"No thanks to you. I'm goin' to see my kin, but know this: we're not done here. You may have got your way, bringing them youngins here, but that was a mistake. Now I've got *two* dogs in the fight, and I'd wager, neither are real fans of you two right now."

THE SECRETS THEY KEEP

Alison Haines

About the Author

Alison Haines is a debut author, with a long-held love for writing. Her career has taken her in several directions as a registered nurse and professor before she settled into the comfortable chair and cozy sweater that is writing.

Alison lives in a small town in South-Western Ontario, Canada with her husband and daughter. When not writing, she loves to travel, be outdoors, and gaming.

Learn more at www.alisonhaines.ca